The Double Blind

❊ ❊ ❊ ❊ ❊ ❊ ❊ ❊ ❊ ❊ ❊ ❊

Doubleday & Company, Inc.
Garden City, New York

THE DOUBLE BLIND

❖

❖

❖

❖

by JOHN ROWAN WILSON

The Double Blind

1

I was sitting at my desk in the Ministry of Health when the telephone rang.

"Dr. Mayne here," I said.

"This is Stratton, Colonial Office." I had a vague memory of Stratton. I had met him once or twice momentarily at official receptions. He was secretary to various committees connected with research into tropical diseases. He spoke in a clipped, self-important voice which inferred that time was valuable to him if it wasn't to me. "I have something I'd like to ask your advice about. I wonder if we could have a talk sometime."

"Now, if you like."

He sounded shocked. "Not on the telephone. It's all rather confidential. Do you think you could manage to call round at my office?"

"When?"

"I'm tied up for the rest of today, I'm afraid. What about tomorrow at eleven-thirty?"

I have one fatal disadvantage as far as the Civil Service is concerned. I am no good at pretending I am busy when I am not— and I wasn't. So I said, "All right. I'll be there."

After I put the telephone down, I began to think that I had perhaps made a mistake—I should have asked Stratton to come and see me. He was not my superior in rank and there is a convention in these matters. He had managed, in a minor way, to score off me.

I was still smarting a little over this when I called on him the following morning. I made my way through the usual dingy Whitehall corridors and up in a small, clanking lift. Evading an attempt by his secretary to detain me in the waiting room, I walked through into his office.

Stratton was sitting at his desk, almost hidden by a mass of papers in his "in" tray. He was a thin, melancholy-looking man, with a brown, wrinkled face. He was almost bald, though he brushed his hair carefully across to conceal it as much as possible. However, there was a naked patch left, which had caught the sun and was beginning to peel. I visualized him as spending a good deal of time gardening down at his home in Thames Ditton. His head was a curious shape, broadening down to the base. This was due to an enlargement of the muscles of his jaw, caused by constantly chewing on a pipe. The office was half of what had once been a finely proportioned room, now ruined by a wall of plasterboard that cut across the window. He had a carpet on the floor, but then so had I—we were equal there.

He shifted a heap of minutes to the side of his desk, got up, and shook hands with me. "So good of you to come and see me, Mayne." When we had both sat down, he made a small performance of lighting his pipe and said, "Has Mackenzie spoken to you about this affair?"

Mackenzie was the head of my department at the Ministry of Health. "No," I said.

"I see." He took a few puffs to get things going. I watched the great masseter muscles expanding and contracting as he did so. If he ever left the Colonial Office, he could always make a living hanging by his teeth from the high wire. "I just wondered. I didn't want to go in for unnecessary repetition. Naturally I had to give Mackenzie an outline of the problem when I asked his permission to call you in." Stratton was an old enough hand at the game to know the importance of the usual channels. "He probably didn't say anything, because I told him at the time that it was strictly confidential"—he looked at me importantly—"as I must also tell you now." I nodded solemnly to emphasize my discretion.

"The trouble is"—he hesitated, wondering how to express it—"we find ourselves in something of a predicament."

"Oh?" I looked conventionally sympathetic. At the same time, I was on the alert. There was always a chance that he might be hoping to push his difficulties off onto me.

"Yes. And it's over a medical matter." He picked absent-mindedly at the loose skin on the top of his head. "Are you familiar with a disease called South Atlantic encephalitis?"

"Well, not directly. I've never actually seen a case. But I have a theoretical knowledge of it."

"Could you tell me something about it? Fairly shortly, that is. And in comprehensible language."

I was accustomed to this kind of request. A good deal of my job nowadays consisted of making *Reader's Digest*-type summaries of scientific matters for lay people. It was not too difficult once you got the hang of it.

"It's a virus disease," I said. "Like polio, or yellow fever. It mainly affects the higher centers of the brain. They get a chronic mental deterioration together with other symptoms, like drowsiness and muscle weakness. It has a tendency to improve and then relapse again. There isn't any cure so far. I believe it's mainly confined to certain groups of islands off the west coast of Africa." I hesitated. "The virus was isolated about three years ago."

Stratton looked at me with unaccustomed respect. "You seem very well informed," he said. "I didn't know you were an authority on tropical diseases."

It seemed a pity to destroy the impression I had made, but I decided to be honest. "I'm not," I said. "The truth is that I have a special interest in this disease. The man who isolated the virus used to be a friend of mine."

Stratton looked at me sharply. "Dr. Farrell?"

"Yes." I saw Stratton nod as if things were going according to plan. I had the impression that he had worked out this conversation beforehand, and that he knew most of the answers to the questions he was asking. I said, "Do you know him?"

"I do indeed," he said, with some feeling. I could not resist a smile. He spoke like a man with bitter memories. "He is, in fact, the problem I wish to discuss."

"Yes?" I was interested. Martin Farrell had, in the time I had known him, always been somebody's problem, and for most of the formative years of my life he had been mine. It was nice to feel that others were bearing the brunt of it nowadays. I said cautiously, "I don't know much about his present movements. We haven't met for ten years. Since we were students, in fact."

"You knew him very well before that, though?"

"Oh, yes. We were at school together. Then we both went to St. Vincent's to do medicine—" He nodded again, glancing at a piece of paper on his desk almost as if making a mental tick against some item. "But you obviously know all this," I said. "It seems to me you've been doing some research."

He was not disconcerted. "We had to find out a few things about Farrell," he said, "and so naturally you came into it. You say you haven't seen him since he qualified?"

"It was before then." I spoke rather curtly. I had done very well up to this point. I had discussed Martin with Stratton in an admirably casual way. But now, suddenly, when I thought of the last time I had seen him, something was beginning to hurt. "He left St. Vincent's halfway through the course, to join the Fleet Air Arm. By the time he came back, at the end of the war, I'd qualified and left."

"I suppose," he said tentatively, "he must have been a very exceptional student?"

"Not in the way you mean." He was not the first person to make this mistake. In view of Martin's present reputation it was understandable. Most medical celebrities show their brilliance quite early. But during the two years we were together at St. Vincent's it would never have occurred to anyone to spot Martin for future eminence. When he packed up to go to the war it caused hardly a ripple of surprise; there were quite a few wild, restless young men doing precisely the same thing at that time. I was not one of them. I wanted to do it the right way, the sensible way. I would qualify, then go into the Army, then work for my fellowship in surgery.

I thought Martin absurdly, if characteristically, reckless. I thought that even if he wasn't killed (the most likely thing to happen), he would certainly never come back to medicine. But he did come back. And a year after he resumed his course he had a surprising break. He made an impression on Professor Hackett. Hackett was a man who liked to discover genius among the students now and then, and when he did so his support was lavish and influential. He was one of the few microbiologists that lay people had heard of. He pushed Martin on every possible occasion. He even published joint papers with him. While I was plodding dutifully up the conventional ladder, Martin went, as it were, up in the lift. Not for him the long, exhausting apprenticeship, the repeated attempts at higher degrees. Within a year or two he became a minor scientific celebrity. In the rather restricted field of virus research, he was regarded as a coming man.

Stratton chewed away at his pipestem as I explained this to him. "Was he just lucky?" he asked. "Or do you think he deserved his success?"

"I don't know," I said. "I never met him again. But I think he probably deserved it. He was always very intelligent and there was something—unusual about him—"

I halted. I had said enough. I wasn't going to start on a character analysis for Stratton's benefit. "His publications are always excellent."

"You never corresponded with him?"

"No." This was not completely true. I had written to him once. It had taken me years to decide to do so. Considering the circumstances under which we had parted, I had thought it better that we shouldn't meet again, but as the years went by, I wondered if this was a little childish. I was also afraid that I might be avoiding him because of envy of his good fortune.

After I had read one of his publications I wrote to him, congratulating him and making a tentative suggestion that we might meet sometime. But he never replied.

I said to Stratton, "What's your interest in Martin?"

"Martin?"

"Dr. Farrell. How does he come into your field?"

Stratton bared his teeth. They weren't very attractive teeth, rather large and yellow, with a good deal of tartar around them. "About six months ago," he said, "he came here to put a project to me." He hesitated, as if remembering something unpleasant. "I might as well say here and now that I didn't exactly take to him."

"No?"

"In our sort of work I think one gets fairly practiced at recognizing what I can only vaguely describe as *difficult* people. I formed the impression that he was impatient and somewhat domineering. Of course, you might not agree with me—"

I shrugged. I had no idea what had happened to Martin in the last ten years, but unless he had radically changed, it was probably quite a fair description.

"What was the project?"

"He claimed to have a vaccine against South Atlantic encephalitis."

"That sounds interesting." It was welcome rather than staggering news. It would be a logical extension of his work in isolating the virus. But if he had done it in the short time of three years, it would be something of a triumph.

"He was very enthusiastic about it," said Stratton with perceptible distaste. Evidently enthusiasm was a suspect emotion. "He claims, on the basis of some animal work, that it will not only prevent the disease but actually halt symptoms already present. Does that seem possible to you?"

I thought for a moment. "Theoretically, just possible, I suppose. If you have a low-grade smoldering infection, the sudden injection of a lot of virus particles might hot up your immunity to a more effective level. And if it works in animals—"

"That's what he says."

"Then he's probably right."

"Maybe." He sounded dubious. "Anyway, the long and short of it was that he wanted to try it out on human beings."

"Naturally," I said. I was beginning to get into the picture now. Practically all the islands where the encephalitis was endemic were British possessions. It would be difficult to do clinical studies there without the co-operation of the Colonial Office. "Where did he want to do it?"

Stratton walked over to a wall map and pointed out a tiny speck about ten degrees south of the equator. He tapped it with the end of his pipe. "An island called Batou. It's a small place. Mixed population—African, Indian, Portuguese, British, and various mixtures of all four. About twenty thousand, all told. It's off the main shipping routes, and there aren't a lot of visitors. According to Farrell, this makes it very suitable for carrying out a trial. Usually, it seems, in rather primitive communities, there's a difficulty in maintaining adequate control over your patients. They tend to wander out of the area. A more or less isolated community is pretty well ideal from this point of view."

"Yes." I could see the attraction of the idea. It was an attempt to bring a clinical study within measurable distance of a controlled laboratory experiment. On the other hand, there might be disadvantages in working in a little hothouse of this kind.

"So Martin wants to go out there?"

"He *is* out there," said Stratton morosely. "He's been out for three months."

"You gave permission?"

"No, we didn't. That's the whole point." Seeing the surprise on my face, he went on, "Yes, you don't have to tell me it's all most irregular. Ordinarily, of course, when somebody comes here with a proposition of that kind, we're in a position to call the tune. But in this case, through no fault of ours, things have got entirely out of hand."

"How was that?"

"Interference," said Stratton bitterly, champing hard on his pipe. "That's what causes ninety per cent of our troubles. When people who don't understand begin trying to cut corners—" He stopped himself. "But I mustn't get annoyed. It doesn't really help. When Farrell first approached me, he did so in a perfectly proper and usual way. He described what he wanted to do and asked for our support. That is, he wanted co-operation from our district medical officer on Batou—use of hospital facilities, and so on. He also wanted financial support, but I gathered he could manage without that, at a pinch. He has backing from some German drug company called Chemiefabriken."

"Are they making the vaccine for him?"

"So I believe. Presumably they hope to make money out of it, if it works. I suppose," he said, without real conviction, "that there's no harm in that. But one aspect of the proposition bothered me a good deal. He said the trial would have to be double blind."

"Double blind?" I was surprised. Blind trials are a device to eliminate unconscious bias when testing out a drug. They involve treating one group of patients with the drug and another with an inert substance made up to appear identical with it. In an ordinary blind trial the patient does not know which substance he is receiving. In exceptional circumstances there may be reasons why this information is better withheld even from the doctor himself. This is known as a double blind. It sounded like an ambitious approach for a trial like this.

"I must say," said Stratton, "that though I'm no expert in this field, it seemed to me a rather unnecessary refinement. I should have thought there were enough difficulties already in a place like Batou without adding complications."

"That's true," I agreed. "On the other hand"—I was trying to see it from Martin's point of view—"if this stuff is good, it's bound to attract a lot of attention. People will be trying to pick holes in the results. If he does it double blind, he couldn't cheat even if he wanted to. He's unassailable."

Stratton thought it over for a moment. "I suppose that might be the answer," he admitted finally. Then he shrugged these technicalities aside. "However, as I told him, it was not for me, as an individual, to make any decision. I explained the drill to him. He'd have to present his idea to the Clinical Research Committee, which would pass it on to the Subcommittee for Encephalitis. I explained that we should want fifteen copies of everything —protocols, animal pharmacology, human pharmacology, background of laboratory research, and full details of his proposals. He was a bit impatient about that, but I explained to him that it was nothing to do with me—I was just a servant of the committee. Then he said, rather rudely, I thought, that supposing he produced all this bumf, how soon could he get permission to go ahead? Naturally, I said—"

I could have repeated this kind of conversation in my sleep. "—that you couldn't anticipate the decision of the committee."

"Exactly. However, I felt I ought to tell him that several members of the committee were abroad at that time and might not be back for several months." I could imagine Stratton threading his way happily through the maze of procedure, enjoying giving this irritable young man a lesson in patience. "After that, it was up to them. There were a lot of items on the agenda. However, I hoped that they might reach his proposals at a first meeting. He said, supposing they didn't? I said, well, that would probably mean holding it over for another six weeks or so. At that stage they might give a definite decision for or against—or, then again, they might refer some part of the scheme for a specialist's opinion—" He stopped and shook his head with the expression of a man remembering a bewildering experience. "Then he walked out."

"Did he say anything?"

"Nothing at all. He just picked up his papers and walked out of the door. Appalling bad manners."

He looked up at me, as if expecting some formal demonstration of agreement. I tried to arrange my features into a grave but essentially noncommittal expression. Something in Stratton's manner told me I had not been successful.

"Anyway," he went on testily, "that was how I looked at it. It was the end of the matter so far as I was concerned. I wasn't going to get in touch with him again after that. It was up to him to send in his protocols. I regarded the whole question as closed."

He added with sudden bitterness, "And so it would have been if it hadn't been for that old so-and-so Hackett."

"Sir Francis?"

"Yes."

Since Hackett had first taken up Martin, he had acquired a knighthood and a seat on innumerable committees. He had also, so far as I knew, done no significant laboratory work for at least five years. As a virologist he was no longer taken seriously by the modern generation. But he was a man of great charm and sudden wild enthusiasms. He had a reputation of interfering, in the most amiable possible way, with all kinds of matters that were none of his business.

"I must say," I said rather apologetically, "I can't help liking the old boy."

"Oh, yes," said Stratton bitterly. "I'm sure you do. Everybody likes him. But the fact remains that he's got himself, and us too, into a fearful mess."

"How does he come into it?"

"He's the chairman of the Encephalitis Committee. When your friend Farrell"—he spoke with venom, and as if I, by my previous acquaintance with Martin, could hardly escape some part of the blame—"when your friend Farrell left me he decided to get in touch with Sir Francis. The long and the short of it is that he seems to have hypnotized the old boy. After a while he had him agreeing that it was out of the question for him to be held up waiting for an official decision. In the end, Sir Francis told him to go out and get started and he'd square it with the others. He wrote to the authorities in Batou, asking them to give the fullest co-operation. In other words," he said, as if even now hardly able to believe the enormity of the offense, "he bypassed his own committee."

"And so?"

"His chickens have come to roost." Stratton laughed sharply. Under his exasperation there was a note of triumph. He looked at his watch. "Are you free for lunch?"

"Yes."

"I'm due to meet Harold Bainbridge in about ten minutes at my club, and I'd very much appreciate it if you could come along and have lunch with us. He can tell you something about the further developments. Very disturbing they are too, I may say."

He got up and plucked his umbrella from a little stand next to the fireplace. "If only people would realize," he grumbled as we went out, "that procedure, no matter how time-consuming it may seem to an outsider, is there for a *purpose. . . .*"

2

AS we walked across the Mall to Stratton's club, he said, "Do you know Bainbridge?"

"Not personally. I remember he once came and gave a lecture when I was at Breckenhall. About the Spanish Civil War."

He nodded understandingly, "Pro-Franco?"

"Yes. Of course, that was nearly twenty years ago." Though I didn't suppose he had changed. Any more than the Jesuits at Breckenhall would have changed. The old hysteria of the civil-war days was long since gone. Through the difficult years of World War II they had waited patiently, saying little but always utterly convinced of being in the right, until the pendulum swung back again, as indeed it was already doing. The smoke of Hitler and Mussolini had cleared away, and we were back to what they considered the fundamental conflict—of Christians versus Reds. In this context Franco, for all his faults, was a Catholic and a gentleman. Not perhaps in quite the same sense that Robert Bainbridge, M.P., was a Catholic and a gentleman, but they had some common ground. Bainbridge had actually spent several months in Spain, and claimed to know what he was talking about. All this talk of atrocities by the insurgents was just Communist propaganda, he asserted. The Moors—well, perhaps they had a tendency to loot, nothing more than that. It was unavoidable with native troops. As for the other side—he couldn't bring himself to sully the ears of young Catholic boys with stories of the things they had done. However, it ought to be more generally known, and for the instruction of the older boys he was donating a book to the upper-school library that would be available for reference by serious students of politics. We could read that, and judge for ourselves.

I had been impressed by Bainbridge. He was transparently sincere, and I am sure he made a big impression on his lecture tour. Unfortunately for him, events moved against him. Mussolini, in particular, let him down badly. World War II began, and that was the end of Bainbridge's political career. He had been a backbencher ever since.

"He's a decent old chap," said Stratton, "and I'm sure he doesn't want to make any trouble. But these damn priests have got hold of him."

"Oh?"

"Yes. It seems that on Batou there's a Jesuit priest called Father de Freitas. Most of the people are Catholics, and he's an influential figure. So far as we can gather, he and Farrell have got across with each other. Now he's written to Bainbridge complaining that the vaccine's dangerous. He claims it's knocked off two of his parishioners."

We had reached the club by this time, and as I walked into the hall I recognized Bainbridge standing by a notice board. He looked smaller than he had twenty years ago. His hair was white now, and his face appeared to have changed shape—false teeth, probably. But he was erect and red-faced, more like a distinguished soldier than an undistinguished businessman and politician.

Stratton introduced us, and then took us fussily up to the dining room. I told Bainbridge that I remembered his lecture at Breckenhall. He seemed pleased. "I still stand by what I said then," he said. "I always have done. Never made any secret of it. Didn't do me any good politically, of course—but I can't help that." He didn't seem much concerned. "Now they're beginning to see sense again. The trouble with those Left Wingers is that they're obsessed by economics. So long as a man waves a red flag and talks

* 19 *

about public ownership of industry, he can murder his grandmother, so far as they're concerned."

Stratton looked at me nervously. He had no idea what my political views were, but was obviously anxious that I shouldn't upset the old man by starting an argument. Bainbridge's goodwill was evidently important. I gave him a reassuring glance. Bainbridge became increasingly benign under the influence of a bottle of Burgundy (the food, as always in that particular club, was execrable). He held forth on general matters for some time. Then, when there was a slight pause in the conversation, he turned to me and said, "I gather from Stratton that you're able to help us out with this business on Batou?"

I made a noncommittal sound. So far, no proposition had been made to me. Stratton was busy chasing a piece of gooseberry tart onto his spoon. After he had trapped it successfully, he looked up and said, "I haven't yet given the full details of your—ah—suggestion to Dr. Mayne."

There was a reproachful expression on his face, as if he found Bainbridge somewhat lacking in finesse. Presumably the idea of the luncheon was that I should be brought along for Bainbridge's inspection and approval before being asked to do whatever it was they wanted of me. I could see that, as far as Bainbridge was concerned, I had passed. He wanted to get down to business right away.

"Perhaps I'd better explain the situation," he said to me. "Have you heard about this letter I received?"

"Stratton mentioned it to me."

"You might like to read it."

He took a letter out of his pocket and handed it to me. It was written in a rather precise, spidery hand, and from the way it was phrased I guessed that Father de Freitas had spent a long time and a great deal of care composing it. He began by introducing himself, and reminding Bainbridge of an occasion a year or two ago when they had met at some function organized by the Catholic Truth Society. He wrote stiffly and with dignity, making no attempt to enlist support by flattery. His case was fairly simple.

He was the parish priest of a remote village on Batou named Cajara. Dr. Farrell had come with a team of workers and proceeded to vaccinate several hundreds of his parishioners. Two of these people had since died. So far as he could find out, no post-mortems had been carried out and no official explanation had been given as to the cause of death. Attempts to elicit further information had been unsuccessful. Dr. Farrell had been offhand and unco-operative. He was not (he was very careful to emphasize) inferring that these deaths had necessarily been caused by the vaccine; he was not qualified to make any statement on a purely medical question. But the people were growing concerned, and he believed there was at least prima-facie evidence for investigation into the matter. Having received no help from the authorities on the island, he felt he had no alternative, etc., etc.

I handed the letter back to Bainbridge and said, "Of course, there may be nothing in this."

"I quite realize that. As a Member of Parliament I have a pretty wide experience of crackpots. But I don't see how we can just let it go."

"No—obviously not." I thought for a moment. "Is anything known about de Freitas?"

"Not a lot. He's been out there for some years. I've been in touch with the Jesuits here and they say he's a very levelheaded fellow. But then they tend to stick together, as of course you know." He added gloomily, "They're liable to pester the life out of me if we don't give them some sort of an assurance that all's well."

"Which we can hardly do in our present state of knowledge," said Stratton. "The truth is that we don't really know what Farrell's up to. Now, if the plan for the trial had been passed through the committee in the usual way. . . . However, there's no use crying over spilled milk. The question is what to do now. Mr. Bainbridge and I think it's essential that somebody should go out to Batou immediately to make an assessment of the position."

"I see." I was not surprised. I would have been stupid not to see it coming. "You want me to go?"

Stratton nodded urgently. "You're the obvious person. You seem to know a lot about this form of encephalitis."

"There are a great many people who know more."

"Possibly. But this isn't just a question of assessing a disease. There's obviously a big personal element. It's liable to need considerable tact and understanding. Now, you know Farrell. It's true you don't know de Freitas, but at least you have some experience of the Jesuits. . . ."

I said reluctantly, "Farrell was a good friend of mine at one time. It might be embarrassing—"

"Well, I can't see that—"

"I can," said Bainbridge suddenly. My heart went out to him at that moment. No doubt he was sententious and out of date, but he understood about certain things—things like honor and loyalty and the value of old friendships. "But I still think you should go. We're not asking you to spy on the fellow. It's all perfectly aboveboard. We're not hostile to him. We just need to know the facts, that's all. You can explain that. He'd probably prefer it to be somebody he knows. . . ." When I said nothing, he went on, "We can give you a few hours to think it over, but I ought to reply to this letter tomorrow." He looked at his watch. "It's time I was back at the House."

As we walked out, Stratton stopped at the cash desk to pay the bill, and for a few moments I was left with Bainbridge alone. He took my arm and said confidentially, "I'm sorry to wish this job on you, my boy." I could think of nothing suitable to say in reply to this, particularly as I had not yet committed myself to accepting. He went on in the same apologetic tone. "You know how it is with these Jesuits. I couldn't say so in front of Stratton, but they can be the most confounded nuisance. Too intense altogether. After all," he said querulously, "why write to me? Just because I'm a Catholic doesn't mean that I'm the political mouthpiece of the whole Society of Jesus. I'm the member for Dinsdale South, not Farm Street. Why me? But nowadays everything's Catholicism. It's all these damn converts. . . ." He lowered his voice. "Do you know," he said, "the other day some confounded fellow came sidling up to me and said in a whisper, 'I hear you're one of us.' As if I was a member of some blasted secret society. And the J.'s encourage it," he asserted with indignation. "Sometimes I think they actually *prefer* converts. . . ."

"Well?" said Stratton. We were back in his office. "How do you feel about it?"

I really wasn't sure. I hedged, "Of course, it's partly up to Mackenzie."

"He's quite agreeable to your going. I asked him before." Naturally he would have done. "We can't do more than ask you to do this, but I can assure you it would be regarded as a great favor. It would get us out of a very difficult position."

He seemed to me to be taking the matter rather too much to heart. "At least your department's in the clear," I pointed out. "Nobody can blame you."

Stratton sighed and picked at his scalp. "Mayne, when you've been in the Service as long as I have, you'll realize that it doesn't pay to be associated with trouble, no matter how blameless you are personally. The time comes when the people on top get tired of trying to find out who's at fault, and give everybody a kick in the pants, regardless. Sir Francis Hackett may be a bloody old fool, but he's a big name and has a lot of important friends. I'm afraid we've got to cover him."

There was something I wanted to know badly but I did not want to ask Stratton directly. "Is there anyone else," I asked, "out there with Farrell?"

"He hasn't taken a team with him, if that's what you mean." It wasn't, in fact, what I meant. "The local senior medical officer is a man called Das. He's half-Indian. A very good man, quite young but very keen and conscientious, so our people say. He's very much on Farrell's side and has been helping him with the trial. We got in touch with him and he says there's nothing to worry about. We've also written to these Chemiefabriken people, incidentally. I have a letter from a Dr. Grune, which I'll show you. Not surprisingly, he says the stuff's as safe as houses. He keeps referring to some long-term toxicity studies in chimpanzees. That's all very well, but chimps are one thing and men are another, as I think you'll agree—"

I agreed. "As a general principle—"

"Of course," said Stratton, anxious to be accurate, "I haven't any definite information as to how much he's mixed up with these Germans. It's just a guess that they're financing him. He may have money of his own."

I shook my head. "He hadn't when I knew him."

Stratton glanced down at the notes on his desk. "His wife," he said carelessly, "is said to have inherited thirty thousand pounds about five years ago."

"Really?" I did my best, but I had a suspicion that my voice didn't sound entirely natural. I felt my palms sweating slightly as I gripped the arms of my chair. But even if I was giving myself away, I had to ask the next question. "Is she out there with him?"

"Yes." He looked up at me. "You know her?"

"Yes."

"Well?"

"Fairly well."

I was doing fine. Stratton closed the file in front of him and gave a yawn. It came to me that he wasn't watching my reactions. He wasn't really interested. "I hate drinking wine at lunch," he said. "It puts me to sleep in the afternoon. Well—can I take it that you agree to go?"

3

*

*

*

*

*

*

I agreed, in the end. I had a suspicion that it would be wiser to refuse, but I was not feeling particularly prudent at that time, and the truth is that I wanted to go to Batou. The job sounded interesting, but it was not only that. Talking about Martin had made me realize how much I had always secretly longed to meet him again, to see him as he was now, a mature man with success and achievement behind him. And to see Barbara too. For the sake of that I was prepared to take a chance on arousing old and painful memories.

Most of my memories of Martin were painful in some way or other, and our first meeting had perhaps been an appropriate beginning to our relationship. We had found ourselves together outside the room of Father Brewer, the First Prefect at Breckenhall, waiting to be beaten. At that time we knew each other only by sight. He was a year older than I was, and that makes a lot of difference at school. I had seen him walking up and down the corridors with his friends, hands in pockets, to my eye immeasurably adult and distinguished, wrapped in the aristocracy of age. He was a tall, fair boy and had been fortunate enough to escape most of the defacements of adolescents. He had no pimples and his hair, unlike mine, stayed flat on his head instead of rising in ungovernable spikes. I was somewhat in awe of him.

I was afraid of being hurt, and I was conscious that the smile on my face was a little sickly. I rested my hands dejectedly on the hot-water pipes that ran along the wall. Martin regarded me with amusement.

"It's no use sticking your hands on the pipes," he said contemptuously. "They aren't even hot."

He was quite right, of course. There was a strongly held theory that heating up one's hands before a beating had a valuable anesthetic action, and it was customary to use the pipes for this purpose. In summer the heating was turned off, but curiously enough we still used to rest our hands against the pipes—on the grounds, I suppose, that it is always pleasanter in a trying situation to do something, however senseless, than to do nothing.

I explained this to Martin. Or, rather, I said, defensively, "Have you any better ideas?"

I little realized what a challenging question that was to a person of his temperament.

"As a matter of fact I have," he said with enormous confidence. When I looked doubtful, he said, "I got it out of a book. It's the method those Indian chaps use when they lie down on beds of nails. It works too. This isn't going to hurt me a bit."

"What do you do?"

"There's hardly time for you. Old Boozer should be along here in a minute or two. You need much longer than that. Still, you can do part of it. Just breathe deeply in and out. Let your shoulders go slack. Try to imagine that your hands don't belong to you at all."

I tried. I breathed. I slumped forward, dangling my arms. Martin did it with me, to show me how, and we must have presented a curious spectacle. Then Martin went in for his dozen. I heard the cracks, like pistol shots, very fast, in four groups of three. He came out, debonair as ever, with a thin, contemptuous smile on his face. Yet his lips, it seemed to me, were a little pale. . . . I went in myself. The room smelled, as always, of dust, leather, cricket-bat oil, and pipe smoke. Father Brewer stood just around the corner of the door, a grim black figure, holding his weapon down at his right side, behind a fold of his gown. I said, "A dozen please, Father. Ordered by Mr. Felloes." He gave no sign of recognition. He just reached out with his left hand and took hold of my wrist. I tried to relax, to breathe deeply, to pretend it was not my hand he was holding. Then I heard a swishing through the air, and all my instructions were forgotten.

When I walked out, Martin was leaning against the wall, waiting for me.

"Did it work?" he asked.

I shook my head. My hands were hurting very badly and felt the size of boxing gloves. But he seemed genuinely interested and I didn't like to disappoint him. "I don't think so," I said.

"No? Well, you didn't really have long enough, did you?" He thought for a moment. "Also, it isn't too easy to be sure. I mean, it might have hurt a good deal more if you hadn't done anything." It was perhaps his first encounter with that major bugbear of the scientist, the valid standard of comparison.

"Did it work with you?"

"Oh, Lord, yes." He showed me his hands. The palms were livid and already heavily swollen; the deep-black bruises were beginning to appear around the fleshy part of the thumb. "I just don't feel a thing." He pressed his finger against the bruised area to show how anesthetic it was. I should have liked to have carried the experiment further and had a little squeeze myself, but I felt I hardly knew him well enough to suggest it, and he made no sign of inviting me. Even so, I was impressed.

It was a beautiful summer evening, and the rest of the school had gone out to the cricket fields. As we walked out to join the others, we talked idly and pleasantly, drawn together by a shared experience. I have no idea what we talked about, and it was probably nothing of any significance. But the ice was broken. When we came across each other after that, instead of passing by we would smile or even sometimes stop and chat. I was attracted by his liveliness and ease of manner. What attracted him to me I cannot say. I was a shy and diffident boy, without, so far as I can recollect, much in the way of personality. I was always a little surprised when people liked me.

At the end of that term I did well in my examinations, and when I came back in the autumn I was promoted. I found myself in the same class as Martin. After that, I began to see a good deal more of him, and our acquaintance developed very rapidly. It was as if from the start we filled some need in each other. I discovered, to my surprise, that he had few close friends among the boys of his own year. He had a reputation of being difficult to get on with.

I suppose that was because he was dogmatic and argumentative. He was accused of "showing off." He was, I soon discovered, ill at ease in any conversation he could not dominate. But I had no objection to this. I had no compulsion to assert myself for the sheer sake of it, and I found him entertaining. I was attracted by the violence of his personality and the luxuriance of his ideas. In return he developed a certain proprietary affection for me. He had discovered me, and regarded me, in a sense, as a sort of possession of his. He introduced into my life an element of adventure, which I have always craved but usually lacked the initiative to discover for myself. It was mainly an intellectual rebellion, a revolt against established ideas of all kinds. Looking back, there is nothing very revolutionary in what we thought and declared. Indeed, many of our ideas have since been accepted and become just as dull and ossified as the old ones they displaced, while others have been tried and rejected as naïve oversimplification. Another generation has come up and is, in turn, reacting fiercely against accepted beliefs. And here am I, the rebel of yesteryear, a member of the so-called Establishment. . . .

But my own resistance to authority was to some extent a sham. Martin's was genuine and deep-rooted. He was in revolt, not only against authority, but against the complexity of human affairs as a whole. The people who enraged him most were those who said, "Ah, but it's not as simple as all that." He believed passionately that, given a little goodwill, things could be as simple as all that. If they were not, it could only be explained by sheer malevolence and obstructiveness on somebody's part. He had the greatest difficulty in adjusting himself to the idea of an honest disagreement.

Always he was searching for the rapid, violent solution of a problem, the short cut. He saw himself as Alexander, sword in hand, looking for a Gordian knot to chop across. Though filled with limitless skepticism by the pronouncements of authority, he was in many ways a very credulous person. He would believe almost anything that supported his own conception of life. He was wide open to dubious advertisements and travelling salesmen. He was perpetually sending postal orders to organizations that undertook to teach idiomatic Spanish on gramophone records in three months, with a money-back guarantee, or sold government-surplus binoculars, by post, at half price. His vision of the world was expansive. Why shouldn't there be something just around the corner to solve all our problems? Why shouldn't there be some method, so absurdly obvious that all the old gang, the shiny-bottomed second-degree pimps ("pimp" was a very fashionable word at Breckenhall around that time), simply hadn't the vision to see, by which you could stop unemployment, or cure cancer, or devise a fountain pen that never needed refilling with ink?

Once converted to a proposition himself, Martin felt a compelling necessity to pass his convictions on to others. His air of absolute certainty (together with a certain carelessness in mentioning the arguments adverse to his case) made him most convincing to a person such as myself. Being of a cautious and precise disposition, I never made categorical statements myself unless I was certain they were right. One always tends to assume that others are governed by the same inhibitions as oneself, and when Martin swore that something was so, even if it sounded surprising to me, I tended to believe him.

It was perhaps inevitable that this general attitude of resistance should eventually become directed into some particular channel. The great event of my schooldays was the Spanish Civil War. The Jesuits felt personally involved and were determined to make us feel personally involved also. In addition to this there were the refugees. These were not refugees of the kind to which we have become so regrettably accustomed since. They were the sons of wealthy Spanish families who had been forced to evacuate their homes by the fighting, and had consequently been sent over to England to finish their education. I suppose there were about thirty or forty of them. Some spoke English well, some hardly at all. With the South Americans, they formed a little community of their own. They felt proud and important about the civil war in their country and talked of it with a certain lofty *expertise*. Some of them had grandiose titles, which impressed the masters, and at least one used to go back to Spain every summer holiday and fight on the Bilbao front. Or so he claimed. He used to show us a khaki drill uniform with exotic badges on it, and during the summer holidays his friends would be delighted to receive letters from him stamped "Passed by Censor" and inscribed "Viva Franco Viva Franco" all over the envelope.

Martin's reaction to all this was inevitable. He declared openly, to anyone who would listen, that the war was the outcome of a Fascist conspiracy and the refugees a collection of phonies. He was not totally devoid of support—nobody much liked the refugees, and there was a body of opinion, basically non-political, which distrusted Franco on the ground that if the J.'s were so heartily in favor of a man, there must, in the nature of things, be something wrong with him. Even among the Jesuits themselves there was a faction that regarded Martin, if not with approval, at least with indulgence. They had some experience of obstreperous young men and felt that he would grow out of it in time. Also, he had a certain prestige socially. His father was a director of a firm of merchant bankers in the City, and lived in considerable luxury. He kept up a flat in town, and a country house in Sussex. More important still, he had artistic pretensions and a wide acquaintance among current celebrities. He had entertained at one time and another such figures as Chesterton, Belloc, Baring, and Wyndham Lewis. In spite of their very restrictive vows, the Jesuits were not above being impressed by worldly distinction.

I went to stay with Martin at Fernfield House during one summer holiday. It was a rambling place with a great many unexplained rooms, and I particularly remember a large drawing room opening onto a terrace. There was also a green baize door leading to the servants' quarters, and this perhaps impressed me most of all. My father was a G.P. in a northern industrial town. We had only one maid, and it was usual to go into the kitchen to shout for her, rather than hurt her feelings by ringing the bell. I was thoroughly intimidated to find that the Farrells actually employed a butler.

That was only a few months before the catastrophe. Looking back, I have tried to remember whether Mr. Farrell showed at that time any sign that all was not well, but I think the truth is that I did not observe him very closely. I have a picture of a tall, stooping man with a mustache, soft-voiced and polite, but very busy and with little time for us. I envied Martin, thinking how wonderful it would be to have such a rich, distinguished, and above all unobtrusive parent; my own mother and father embarrassed me by what I considered an excessive interest in my affairs. Mr. Farrell was a widower, and one of his sisters, a colorless, fussy woman, acted as housekeeper. Both Martin and his father regarded her with barely concealed contempt.

During that summer the talk was mostly of careers. We should be leaving Breckenhall shortly and it was becoming necessary to decide what we wanted to do afterward. There was not very much to discuss as far as I was concerned. By both tradition and inclination, I was obviously cut out for medicine. At that time Martin regarded this as a prosaic ambition. While of an experimental turn of mind, his interests lay mainly along the lines of experimenting with his own life. He was not sure what he was going to do, but it would certainly be something rather unusual. Fortunately he was not so dependent on earning money as I was. He would probably go to Oxford, make a name for himself in some way or other, perhaps at the Union, perhaps in literary circles. He had the brains and, through his father, some very useful connections. He might end up in Journalism, the law, politics, wherever his fancy led and the opportunity offered. A man of ability, he propounded, should not be too hidebound with plans for the future—he should be an opportunist. To have everything laid out ahead as I had—medical school, hospital, qualification, house jobs, then a partnership in my father's practice—was altogether too dreary for a person of his (and, he implied, my) potentialities.

He began to worry me after a time. I was desperately anxious to live up to his flattering opinion of me, but I didn't see offhand what I could do about it. I went back for the winter term like a novice troubled by doubts about his vocation. But within a short time the pressure of events drove my own problems completely out of my head.

Martin's hostility to what he referred to as "Fascist propaganda" had been becoming increasingly vocal as time went by, and recently he had begun to refer darkly to the possibility of some form of direct action. His first attempt at this came as a result of Bainbridge's lecture. As I have said, I was impressed by the lecture, and so were most of the others. Martin was not. He even made one or two violent attempts at heckling, which were suppressed with almost contemptuous ease by the First Prefect.

After the lecture, Bainbridge's book appeared in the school library. It was a striking red-and-yellow paperback production entitled *Communist Atrocities in Spain: A Factual Account*. It contained descriptions of a series of rapes, tortures, crucifixions, disembowellings, and so on, unrivalled since the publication of the Lives of the Saints. For several months it was the most sought-after book in the library. Even the "Prostitution" section in the Encyclopædia Britannica (an old favorite) was pushed temporarily into second place.

"Of course, you appreciate," said Martin loftily, "that it's all a pack of lies."

"Even the photographs?"

"Of course. It's terribly easy to fake photographs, you know. I was talking to a journalist who came down to Fernfield last holidays. He knew all about this book. You know all those raped nuns? They just dressed up prostitutes in black habits, chucked red ink on them, sprawled them on the ground, and took pictures of them. Too easy."

I thought for a moment. "Why prostitutes?" I said.

He shrugged his shoulders impatiently. "Well, really, if you can't see *that*—"

I couldn't, but I was too much under his influence to argue about it, and put it down to my own lack of knowledge of the world. I was ill equipped to argue with someone who was on conversational terms with knowledgeable journalists from Fleet Street. And it may well be that he was right. There was no doubt that he did hear a great deal from his father's friends. But it is also possible that he succumbed to a temptation to round a story off by adding a few details from his own imagination, particularly when he was anxious to prove a point, as a policeman might plant a little stolen property in a burglar's house before arresting him, just to make absolutely sure.

A few weeks later, Martin hit back. An anonymous work began to circulate privately among his friends, entitled, "An Account of the Atrocities Committed by the Athenians Against the Helpless Spartans During the Peloponnesian War." It was rather badly typed, and bound in an ordinary buff folder. Perhaps nowadays I should think it poor stuff, its style derivative, its violence synthetic, even its obscenity a little naïve. But it attracted a good deal of attention at the time. It was regarded as a very dangerous document, if it should come into the hands of authority. The authorship could hardly be in doubt. Everybody knew that Martin was the possessor of a typewriter, and had been hammering away at it every evening in the seclusion of his room for several weeks.

One morning, Martin failed to appear in class. He had been seen at chapel and at breakfast, looking and behaving quite normally, and so was presumably not ill. He was absent all morning and (an ominous point) his class master made no comment on the fact. Evidently the J.'s knew why he had disappeared. Throughout the day excitement mounted. A public school is like a prison at least in this respect—any disturbance of routine, any unexplained incident reverberates through a closed, bored community, leading to reaction totally out of proportion to its importance. Discussion was rife. The most popular view was that Martin's atrocity book had finally been discovered, and that the J.'s were holding him incommunicado in the sanatorium, a habit they had when anxious to extract a confession.

We were wrong, as it turned out. When I went to my room after supper that evening, I found Martin there. He was standing by the windows, looking out onto the quadrangle in what I can see now as a consciously dramatic posture. He was wearing his best suit, which in itself made him look strange. Most of the time we all wore sports coats and slacks, but it was customary to keep a formal suit for special days, visits of parents, going home, and so on. One's best suit was so often associated with outside events that the fact of putting it on seemed always to separate one from the college. My first reaction was to wonder if Martin had been expelled.

"What happened?" I asked. "Where have you been all day?"

"In the san." His face was pale and his voice curiously flat, as it often was when he was in trouble. He made a wretched attempt at a smile.

"Was it the atrocity book?"

He looked at me as if he had no idea what I was talking about. Then he seemed to remember. He gave a short laugh. "Oh, God, no. Nothing like that." It was as if he despised me for thinking of anything so trivial.

"That was what everyone thought," I said defensively. But he hardly seemed to hear me. He was totally preoccupied with his own position.

"My father's dead," he said.

"Oh, I say, I'm dreadfully sorry—"

"He committed suicide."

"God!" Boys are not very sympathetic at heart, and my reaction to the news was a mixture of acute embarrassment and fascination. I had not known Martin's father well enough to feel any personal sorrow. "How?" I asked.

"He shot himself last night." Martin gave the words every

ounce of tight-lipped drama they could carry. The fact that he did so was no indication that he felt less or more about his father than anyone else might have done. It was simply his instinctive way of reacting to a situation.

I could not help being impressed. I had known bereavement myself but always in a more prosaic context. Members of my family tended to die of diseases like dropsy, or to have strokes while sitting on the lavatory. None of them had ever taken his exit in such a dashing way as this.

"Of course," said Martin, "he and I hadn't very much in common." He spoke rather loftily and I knew now how he had decided to take it—very scientific and detached. "As you know, he was a liberal intellectual of the old school."

I nodded, though it was not how I had thought of Mr. Farrell. I had been far too much in awe of his wealth and position and assurance of manner to take up such a patronizing attitude.

"I won't deny that I was fond of him, but we tended to live our own lives, you know." I might have been interviewing him for a newspaper. But I could see that he was giving the story not to me but to himself. "He allowed me a great deal of freedom. I shall always be enormously grateful for that. Life at Fernfield was an education in itself—far more so than here." He gave a shrug of the shoulders. "Anyway, that's all over now."

"All over?"

"Yes. It seems there isn't any money any more." He was managing to maintain the same rather clinical detachment, but only just, I thought. His mind was to some extent adjusted to the idea of a life without his father. The possibility of a life without money had never entered his head. "So far as I can gather," he said vaguely, "something disastrous happened at the bank—I'm not quite sure what. I think they invested in some dud securities or something. Anyway, the upshot of it is that we're bust."

"Perhaps it won't be as bad as all that."

"Oh, it's definite, all right. I've spoken to my father's partner, McEnnery, on the telephone. I've arranged to take the first train home tomorrow morning. The Rector suggested that I should sleep over in the san—I didn't want to meet a lot of people who'd ask questions. But I wanted to see you before I left." There was an awkward pause. Then he said, "It's quite likely that we may not see each other again."

"Oh, surely not. I mean, you'll be coming back, won't you—?" I could hardly believe the financial position could be as bad as that. He had, after all, only a year or so to go at school.

"I doubt it. Even if we can afford it, I can't really see much point in coming back." He burst out angrily, "All this public-school and Oxford business is a lot of damned nonsense anyway. It never did have much relation to reality. But to a generation like ours, living all the time under the threat of a Second World War—"

He became rhetorical. In the thirties, as in the fifties, it was fashionable for youthful rebellion to take the form of a resentful, rather humorless self-pity. The time was out of joint, and the various painful attempts at reduction without anesthesia were not reassuring to us. We tended to regard ourselves, in our gloomier moments, as impotent victims of an impending blood sacrifice. Martin had always been a strong proponent of this way of thinking. Now he had the stimulus of being literally as well as figuratively disinherited.

"Then what will you do?" I asked.

He looked evasive. It seemed to me that he had some plan in his mind which he was not yet ready to discuss. "I'm not sure just yet. It will depend to some extent on conditions at home. I shall probably write and let you know when I've made up my mind."

4

❁

❁

❁

❁

❁

❁

A week later I received a letter from him.

Fernfield House,
Wednesday.

My dear Peter,

Things here are pretty much as I expected. Fernfield is like a Wailing Wall. Aunt Alice is running around bleating like a startled sheep, and McEnnery is also here, trying to restore some order into the family finances. Each morning he takes me for a quiet talk in my father's study, to give me some depressing tidbit of news. When he has finished, he sighs heavily and says, "It's a ba-ad business—a ba-ad business. But we've just got to grit our teeth." Yesterday I had a row with him. I told him that I was sick of gritting my teeth, and that I didn't give a damn about the money since in my opinion the capitalist system was doomed anyway, and that I looked forward to the day when chartered accountants would be hanging from lampposts down the length and breadth of the City. I hoped this would send him away, but he seems determined to save me in spite of myself, and he is trying to work out some sort of trust fund so that I can finish my education. He is even trying to enlist the co-operation of the J.'s in this project. As you can imagine, I have not the slightest intention of accepting charity from *them,* and have told him so.

The whole idea is stupid, of course. I refuse to be salvaged in this dreary fashion. The great advantage to be gained from this disaster is that it is now relatively easy for me to break away from the bourgeois pattern of life. The university of our time is not Oxford or Cambridge—it is Spain. And I intend to go there. If that pimp Romirez is old enough to fight for the Fascists, they should take me in the International Brigade.

Needless to say, I haven't told Aunt Alice or McEnnery about this, since they would prevent me going. I have agreed to come back to Breckenhall, but when I change trains in London I shall take the boat train for France. I have a passport and some money.

By the time you receive this I shall already have made my escape. However, I know I do not need to emphasize to you the importance of the *utmost secrecy*, especially with regard to the J.'s. Please tell nobody that you have received any communication from me, and destroy this letter immediately.

Martin.

I did not destroy it, of course. I have the letter in front of me as I write. It would have required more self-discipline than I possessed to do away with such a dramatic document. I simply hid it as effectively as I could, and waited for further developments.

They were not long in coming. Only forty-eight hours later, as we were filing out after early-morning Mass, I found my path blocked by the First Prefect. He smiled at me. He was a big, bluff man and he smiled all the time, whether there was anything to amuse him or not. His conversation was punctuated by loud, pealing laughs. Parents were always reassured by him. He seemed such a jolly, benevolent, well-fed fellow, a sort of Friar Tuck. He said, "Peter." He was one of the few J.'s who ever called us by our Christian names. This also had a favorable effect on parents. "I just want to talk to you for a moment." He wagged a finger and I followed him into one of the bays off the main corridor. We were suddenly very close together. I could smell the odor of tobacco clinging to his gown. He pushed his hands into his sleeves and leaned up against the wall, regarding me closely. He had stopped smiling now, and that seemed to me particularly alarming.

"Have you any news of Martin Farrell?" he said.

I had anticipated an ordeal of this kind, but even so I had not finally made up my mind what my response should be. When it came to the point, only the simplest seemed at all feasible. "No," I said.

"No?" The First Prefect's eyebrows went up almost to the top of his head. "Come, come, Peter. If I'm not mistaken, you received a letter from him a day or two ago." He always handed out the letters himself, calling out the names in alphabetical order, at the beginning of the midmorning break. He might easily have recognized Martin's handwriting. "Isn't that so?"

I shook my head. Around the corner of the corridor I could hear the sound of the boys clattering across the wooden floor outside the chapel toward the dining room, interspersed with a sort of thumping noise as some of them genuflected before the Lady Statue; it wasn't compulsory to do so, but showed devotion. I was a hundred miles away from them now. The noise died away as the last boy went into the refectory and closed the door behind him.

The First Prefect was saying, "I didn't think you would lie to me, Peter."

This was humbug. He must have known that all the boys lied to him whenever they thought they had a chance of getting away with it. I said nothing.

"Haven't you anything to say?" I shook my head again. "I know you received the letter. I haven't even asked you to tell me what was in it. I don't understand why you're taking up this attitude."

I was conscious myself that it was not a very dignified attitude. What I should have done, in theory, was to admit receiving the letter but refuse to disclose its contents on the ground that they were private. But I was only sixteen. At that age it is not easy to take a stand on a matter of principle. Lying comes more naturally.

"It's possible," he said, "that you may be taking the view that it's no business of ours what he wrote to you. Well, as it happens, it is. Martin has run away from home. His guardians are in a state of great anxiety—as you can imagine, particularly in view of the trouble they've had recently. It's even possible that his father's death may have unbalanced his mind." He paused for a moment to allow this to sink in. "So you see how important it is for us to find him as soon as possible. We don't want to bring the police in if we can possibly avoid it."

I did not think Martin was mentally unbalanced, and I had long since formed the habit of disbelieving most of what the First Prefect said. So I stood firm. When he realized he was not going to get anything out of me, his mouth tightened.

"Very well, then. If that's all you're prepared to say, we shall have to see what other steps can be taken. I shall discuss the matter with the Rector." I almost smiled. The Rector was a mild, vague man mainly preoccupied with astronomy. He did not, on the whole, know one boy from another. Presumably it was necessary for the First Prefect to consult him occasionally when he required a formal extension of his powers, a sort of *lettre de cachet*. "In the meantime, perhaps you'd better move over to the sanatorium." As I turned to go, he said, "I'll come with you and help you collect your things."

He stood over me while I collected my night things, and then we went over to the sanatorium together. When Martin's father had died he had been sent over there to protect him from prying eyes. In my case the reason was different. It was obviously an attempt to frighten me, and soften me up. It would also give them an opportunity to search my room. Fortunately I had anticipated this and was carrying the letter on me. I did not imagine they would dare to strip me and go through my clothes.

The rooms in the sanatorium were small, white, bare, and antiseptic-looking. They had a linoleum floor with a strip of carpet, a chair, and a hospital bed. I was not locked in, but the only way out was by a narrow staircase that led past the Matron's room. There were a few books beside the bed, of a devotional kind— meditation on the significance of Advent, biographies of St.

Ignatius and St. Stanislaus Kostka, also a piece of cautionary moral fiction about a small boy who used to beat himself with a hairbrush to simulate measles and thus get out of going to Mass. It was intended for a rather younger age group than mine.

I was left alone until lunchtime, and after that I began to have visitors. First there was my class master, a pleasant young man for whom I had considerable respect—he brought me close to weakening. I was strengthened in my resolution again by a visit from the Spiritual Father, who intoned at me from the bottom of the bed and professed himself ready to hear my confession at a moment's notice at any hour of the day or night. Then the First Prefect returned. This time, ominously, he said very little. When I again refused to tell him anything, he nodded as if this was no more than he expected. He gave the impression of having some trump card up his sleeve which he had finally decided to play. After that I was left alone for the night.

The next morning nothing happened till eleven o'clock. Then there was a knock on the door and Matron showed in my father and mother. They looked frightened and ill at ease—and, as always at Breckenhall, rather smaller than they looked at home. When Matron had gone, my father said abruptly, "I suppose you know why we're here?"

"I can guess," I said. "Though nobody told me you were coming."

"The First Prefect rang us up on the telephone last night. He said it was urgent, so we drove over this morning."

"Have you seen him?"

"Yes. Just now."

I said bitterly, "I suppose he convinced you?"

My father shook his head. He was never a man of great presence—an ordinary G.P., a little rusty in his medicine, harassed by family and financial responsibilities—yet anxiety gave him a certain dignity. "I haven't heard your side yet. He told me that this boy Farrell had run away and you know where he is, but you won't tell anyone." He paused, waiting for me to deny it. "Do you know where he is?"

"No."

It was a quibble, and my voice must have shown it. He said, "Did you have a letter from him?"

"Yes."

"So you have some idea?"

I hesitated. "Yes."

"Then why won't you tell them?"

"Because he asked me not to. It was confidential."

As soon as I had said it I knew how childish and pretentious it must sound to them. A boy of my age had no right to confidences on matters of importance which concerned his elders. My mother said gently, "But Peter, this is serious. You must see that."

She spoke as if Martin and I had been playing some game that had accidentally resulted in disaster. "Of course I do," I said.

"Well, then—" She looked at me helplessly. "I don't understand you. You don't seem to realize—your whole career's at stake."

"My career?"

"Yes. The First Prefect told us that if you won't co-operate, the Rector may ask us to take you away. We have to go and see him when we've finished talking to you."

"That's just bluff."

"I don't know. He seemed very serious. I don't think he's the sort of man who'd try to alarm us unnecessarily—"

My father cut in. "I'm asking you to act sensibly. I think I'm entitled to. Your education has cost me a great deal of money. I've made sacrifices—"

I nodded miserably, filled with shame. I knew it was true. It was all very well for Martin. The sons of the rich are to be envied —they have a freedom from obligation denied to the rest of us. They owe no gratitude, they are not tormented by the memories of pinching and saving, of new clothes and summer holidays cheerfully foregone to pay school fees. All through life I have been shackled by a compulsion to pay my debts, both material and emotional. To my parents it seemed a little thing they were asking, in return for all they had done for me. I am not naturally a strong or ruthless person. I can see that my behavior may seem weak and unheroic. I should perhaps have stood by my friend and damned the consequences. But this is not a romance and I am not a hero. I handed the letter over to my father.

"Here it is," I said. "Do what you like with it."

As soon as they had left me, I lay on my bed and began to sob. I knew that I had lost something, something important and irreplaceable—though I could not at that time have told anybody what it was.

They caught Martin at Poitiers, by circulating his description to the French police. He had been trying to hitchhike down to Perpignan, where he had heard there was a recruiting center for the International Brigade.

When they brought him back to Breckenhall, he was thinner than I had remembered him and filled with bitterness, mainly against myself. "I was a fool to write to you," he said savagely. "I ought to have known you'd let me down."

5

ONE might have imagined that, following this, every-thing would have been over between Martin and myself. Cer-tainly he blamed me, equally with the Jesuits themselves, for what had happened. I do not think of the episode now as much as I used to, but the recollection of it still fills me with shame. By the standards of any mature, sensible person, of course, I had done the only possible thing. I had not even been bound by a promise, for I had made none. It could be argued that I had probably saved Martin's life. Yet in my heart I could not escape the conviction that I had acted dishonorably. I felt miserably guilty and Martin knew it. He never let me forget it.

For a week or two we hardly spoke to each other, but when one lives in such close contact with others it is difficult to maintain attitudes of this kind for very long. Without either of us making any definite overtures, we drifted together again. At first we passed the time of day, then we talked of minor school matters. In a surprisingly short time, we were confiding in each other once more. The Breckenhall authorities were pleased at this de-velopment and made a point of telling me so. They had handled Martin very gently since his return. His escapade was never men-tioned—they had presumably decided to put it down to the shock of his father's death. He was very morose at first, walking the corridors of the school with downcast eyes as if he was a prisoner. In a sense he was, but the Jesuits showed their very best side in their handling of him. Their reaction to transgression was never very easy to predict, based as it was on an attempt to reconcile an authoritarian rule of Latin origin with the British public-school system. St. Ignatius ran in uneasy harness with Dr. Arnold. The fact is, I think, that Martin's emotional extremism appealed to them. It was something they understood. They yearned to harness it in the right direction, to govern it by discipline. It could happen; it had happened to many of them, to their own Founder. If a man felt strongly, they had hopes of getting him to feel as they felt. Apathy was the real enemy.

It is curious now to remember that Martin only went in for medicine because I did. Now that his father was dead and he was relatively poor, the question of a career became urgent. Obstinately, he refused at first even to discuss the matter. In the end, after having been goaded for several months by his trustees, he made his decision.

"Just to keep them quiet," he explained to me. "Perhaps now they'll let me have a little peace."

"Don't you want to do medicine?" I asked. I was a little shocked.

"I don't really give a damn what I do," he said carelessly. "I might as well do the same as you. And at least a knowledge of medicine always comes in handy. Not that either of us will ever finish the course. There's bound to be a war within the next few years."

I agreed. My recollection is that in those days we all took the coming war for granted. We were only seventeen, and Danzig and the Sudetenland were just names to us. But since all these detailed issues were purely fictitious anyway, we had in fact a much clearer idea of what was likely to happen than those who had dedicated their lives to the study of diplomacy. This was not diplomacy, it was melodrama; at seventeen, one has an instinctive feeling for melodrama.

We left Breckenhall in the summer, and started our premedical course at St. Vincent's in September. In those days it was traditional for medical students to behave in rather a disorderly fashion, and this was intensified by the unsettled nature of the times. I have always been amazed at the tolerance shown to us by the authorities. Unpopular lecturers were barracked and pelted. Laboratory sessions took place to the accompaniment of a series of detonations, as fireworks exploded in the wastepaper baskets and mixtures of gases were ignited in glassware, supposedly by accident. In such an atmosphere it would have been difficult to settle down to work even if we had wanted to—and we did not really want to. What we were learning in the physics and chemistry laboratories seemed a far cry from human medicine, and it was fashionable to do only enough work to secure a bare pass. The rest of the time we dedicated to enjoying ourselves in the short period of time remaining to us. Martin and I shared lodgings in Hampstead; there was an idea current among his guardians that I would exercise a steadying influence on him. My parents, who suspected, perhaps more accurately, that he would have an unsteadying influence on me, were not enthusiastic about the arrangement, but they accepted it philosophically. They even put up twenty-five pounds for a half share in a secondhand Austin 7.

We were a little feverish in our enjoyments, anxious to pack in as much experience as possible before it was too late. We got drunk, we stayed up conscientiously until daylight, we quarreled and talked and made love to girls as eager for sensation as ourselves. After the first year we moved into the dissecting room. The bodies there, waxy as they were, seemed more real than physics and chemistry. Some of us began to take life a little more seriously, but not many. Then, suddenly, three months later, the party was over.

My recollection is that we hardly felt even a twinge of regret; our feeling was more of relief that the moment had finally come. It was, after all, what we had been waiting for.

I do not know what we had been actually expecting from the war. Whatever it was, we didn't get it, certainly not at first. This was neither a romantic crusade nor the cosmic explosion predicted by H. G. Wells. It was inconvenience, blackout, a listless preparation for an eventual clash of arms that would possibly occur at some future date, no one knew when. As medical students, we were exempt from military service until qualification, three or four years hence. It appeared unlikely that we should ever take part in the war at all.

One fortunate result of the war was that Martin's family house, which had been lying empty since his father's death for lack of a purchaser, was at last sold. The market in country property, situated in areas remote from centers of population, was booming. Martin would occasionally drive over there to attend to business details in connection with the sale.

"They're some people called Kalash," he said. "Lots of money. Polish origin, I believe. But they've been here in England ever since the end of the last war."

"Any family?"

"A daughter about our age."

"Any good?"

He hesitated for a moment. "Not bad," he said carelessly, and changed the subject.

During the next few months there were indications that in the course of his business negotiations Martin had become quite friendly with the Kalash family. Every now and then when I was working, he would take the car and drive out to the house on his own. I had a suspicion that he might be interested in the daughter and occasionally taxed him with this, but he always denied it, sometimes irritably. There was no suggestion that I should meet them, until one day he informed me that we were both invited for the weekend. He told me about the invitation rather late, and made it sound as unattractive as possible. I had the impression that he did not really want me to go. Perhaps he had mentioned my name in an unguarded moment, and somebody had suggested me as a spare man.

His reluctance only increased my interest and I accepted the invitation. I liked the Kalashes from the very beginning. The mother and father still had strong foreign accents and gave the impression of being, even after twenty years, incompletely assimilated into British society. They inhabited Fernfield in a curiously temporary way, as if encamped there on their way to somewhere else. Meals occurred irregularly, sometimes sumptuous and sometimes inedible, according to the success of their dealings on the black market. They were careless, emotional, and extravagant.

Barbara Kalash was a slender, fair girl with an oval face and slightly slanting eyes that one could easily imagine to be Slavic in origin. She was more Anglicized than her parents, but there was something about her laugh and her gestures that suggested a less inhibited civilization than ours. She greeted Martin with a kiss, but she did the same to many of her other guests, and I took it that this was probably no more than the convention of the household.

In many ways it was a fairly usual sort of weekend house party. There were about half a dozen young people staying in the house, and more who came in to play tennis in the afternoon. Then we drove out in cars to a roadhouse and danced. On the way home we stopped the cars in remote spots by the roadside and indulged in amorous play until it was time to go home. There was a cheerful, innocent promiscuity about it all, and the partners were by no means the same each night. It was tacitly accepted that we were all engaged in the process of gaining experience about sex. According to the rules of the game, the young men tried to see how far they could get, and the girls decided how far they would let them. It was good wholesome exercise and little sentiment entered into it. On the second night of the weekend I found myself in the back of somebody's car with Barbara Kalash. When eventually I attempted to kiss her, she came into my arms and returned my embraces as if I had just invited her to dance—with the same air of concentrated enjoyment in a physical pleasure, the same air of impersonality. It would probably have been just the same if she had found herself with any one of another half dozen personable young men. I noticed this without resenting it. What she was prepared to give me on this purely physical plane was enough for me at that stage.

On questioning her, I found that she spent most of the week in London, living with a friend who had a flat in Kensington. She had some more or less useless job as a chauffeur for a higher civil servant. We arranged to meet one evening, and after that we saw each other fairly regularly several times a week. She seemed to consider herself free, and I had had no official intimation that she was Martin's girl. When he had mentioned her to me, it was in an unenthusiastic, offhand fashion. We all took the attitude at that time of being more or less immune to emotional involvements.

I grew fonder of her each time I saw her. She was gay and cheerful and demonstrative. You felt that her affections were scattered widely and she had no constraint in giving expression to them. For her, an embrace had not the same exclusively sensual implication as it had for me—it could be no more than a token of warmth, of friendliness. When I tried to press on further, she showed a disappointing degree of self-control. She was used to predatory young men of my sort and had clear ideas as to how to deal with them. She had no intention of abandoning herself, either physically or emotionally, to any frivolous young medical student who was mainly occupied in acquiring another specimen in his collection. Occasionally I found it exasperating that I was not able to elicit from her any more than I myself was prepared to give. If she was a specimen in my collection, she implied, I was equally a specimen in hers. Once, trying to burst my way past her defenses, I said more or less dishonestly, "I love you, Barbara."

She pushed me away.

"Don't be silly," she said.

"Don't you believe me?"

"Of course not. What you'd like to do is to fool me into falling in love with you."

"Why should I want to do that?"

"So that I'd sleep with you, of course," she said equably.

I felt humiliated and exposed. For what she said was true. Up till then I had felt for her only a close friendship, intensified and dramatized by desire. I valued my freedom, and the thought of becoming attached permanently to one woman, no matter how attractive, was repellent to me. But the curious thing is that from that moment I began to feel quite differently about Barbara. It was as if as soon as I was brought face to face with my own attitude, I automatically rejected it. And in its place came something else, something deeper and more protective—a little anxious, more than a little sad. I was too inexperienced to know whether this was the real thing or not. I knew only that whatever it was, it could lead nowhere, for the present at least. I was penniless and would be for many years. I wanted to become a surgeon, and in those days it was taken for granted that there was no question of a surgeon marrying under thirty. There has been a great deal written about the tragedy of meeting the right woman too late. It seemed to me that I might well have met her too soon.

I was never exactly certain how Barbara felt about me after this. I think she suspected that my attitude had changed, but I was too overcome by a sense of futility to talk to her about it. It was foolish of me. Perhaps, given time, it would not have mattered—she might have known without my telling her. But time was the thing which was not to be granted to us.

One evening I was sitting in front of the gas fire in my room, reading (the incident is still very vivid in my mind) about the course of the vagus nerve in the neck, when Martin came in. He looked unusually grim. One glance at his face told me that I was in for a scene of some kind.

"Peter," he said, "I want to have a talk with you."

"All right." I closed my book.

"It's something rather serious."

I got to my feet. Even in those days I was aware of the necessity to stand up for myself and not allow him to play it entirely the way he wanted. "If you're going to quarrel with me," I said, "the least you can do is to buy me a beer first. Let's go round to the pub."

We marched stiffly round the corner to The Grapes. Martin refused to speak on the way; he was obviously determined not to be appeased. When we had settled down in a corner of the saloon bar with a couple of pints of bitters, he said, "It's just come to my knowledge that you've been seeing quite a bit of Barbara."

I raised my glass. "Cheers," I said. He didn't reply. "Yes, that's right."

"Behind my back," he added bitterly.

"Now, Martin, don't be absurd—"

"Why did you keep it secret? Why did you never tell me about it?"

"It was no secret. I didn't mention it to you because—" I hesitated. It was not easy to explain. I hardly knew myself. I said defensively, "Was there any reason why I should?"

"It would have been the decent and honorable thing to do. Perhaps that was too much to expect of you." He spoke loudly, and I saw the barmaid give us a curious glance. We must have looked rather absurd, so young and solemn, with our pints in front of us, talking about honor.

"I didn't even know you were particularly interested in her."

"Don't lie about it, for God's sake. It only makes you sound more despicable." His voice trembled. It was impossible to doubt his sincerity. He genuinely believed at this moment in every word he said. What one could never tell was how much his emotion was self-induced, how much a more or less conscious surrender to delusions of persecution. My conscience was not entirely clear. Though I recognized no obligation to tell him about myself and Barbara, it would certainly have been more usual to do so. If I had really thought he had no interest in her I should probably have told him.

I was also impeded in my handling of the situation by the knowledge that not only the barmaid but also one or two other people were listening now. This did not worry Martin in the least. He was indifferent to the opinions of strangers. I realized too late how foolish I had been to insist on coming out to the pub.

"Look," I said in a low voice. "You don't have to tell the whole of Hampstead about it. Let's talk quietly."

He looked over his shoulder. "Do you suppose I care if those fourth-rate pimps have nothing better to do than listen to our conversation?" he said, very audibly.

"Perhaps not—but I do."

"Must you be so bloody lower-middle-class?"

I managed with an effort to finish my pint. "If you feel you can't talk about it without shouting, at least let's go back to the digs."

"I'm damned if I will. It was your idea to come here." He glared at me. But I was relieved to note that he had dropped his voice a little. He stopped ranting and said seriously, "Do you really care a damn about Barbara?"

Suddenly I felt afraid. The real attack was coming, the one that mattered. Something important to me was threatened and I did not know how to defend it. "Yes," I said.

"I don't believe you. You can't really pretend you're in love with her. You're just playing around trying to seduce her."

"No," I said painfully. I would not have believed that it could have hurt so much to hear him say it. Perhaps it was because only a few weeks ago it would have been true. But not now.

"You are," he persisted, leaning forward, willing me to agree with him. "You know you are. What else are you prepared to offer her?"

"And what about you?" I was stung into asking. "What can you offer?"

He hesitated for a moment. "Marriage," he said. "I'm in love with her."

I was dumfounded. It had never entered my head that people like Martin or myself could even think of marriage for at least another five years. To this day I cannot be sure whether Martin had contemplated such a step before he began this conversation with me or whether, determined to secure Barbara from me at all costs, like a man in the excitement of an auction, he threw in a bid that he knew I could not hope to match.

"How could you possibly marry her?" I said.

He paused again, but only momentarily. The idea, I could see, was beginning to grip him—an adventure, something new, a complete change in the direction of his life. "I'm giving up medicine," he said. "I can't see myself spending the war sitting round mugging up the relations of the lesser omentum." This, I knew, he must have thought out before. Many of us had the same doubts. It was only a few months since the fall of France, and the febrile excitement of those days made us impatient with routine tasks. Several members of our year had already left to join the services. Martin said, "I'm told there's no problem about getting into the Fleet Air Arm."

I could well believe it. The Fleet Air Arm was generally regarded as the most fatal of the services at that particular time. It would have a natural appeal to Martin in his present frame of mind.

"Have you told Barbara?"

"Not yet."

We sat in silence. The moment had a certain genuine solemnity. I knew Martin was not bluffing; he would do what he said. He was prepared to pay for Barbara not only with his career but, in all probability, with his life. And I was prepared to give—what? Nothing comparable to that, certainly. I felt helpless, and more than a little bitter. I knew then that I could not win; I did not deserve to win. Just then I hated Martin and yet I admired him because he seemed to me to be a character of greater size than I could ever be. He made me feel insignificant. I was ashamed, at that dramatic time, that I was not of the stuff to make grand gestures. I was everything that Martin had accused me of being, at one time or another—cautious, sensible, calculating. It was in my nature, no matter how deep and sincere my feelings, to count the cost. I knew in my heart that it would always be the same. There was nothing I could do about it.

He said, with great intensity but without bombast, "This matters to me more than anything in my whole life. It doesn't really matter a damn to you. I sometimes think you were only attracted to her because you knew I wanted her—"

"That's not true."

"I think it is. It may not be obvious to everybody, perhaps not even to yourself, but you're a spoiler, Peter. You don't really want anything unless you can take it from someone else."

Quite abruptly he got up from his seat and walked out of the pub, leaving me there. He had won, and he knew it. If I tried to take her from him now, with nothing to give her at the end of it, I should prove that he had been right, that I *was* a spoiler. I owed him that at least—not to deny him his heart's desire for the sake of a love that could lead nowhere for either Barbara or myself. And deep within me I was still racked with guilt about my betrayal of him at Breckenhall. I could not let him down again.

I stopped seeing Barbara after that. I never discussed the matter with her. Perhaps I should have done, but I was young and awkward and I could not think how to explain my behavior. I could not tell her that I loved her, but that in the last instance I could not compete with Martin in making sacrifices for her.

Martin kept his word. A few weeks after our conversation he resigned from St. Vincent's and joined the Fleet Air Arm. He had a farewell party at which we got ceremoniously drunk together and he informed me that Barbara had promised to marry him. I offered him my congratulations.

I was not invited to the wedding. What Barbara thought of my sudden abandonment of her, I never knew. Perhaps she told herself that it had been just another casual affair, and that I had become attracted by someone else. It was the sensible attitude to take, and I had been trying to think of it in that way myself. For ten years now, I had been trying.

6

❈

❈

❈

❈

❈

❈

A week after my meeting with Stratton I left for Batou. There was no direct service with the island either by air or by sea, and in the end I had to fly to Lagos and then wait for the mailboat, which departed once a week for Flores Blancas, the only port of any size on the island. Besides mail it carried a certain amount of miscellaneous light cargo and an assortment of passengers, mainly Negro or half-caste. The captain was a plump, sweating Portuguese.

Almost all mountainous islands look picturesque on approach, especially in the tropics. Flores (as it was generally called) had a good natural harbor, and as the mailboat slid gently round the corner of the bay, the houses appeared perched in white rows on the cliff, like pigeon cotes. At the center of the bay there was a small plaza, with fishing boats piled on the sand and nets spread out to dry. The steamer advanced a little way and then stopped; evidently the bay was shallow. After a while there was a rumbling of the anchor chain. Rowing boats, piled with fruit, baskets, and leather suitcases, began to pull out from the shore. Immediately afterward they were overtaken by motor launches containing customs, immigration, and health officials. Almost certainly there would be somebody in one of them to greet me. I went down below to complete my packing.

When I returned on deck five or ten minutes later, the bumboats were all around the ship, and the rails were crowded with trading passengers. It was very hot now that we were stationary in the bay; the breeze that had kept us comfortable at sea was either cut off by the cliffs or had been no more than an illusion of motion. As I mopped the sweat from my face, a sharp voice said, "A little sticky today?"

She was a woman of thirty or so, in a severe white linen suit. Her jet-black hair was bobbed in a style that was either very old-fashioned or very new. She gave me a thin-lipped smile. "It's always unpleasant down in the bay at this time of year. But you'll find it cooler up in the hills." She seemed to think for a moment, and then decide that the weather as a subject was satisfactorily disposed of. "You're Dr. Mayne, I imagine?"

"Yes."

She pushed out a dry brown hand. "How do you do? I'm Mary Paston." She explained, "I live here. I came out on the launch to pick up some things."

The explanation still appeared to lack something. I said, "You knew who I was?"

She laughed dryly. "My dear fellow, this is a very small community. Everybody knows everyone else's business." She straddled her legs and leaned mannishly against the rail, puffing at a cigarette. "I believe you're connected with Martin Farrell's encephalitis trial." I smiled and said nothing, but she was evidently not so easily put off. "Is that so?"

It is always hard to refuse a direct question of this sort. I had no idea who she was, and I recoiled from the idea of being openly offensive. "Substantially, yes," I said.

"Are you a virologist, too?"

"Not exactly."

She raised her eyebrows. In her sharp voice, she said, "He's doing wonderful work, don't you think?"

"Farrell?"

"Yes."

"I don't know much about it yet. I've only just arrived."

"Haven't you read the press reports?"

"No."

She looked at me with obvious disbelief. I was indeed lying. Stratton had shown me two feature articles in the *Universal* magazine before I had left. They had been rather alarming—absurdly overdramatized and quite unscientific in the claims they made for the work. There was even an inference that the vaccine might be of value in other diseases besides encephalitis. The trouble was that there was enough fact (and enough photographs) to give the impression that Martin had co-operated with the author in their composition. This could be disastrous for him. It would do him little good to become a national celebrity if in the process he antagonized the Encephalitis Committee.

"Well, anyway," she said defiantly, "we think he's doing a simply marvellous job—"

"We?"

"The people on the island." She leaned forward and went on solemnly, "This encephalitis is a terrible thing, you know. People in England simply haven't any idea. It's a scandal that the Colonial Medical Service hasn't made any effort to tackle it before. In the end, it has to be done by a private individual, single-handed, running all kinds of risks. . . ."

I was overcome by the usual sense of fatigue that one always has when hearing medical matters discussed in lay terms. She obviously had a superficial knowledge of science, which made it possible for her to use technical terms and give an impression of being an authority on the subject. This only had the effect of making the emotional content of her discourse more distasteful. Familiar phrases began to appear—"dedicated scientist," "bureaucratic stupidity," "alleviation of human suffering"—and the usual O.K. names—"Fleming," "Koch," "Schweitzer."

This last was too much for me. I had not seen Martin for a long time, but I could not believe he had changed as much as that. "Schweitzer?" I asked, with a grin.

It threw her a little. She flushed.

"Dr. Farrell is a very dedicated man," she said.

"You know him personally?"

"Very well indeed," she said significantly.

It occurred to me that some of the phrases she had used were quite unusually familiar. A suspicion entered my mind.

"You didn't by any chance write those articles for *Universal?*" I asked.

She nodded.

God, I thought, what is Martin getting up to? A picture of him came into my mind, scenting opposition and deciding to counter it by some unexpected but reckless stroke of policy. Where else, after all, could she have got all her information from? He must have helped her. It was the kind of action that fitted into my knowledge of his character as it used to be, when we were students. But we were no longer students. Had he learned nothing in the meantime?

I said coldly, "I think perhaps you should have told me you were a journalist."

"Perhaps I should." She tossed her cigarette into the scuppers. "But then you lied to me when you said you hadn't read my articles, didn't you? So in a way we're quits."

She had barely left me when I was called to see the Captain. In his cabin was a slight brown man with a tentative, anxious expression. The Captain made a perfunctory introduction.

"Dr. Das," he said, in his deep, grating voice. He belched slightly. "Dr. Das is the senior medical officer on Batou."

I smiled at Dr. Das and he smiled back, but thinly, cautiously. In a precise, formal voice, he said, "Welcome to Batou, Dr. Mayne."

"Thank you."

We looked each other over. His light-fawn tropical suit was crumpled, even at this hour in the morning; it was the sort of suit that would always look crumpled, even when it had been worn for only ten minutes. His chest was narrow, and the shoulders of his coat too wide: they drooped despondently in two ledges of padding with hollows beneath, as if he had bilateral dislocation of the joints. His face was refined, sensitive, and intense, his thin hands constantly in movement. With a little more stature he would have been a good-looking man, but his skeleton had let him down.

He said, "Dr. Farrell asked me to meet you on his behalf. He is upcountry at the moment, inoculating one of the villages. He said he was sure you would understand."

"Of course. It was very kind of you to take the trouble. . . ."

"Not at all. It is a pleasure." He spoke rather coldly, as if I had accused him of something. "I think you will find everyone here very ready to help you in any way they can. We are a small community but we take a pride in our hospitality."

"So I believe. I've already been talking to a Miss Paston—"

He looked somewhat concerned. "You spoke with her?"

"Yes."

"Did she tell you that—"

"That she wrote those articles? Well, not exactly. But it came out in the course of the conversation. Whom is she employed by?"

"She is a free lance. She has private money, I believe. She came here several years ago. She lives in a house on the cliff with a"—he hesitated—"with another lady. When anything interesting happens here, she writes it up for the London papers. She has contacts in the London journalistic world." I nodded and said nothing. He was nervous and it made him talkative. "The whole thing was most unfortunate. As you can imagine, Dr. Farrell was extremely angry when he saw the articles. He himself had nothing to do with them—nothing whatever."

He looked at me intently, determined to make me commit myself to Martin's side. Already, it seemed, the advance guard was making contact, the pickets were out. First Miss Paston, now Das. Evidently Martin had his disciples. It was an old pattern. Always he had aroused strong emotions, either of devotion or enmity. "I have the impression," Stratton had said to me before I left, "that everyone on the island is beginning to get a little unbalanced about this affair. We see you as introducing a cool breath of sanity from the outside world." That was how I had, intermittently, seen myself. But I was already beginning to sense the tensions that had been building up on Batou. For me, I reminded myself,

this was a routine job—the assessment of a clinical experiment.
I was determined to keep it on that footing. I said, "Perhaps I'd
better get up my luggage. . . ."

As we bobbed toward the shore in the launch, Das said, "I have
a car at the landing stage. When you are through the customs, I
will drive you up to Dr. Farrell's house. It is on the hill on the
other side of the bay."

"You mean—it's been arranged for me to stay with Dr.
Farrell?"

"Yes, naturally. I believe you are an old friend of his."

"That's true, but just the same—" I said firmly, "I'm afraid I've
already arranged to stay at a hotel."

"A hotel?" He sounded not only surprised but a little shocked.

"Yes." I had decided this in London. If I was going to have to
act as an impartial assessor, it was important not to accept too
much hospitality from either side. "I booked a room at the
Clanricarde. I believe that's the best place?"

Das looked gloomy. "I do not believe you will be very comfortable at the Clanricarde."

"They told me at the tourist agency—"

"I imagine that nobody at the tourist agency has ever actually
been to Batou, Dr. Mayne. The Clanricarde is indeed the best
hotel. It is, for all practical purposes, the only hotel. Most people
who visit here stay with friends."

This sounded discouraging, but I found it hard to believe that
the Clanricarde was as bad as all that. I had stayed at second-
class hotels before in my life. I said firmly, "Just the same, I think
I'll stay at the Clanricarde."

Das sighed. "Mrs. Farrell will be expecting you."

"She'll understand, I'm sure. I'll explain to her later."

When I first caught sight of the hotel I cheered up a little. It
seemed to me that Das had been exaggerating. The building
looked rather picturesque from outside. It was of white timber,
very Old Colonial, with a balcony running all the way around the

first floor. But the nearer you got to it, the worse it looked. The white paint was peeling, and inside the lobby it was dark and musty-smelling. There was no one about. A curling menu stuck on the wall with drawing pins announced that luncheon would consist of brown Windsor soup, roast mutton, and bread-and-butter pudding. It didn't say which day, and the menu looked as if it had been there for some time. No wonder Africa was so eager to shake off the shackles of colonialism.

There was a brass bell on the counter, and Das banged his hand on it several times. In due course a fat brown man appeared out of the inner recesses of the building. He was listless and indifferent and seemed to have no knowledge of my reservation. Not that it mattered, since the hotel was almost empty anyway. I could have one of their best rooms.

The room was on the first floor and was in almost pitch darkness. Even so, it was very hot. As the fat man opened the shutters to let the light in there was a soft rustling sound as about half a dozen cockroaches scuttled away toward cover. The fat man casually put out a foot and squashed one of them as it tried to pass him. He switched on the ceiling fan, which gave a few slow, unhappy turns, then creaked to a halt. The walls were covered with little smears, a few black, mostly dark red—the mosquitoes had at least died replete. I began to regret my decision.

I said to Das, "Have you had many cases of encephalitis in the town?" The disease was thought to be spread by mosquito bites.

"Recently, yes. It seems to be spreading in from the villages."

There was a silence while I struggled with my pride. I was going to look a fool if I changed my mind at this point. However, I decided that I would sooner look a fool than catch encephalitis.

"If you don't mind," I said to Das, "I think I'd prefer to go to Dr. Farrell's after all."

"I'm sure you will find it better," he said.

He smiled and I felt ridiculous. But I was not, after all, there to run unnecessary risks. Heat and cockroaches were one thing, disease was quite another. The fat man did not appear in the least surprised at my decision. As I got back into the car, I realized that Das had known all along what would happen. He had never even bothered to have my luggage brought in.

The car was an old battered Vauxhall, covered inside and out with a film of thick yellow dust. The dust rose in clouds from the narrow twisting mountain road as we struggled noisily upward toward the top of the cliff. Outside the town the vegetation was luxuriant, and the air was alive with the twittering of cicadas. Das drove with great concentration, dragging viciously at the wheel and jerking his foot on and off the accelerator. Occasionally he would blast his horn at some completely deserted bend.

"You will like Dr. Farrell's house," he assured me. "It is in a very beautiful position on the hill."

"He's managed to make himself comfortable?"

He caught the irony in my tone, and became immediately defensive. "Why not? He has money, I believe. And half the time he is away in the villages, where things are not so pleasant. He runs great risks."

"Really?"

"Yes." He said rather spitefully, "Life in the villages is very rough. Even the Clanricarde is luxurious by comparison."

He grabbed the wheel and piloted us fiercely around another corner. It was obvious that he disliked and resented me. He saw in me a threat to his hero. I could sympathize with him. I had been a worshiper myself in my day. I said, "Do you live up on the hill, too?"

"Oh, no, it is very expensive there. I have a house down in the town." After a slight pause, he added, "My wife and I would very much like you to visit us."

"Thank you very much."

The invitation had not been very enthusiastic, but, once made, he seemed to feel it should be followed through with determination. "Perhaps for tea tomorrow—if that would be convenient?"

"I imagine so. I'm not exactly sure of my program—"

"We would have liked to have you for lunch or dinner, but,

you understand, there are domestic difficulties. We have a baby, and also my parents live with us—they are getting on in years—"

"Please don't put yourselves to any trouble."

He regarded me severely. "There is no trouble. My wife is very much looking forward to meeting you."

He spoke in a tone which admitted of no argument. I did not think he liked me or wanted me to visit his house, but protocol demanded that a formal invitation should be given and accepted. I imagined that any evasion on my part would give rise to offense. I looked forward with misgiving to the tea party, but there was nothing much to be done about it.

We turned through a gate into a private road, and then drove for perhaps half a mile through thick forest. Suddenly we emerged into the sun again, with the trees behind us and the top of the cliffs in front. In the clearing between the two stood the house, a large, opulent, sprawling bungalow in what the Americans call "ranch-style." It was on the point of a bluff between two bays; down on the left was the harbor and the town of Flores, on the right a narrow inlet filled with forest, and a small strip of sandy beach. The view was magnificent and the air was cool, with a slight breeze blowing in from the sea. There was a small swimming pool and a Jaguar 2.4 parked in front of the double garage.

As the car drew to a halt, I saw a woman come out of the house. She moved across the shadow of the terrace into the sun, and I saw it was Barbara. She was wearing slacks and a shirt, and looked slim and athletic, as always. She raised her hand to protect her hair from the breeze in a gesture which I remembered well. It seemed to me that she had hardly changed at all.

7

NOBODY, of course, ever stays exactly the same over that period of time, even in appearance. There were a few lines about her eyes and mouth that had not been there before, and her face somehow carried less eagerness and more authority. Her figure was unchanged, but her blond hair was paler than I remembered, bleached by the tropical sun, and her skin was deeply tanned.

All the time on my way here, I had been worrying about this meeting. I had no idea how either Barbara or Martin thought of me now. Had they forgotten the past? Would they resent me, either for myself or the part I was now playing? How would they receive me?

As far as Barbara was concerned, I need not have worried. Her manner was as easy as if we had seen each other only a week ago. She put up her face to be kissed, just as she had done in the old days. These, I remembered, were the routine, affectionate kisses, given indiscriminately to all her friends, with which she had tormented me as a young man. Now, as then, I responded clumsily.

She broke away, smiling, not disconcerted by my awkwardness, perhaps remembering as I did, perhaps even pleased that a kiss from her was something I could still not take as a matter of course. Even the scent of her was unchanged, a mixture of freshly laundered silk, Ecusson, and the effect of sun on skin and hair. Smells, I thought, are the most evocative things in the world.

More than any other sensations they have the power of arousing old memories and emotions.

"Darling Peter," she said, "it's so good to see you again!" It was the sort of thing one might have expected her to say anyway, but I had a feeling that she meant it—that she was pleased to see me and at the same time, in some curious way, relieved. She put her arm through mine and squeezed it. I could see Das through the corner of my eye, watching us. He looked a little shocked—also, I thought, resentful and excluded. He began to lift the suitcases out of the car.

"You're later than I expected," she said. "I saw the boat come into the harbor—" She pointed over the cliff. The harbor was set out below us as in an aerial photograph. The packet boat lay in the middle of the blue water, looking from this height like a child's toy. The launches around it were a series of brown dots hardly distinguishable one from another.

"We were slightly delayed," I said. "Before I left England I arranged to have a hotel room booked—"

"Not at the Clanricarde?"

"Yes."

Das said hurriedly, "I told him it was out of the question."

She smiled absently at Das, as if noticing him for the first time. Then she turned back to me. "What you missed! If you were going to pick a brothel, you might at least have chosen one where they change the sheets."

I wanted to forget about the Clanricarde. I said, a little stiffly, "It was good of you to invite me. I hope I shan't be too much trouble."

She laughed. "What trouble? This isn't England, you know. The house is full of servants. We're at our wit's end to find something for them to do. Naturally we took it for granted that you'd stay with us." There was a degree of amiable mockery in her voice. I always had the impression that she found me slightly comic in my more formal moments. "But it was sweet of you to think of it, just the same."

She led me into the house. Das gave instructions to two servants who had appeared and were struggling with my luggage. Then he followed us into the living room of the house. It was a long, low room with picture windows looking out over the bay and sun blinds to protect it from the harshness of the light. It was after five o'clock, and the afternoon sun was beginning its rapid, dramatic fall into the Atlantic. Das accepted a glass of lemon squash, drank it quickly, and then left, not forgetting to remind me of my appointment to visit him the next day. He seemed ill at ease.

"Poor Harold," said Barbara when the car had vanished down the drive. "He's so good and he has such a tough time. He's one of those men nothing ever seems to go quite right for. And one ends up with a feeling that perhaps nothing ever will." She paused. "Don't you think he's rather pathetic?"

I nodded. "I don't think he likes me very much."

"He's suspicious of you, that's all. And he probably finds you oppressive. You're big and self-possessed and you have a sort of —fortunate look. You look like a man that things go well for."

"What particularly went wrong for Das?"

"What can go wrong for a man? Money? Women?" She shrugged her shoulders. "You'll see tomorrow. His wife's English, by the way."

"You don't like her?"

"She's not my type exactly. A bit of a Roundhead," she added vaguely. She was fond of giving these obscure and allusive judgments on people. Usually they meant something to you when you actually met the person. "But don't let's talk about them." From her tone of voice I knew that the Dases were not completely real to her. "Tell me about yourself," she said.

I wanted another drink, and without being asked I mixed one for myself and one for Barbara. It seemed the natural thing to do, as if, in this absurd and pretentious rented house, I was at last at home. I told her of what had happened since we last met, of the hospital jobs, the struggle for the fellowship, my training as a surgeon, and my breakdown in health, which had compelled me to leave surgical practice and join the Ministry.

At the end she said, "Do you miss surgery very much?"

It was a question I was used to by this time. "Naturally I did at first, but that was some time ago. . . ." I described to her as objectively as possible the process of adaptation I had gone through. At first when I left surgery, I had felt very unhappy. There was something absurd in the idea of sitting at a desk all day with a briefcase beside me, dictating letters and reports to a secretary. The matters I had to deal with seemed of no conceivable significance compared to the responsibility for individual human life. It was a new and disagreeable sensation to me to question the value of what I was doing and to be dogged by the suspicion that nobody in the world would be a penny the worse whether I did it well or not. I became aware that most men never even concern themselves over this question, and that most jobs are done purely for the sake of money or power or advancement, with usefulness as a by-product. Now I too was in this group, and I felt somehow degraded. But after a year or two I began to settle down to my new position. I was no longer a protagonist. I was a spectator at the arena of life, comfortably paid and not overworked, being as efficient as I could because efficiency is always more satisfying than muddle, doing a little good here and there if circumstances allowed it, but fundamentally an observer, uncommitted, uninvolved.

Barbara said, "You make everything sound so easy." Before I could say anything, she added quickly, "Oh, I know it wasn't really. But it's very considerate of you to pretend it was."

She had no need to explain what she meant. She was pleased that she didn't have to sympathize or feel sorry for me. Pleased for my sake, because she was fond of me and wanted to feel that I was on top of things, that I had been resilient enough to surmount my reverses. I welcomed her attitude, which fitted in with my own. I had no craving for pity.

We had more drinks and watched the sun go down. We chatted idly about trivialities while all the time unspoken questions hung in the air between us. There were so many things I would have liked to talk about, explanations I longed to give, but I could not bring myself to speak. After all, I thought, the whole affair might mean nothing to her now. I might be reminding her of something she would far sooner forget.

A servant came to fix the mosquito screens and turn on the lights. I said to Barbara, "You live in very grand style here."

She sighed. "Yes. Too much style altogether. I was against it, but what can I do? Martin arranged it. He rented it from some sugar millionaire who had to go to Europe for six months." She gave a helpless little shrug. "This is so like him. He rents a place three times as big as we need, at five times what we can afford, and then spends most of his time away, sleeping in mud huts."

"Do you ever go with him?"

"No."

She made no attempt at amplification, and I did not ask her why she never went with him. I had no knowledge of what relations between the two of them might be, though I was very anxious to find out. There was something in the way she spoke about Martin which made me feel they were not perfectly happy together, and I suppose I have to admit that I was not as distressed about this as I might have been. The truth was that I was still a little jealous of Martin. I still regretted my sacrifice of ten years ago, which had seemed so right then but which appeared to me in retrospect as quixotic and absurd.

"Do you like Batou?" I asked.

"Not much. Of course, it's very beautiful—but I'm never really happy outside Europe. You must know what it's like—small-town colonial society, cocktail parties, dinner with the Governor once in a while. Then you have the islanders themselves. No doubt they're very nice but I don't understand them. They always seem to me secretive and a little deceitful. It's not their fault. Poor and uneducated people are naturally like that—it's their only way of self-protection. But it doesn't make them easy to deal with." She looked around the vast, luxurious room. "I think they must resent us terribly. I know I should, in their position. When I say so to Martin he just laughs at me. I don't think he has any feelings of guilt at all. He feels he's entitled to have more of everything than other people." She paused. "The curious thing is that he seems to get on very much better with the islanders than I do. . . ."

That sounded plausible. Martin had always made his claims to special treatment with such assurance that there was a tendency for people to accept them without examination. I could not help wondering where the money came from to enable him to live in such grand style. Chemiefabriken? Or Barbara? It could hardly be his own.

Dinner was not served until nearly nine o'clock. On long, warm tropical evenings life moves at a slow tempo. One feels shut away in a quiet, remote pocket of the world. It is the perfect setting for desultory conversations, for confidences and indiscretions. Intermittent gin slings on an empty stomach have a tendency to relax the inhibitions and promote a mood of sentimental reminiscence. Gradually we grew more confidential.

Barbara said, "You can't know what a relief it is to be able to talk again. I was so looking forward to your coming. Yet—I was nervous. . . ."

"Why?" I asked this though I knew the answer. After all, I had been nervous, too.

"As a rule, I'm afraid of meetings like this, after a long time. One expects too much—"

"It's not such a very long time."

"Nearly ten years. Has it gone so quickly for you?"

"Yes." Recently, for some reason, every year had seemed shorter than the last.

"For me it's gone quickly—and yet it seems a long time. That's not quite so stupid as it sounds. It's as if I'd been travelling in a car, very fast. Suddenly the journey's over. Yet when you look back, the beginning seems so far away."

I could see that life with Martin might be like that. I said, "You don't look in the least different from the last time I saw you."

She smiled. "I'm over thirty now, just as you are. But I expect you're still looking at girls of twenty-three. It must be nice to be a man." She paused. "I never asked if you were married."

"I'm not."

"I didn't think you were, somehow." She became suddenly serious. "Why did you come here, Peter?"

"Because the Ministry asked me to."

"Don't be evasive. You could have got out of it, couldn't you?"

"I suppose so."

"You must have known it would be rather an—odd situation."

This was true, of course. Indeed, the fact that I accepted the assignment is an indication that I was never really suited to my job. One could not blame Stratton or my chief for asking me to go. So far as they knew, I had simply been on friendly terms with Martin Farrell as a student. The complex relationship that existed between the three of us was unknown to them. If I had asked to be excused for personal reasons, as any correct civil servant would have done, there would have been no alternative for them but to agree. But I was weary of discretion. Sitting here with Barbara, I did not for a moment regret my decision to come.

I said to her, as lightly as I could make it, "If I say I came here because I wanted to see you again, you won't believe me."

"You never know. When you don't get so many compliments as you used to, there's a temptation to believe them."

We were silent for a moment. Then caution left me. I was finding it impossible to talk to her on a superficial plane. I said, "You know I was always in love with you."

"Were you?"

"Yes. Surely you must have known."

"I used to think so. Then—" She shrugged her shoulders impatiently. "That was all a long time ago."

I said, "There's something I'd like to explain—" I started to tell her what had happened, from the moment Martin had walked into my room when I was reading Gray's *Anatomy*. She listened without saying anything. At the end I said, rather bitterly, "It sounds silly now, told in cold blood. But in those days it seemed the only possible thing. I had no experience of life, I didn't know what I felt half the time. I was very young—"

She nodded sadly. "We were all very young," she said.

She looked as if she had been about to say something else and then checked herself. I said, "Barbara, supposing I hadn't acted as I did—would you have married Martin?"

Her voice was suddenly angry. "Do you think you have a right to ask that?"

"No," I said stubbornly. "But would you?"

She paused for a long time. Then she said wearily, "No, of course I wouldn't. But what does it matter now?"

8

⚙
⚙
⚙
⚙
⚙
⚙

SOON afterward I went to bed. The nights were cool on the top of the cliff, and I was asleep almost as soon as I turned off the light. I was awakened at seven o'clock by a servant bearing a cup of tea. It was a magnificent morning. I bathed and dressed hurriedly and went downstairs, to find Barbara already having breakfast on the terrace.

She smiled at me and asked me if I had slept well. Neither of us made any reference to our conversation of the night before. We talked of trivialities throughout breakfast. I was just finishing my toast and marmalade when I was called to the telephone.

"Dr. Mayne?" said a rather harsh male voice.

"Yes."

"I'm Dr. Hume—the pathologist. They tell me you got in yesterday. Have a good trip?"

"Excellent."

"Fine. I hope you enjoy yourself here." His politeness was rapid and perfunctory. "I was talking to the Governor last night and he mentioned he'd like to see you. He asked me if I'd bring you round for a drink this evening. Would that be all right for you—say, about seven o'clock?"

"Yes."

"Good. I'll pick you up at the house and drive you there. By the way, I had quite a business finding you. The story was that you were staying at the Clanricarde."

"I took a look at it and changed my mind."

Hume laughed. "I see your point. Well—I look forward to meeting you this evening."

He rang off. When I went back to the table Barbara said, "Who was it?"

"A man called Hume. He's going to take me up to see the Governor this evening." She nodded, without interest. I asked, "What is he like?"

"Hume or the Governor?"

"Hume."

She buttered a piece of toast. "All right, I suppose. A bachelor, lazy, drinks too much. Fat, rather boring."

"And the Governor?"

"Thin and boring." She added indifferently, "Don't take too much notice of me. I'm no sort of a judge of character."

"You're the only person I've ever known who admits it."

"Yes, it's one of those things like having a sense of humor. . . . But I've found out that unless I really care for people I only get the vaguest idea of what they're like. Perhaps I'm not sufficiently interested."

It was likely. My recollection of her was that she felt warmly and intensely about people who inhabited her own world. But she had never had much genuine understanding of those who lay outside it.

After breakfast she said, "Is there anything special you'd like to do today?"

"Don't think you have to cook up amusements for me. I have plenty of books. And I have some work I'd like to get through—"

"Are you sure?"

"Of course."

She looked relieved. "That's as well, really. Because when you come down to it, there isn't very much to do. Not unless you want to become a temporary member of the Yacht Club."

"How do you spend your time?"

"I ride a little. Swim in the pool." She hesitated, and added abruptly, "And I do some painting—"

"Painting? I didn't know—"

"It's nothing of any importance," she said, with a curtness that obviously covered embarrassment. "Just a hobby."

"Can I see anything you've done?"

She shook her head and said with finality, "I can assure you, you wouldn't find them in the least interesting."

In the end I did no work but spent the morning talking with Barbara on the terrace. We talked mainly of the years we had spent apart, filling in our experiences for each other. She had lived out of England for so long that she claimed to have almost forgotten what it was like.

"Let me see if I can guess how you live," she said. She thought for a moment, regarding me through narrowed eyes. "Bachelor apartments in St. James's."

"Too grand. Victoria."

"One of those lovely, stuffy old clubs where men go for lunch. And a gloomy office in Whitehall—"

"Savile Row."

"A bowler hat—no, that's too much—a black Homburg perhaps." I smiled and shook my head. "Well, then, a trilby—no? And a black umbrella." She saw me blush and clapped her hands in delight. "Oh, Peter, you do! How wonderful. You really carry a rolled umbrella, with a button and a little piece of elastic—and a whangee handle—"

I was slightly nettled. "It's very rainy in London, you'll remember, and it's impossible to park a car—"

"Yes, I know. I'm sure you have the most wonderful logical reasons for it." She looked at me solemnly, biting her lip.

"I shall sulk," I said. "You're laughing at me."

"You don't mind really, do you? It's so good to laugh." Suddenly there was an infinity of sadness in her voice. "Peter, you don't know how wonderful it is to have you here."

"It's wonderful for me, too."

"No. I didn't mean it like that. It's something more than just pleasure in your company." She paused and then said, "I feel as if you're my only hope—my only chance." She paused again and said in a low voice, "And Martin's too."

"I don't know what you mean."

She seemed to pull herself together. "No, of course you don't. And I mustn't tell you just now. You'll see soon enough." As I was about to say something she went on, "No, please don't ask me. Later perhaps." What did she mean? I wondered. Was it something between herself and Martin? Perhaps I was supposed to meet Martin first. It was not at all like her to throw out hints, and then become secretive. She had always been the kind of girl who either told you the whole of something or never mentioned it at all.

I asked, "Will Martin be pleased to see me?"

She thought for a moment. "It's not easy to say what he really feels about anything nowadays." She said, "He believes you've been sent out here to spy on him. Is that so?"

"I can imagine him taking it like that." It was what I had been rather afraid of. "No, of course it isn't true. I was asked to make an interim report on how the trial was proceeding. It's quite a usual thing, particularly when there's been so much public interest—" It sounded good enough. I was almost persuading myself that there was no more to it than that. "How did he take it, when he heard I was coming?"

"Naturally he was furious to hear that anyone was coming. When he heard it was you he was still angry. But in another sort of way—" She paused. "Dramatic situations rather appeal to him, you know."

I knew very well. "Even to the extent of creating them sometimes," I said.

"Yes, indeed." She shook her head sadly. "Those poor Germans."

"You mean Chemiefabriken?"

"Yes. He gave them a terrible time. I always feel sorry for businessmen when they have to deal with Martin. They can't understand him. He breaks all the rules they live by. He lies when he ought to be telling the truth, and he tells the truth when

they think it's normal to lie. He treats important people like no-
bodies. He talks them silly with technicalities and then throws a
tantrum if they raise objections. But he manages to leave them
with an uneasy feeling that perhaps he's a genius and it may be
worth while to give him his head. Even they can realize that there
are only two choices with Martin—you either go along with him
in his own way or else . . ." She hesitated. When she spoke it
was as if she had forgotten about the Germans and was speaking
of something else, herself perhaps. "Or else you cut loose completely. And that takes a bit of doing."

"I suppose so." I was not going to ask what she meant. If she
wanted to tell me she would do so in her own time. "They must
be fairly generous, these Chemiefabriken people," I said. I looked
round at the house. "Are they paying for all this?"

Barbara shrugged her shoulders. "Presumably. Whether they
know about it is another matter. Certainly there's nobody else
who can pay for it. Martin has nothing, as you know. Nor have I
nowadays."

I looked at her in consternation. I had been brought up in a
middle-class world where invested capital had something like a
sacramental value. The idea of the two of them running through
a fortune of thirty thousand pounds within a few years was shock-
ing to me.

"You don't mean that?" I said.

"Yes." She sounded regretful, but not especially upset. "All
gone."

"But where—"

"Some on living. We've both been very extravagant. And Martin's research took quite a lot at one time and another. We weren't
always lucky enough to find German businessmen, you know."

I was surprised that she could take it so casually. "He squan-
dered all your money?"

"Don't look so horrified, Peter." There was a glint of amusement in her eyes. "I'm just as much to blame as he is. I let him
have it. He would have spent it just the same if it had been his
own. He never counted the cost of anything. He has no idea of

value. Always, all through his life, he's decided what he wanted and bought it if he could, with his own money or anyone else's. It's just so much paper so far as he's concerned. When I told him there was nothing left, he wasn't worried and he didn't expect me to be. He'll live in luxury as long as the Germans will stand for it. After that, he'll either find someone else to finance him or he'll just do without. He can manage very easily without luxury, if he has to. And so can I, I suppose."

I could imagine how it had happened. It was difficult to stand out against such a lordly casualness, particularly if, like Barbara, you were a little that way yourself and despised bourgeois calculation about financial matters. I could visualize her being a little alarmed as her inheritance began to fade away so rapidly, and then shrugging her shoulders philosophically and wiping it out of her mind. She had always been rich. She could talk theoretically about accepting a life of poverty. But I was extremely doubtful whether she had any idea what it really meant.

9

◉

◉

◉

◉

◉

◉

IN the afternoon, Barbara drove me down into Flores.
While she went shopping I looked around the town. I had an
hour or so to spare before I was due for tea with Dr. and Mrs. Das.
There was not a great deal to see. There were the usual rows of
small shops disgorging shoddy goods onto the street; the English
department store staffed by half-castes in white cotton suits; the
market, hot, crowded and noisy, where anything could be bought
from buttons to crates of live poultry. There was an Anglican
church in sham Gothic and a whitewashed Catholic church in a
vaguely Moorish style. A black-robed priest came out of it. De
Freitas? I wondered. But, no, he was up in the mountains, like
Martin.

At four o'clock I made for the address Das had given me. The
house was up a narrow street in a part of the town that had perhaps once been fashionable but was so no longer. Probably, with
the laying of the motor road, most of the Europeans had moved
out. It was a stucco house that badly needed repainting. On the
wall were scribbled ill-spelled slogans of a generally seditious nature—"African Union," "No More British Exploitation," and so
on. The garden was overgrown with tropical weeds and loud with
the humming of insects.

When I rang the bell, the door was opened by Das himself. He
looked a little flustered. There was a pram in the hall, and a good
deal of outmoded Victorian-style furniture. As I was negotiating

my way past it, a woman came down the stairs. She was fair, with thin wispy hair and a short, stocky body. On her right arm she carried a small brown baby.

"I would like you to meet my wife," said Das.

Mrs. Das reached the bottom of the stairs and looked me over rather aggressively. "Excuse me for not shaking hands," she said. She had an abrupt, South Kensington type of voice. "You'd better come into the back parlor. It's in rather less of a mess than the others."

The back parlor looked out through French doors onto an overgrown back garden across which stretched what looked like a permanent line of washing. We all sat down. The child began to crawl around on the floor, blowing bubbles of his own saliva. A few flies buzzed against the windowpane.

"Well, Dr. Mayne, it's very nice of you to come and see us," said Mrs. Das. Her tone conveyed that she had half expected me to insult them by refusing the invitation. "Harold tells me you're from the Ministry of Health."

"Yes."

"I must say, it's a nice change to see anybody from England out here—isn't it, Harold?" Harold smiled nervously. "You know what they call Batou?—the forgotten island. Nobody in Whitehall seems the slightest bit interested in it."

"Really? Of course, the Colonial Office—" I was hoping to explain that I had no responsibility for this official indifference, but I was not quick enough.

"Harold constantly sends in reports, and asks for equipment and facilities. Nobody takes the slightest notice. I don't suppose they even read his letters. He's hopelessly short of staff. The standard of public health among the islanders is appalling. Why, if you go out into the country—" She launched out into a denunciation of health conditions on Batou. It was evident, from her fluency and the number of figures she quoted, that she had delivered this tirade frequently before—indeed, it sounded suspiciously like a lecture. Her voice was the high, querulous voice of frustrated idealism. At how many protest meetings had I heard it, stating the case for disarmament or proportional representation or the abolition of capital punishment with such an extreme degree of humorless conviction as to dishearten even the converted. It was a voice guaranteed to arouse reaction in the most progressive heart. Nothing, one always felt, could be quite so certain and simple as it seemed to her. Vice could not be so black, virtue not so white— nor so dull.

I found myself in the false position of almost trying to defend Whitehall. I knew they were often incompetent, sometimes dishonest, and almost always inefficient and lazy—but they were not, to my knowledge, a gigantic, concentrated conspiracy to keep Batou unhealthy and Das in a position of impotence. Nor did I want Das to think so, since nothing can be more damaging to a man's happiness and career than a chronic grievance, real or imagined. I made an effort to protest but she drove over me.

"But what's the use of talking? Harold needs at least two assistants, don't you, Harold?" Das gave a melancholy nod. "The Government won't authorize them. And even if they did, I doubt whether they'd get them, the salary scales being what they are. I can tell you, it's quite impossible to bring up a family decently on what Harold's paid. I've been trying it for five years and it can't be done." She picked up the child and began to mop saliva off its face with pieces of cotton wool that she subsequently tossed into a wastepaper basket. "Let's hope you're going to do something about that."

"Well—" I was interrupted by the arrival of tea. It was brought in by a plump, adolescent colored girl who seemed overcome by the importance of the occasion. Through the open door I could hear high-pitched voices raised in argument and the squeals of children. Das's relatives, no doubt, and his other children. Mrs. Das frowned wearily, as if such promiscuous living was beginning to tell on her.

"Perhaps," I said when she was pouring tea, "I should explain my position. I'm from the Ministry of Health, not the Colonial Office. And I haven't any jurisdiction over salary scales—I wish

I had. I think they're rotten, too. But until the Government does something—"

"The Government!" She scornfully folded a piece of bread and crammed it into the baby's mouth. "It's no use expecting anything from a reactionary gang like that."

"The Governor," said Das, sitting on the edge of the chair and sipping his tea delicately, "is more advanced. He is sympathetic—"

"Sympathy's cheap. What does he get done?" She added irritably, "You're too trusting, Harold. Anyone can deceive you."

I felt sorry for Das. I could see that she would have been attractive once—even now she was not bad-looking, in a crumpled, indignant sort of way. It was obvious that she had no talent for housekeeping or bringing up children, especially on an inadequate income. The room we sat in was tasteless and rather grubby. No doubt she regarded housework as an irritating distraction from the things of the mind. She was more interested in fighting her husband's battles for him.

"Of course," she said, turning on me, "as you'll soon find out, we're not people of any significance here. We're not even socially acceptable to the people who matter. Harold's an Indian and I'm a Socialist. That's the end of the matter as far as they're concerned." I murmured sympathetically. "Not that we care, of course—not in the slightest. I just thought it might amuse you to know." There was, I decided, nothing I could say to this. She went on, "The only person worth a damn on this island is Martin Farrell."

Das spoke solemnly. "I think he is a very fine man."

"Of course, Harold's helped him a lot with this trial. I don't suppose he's told you because he doesn't advertise himself, but Martin would have been lost without him. He freely admits it." She became confidential. "As a matter of fact he's promised to fix Harold up with a first-rate research job if the trial goes well."

I was startled. A job where? I wondered. Das was surely a clinician, not a research worker. He would be useless in a laboratory, and so far as I knew Martin had no influence anywhere else. But I had memories of Martin, his eyes firmly fixed on the present

object of his enthusiasm and ready to use whatever means came
to his hand to attain it. I could picture him "taking up" Das as he
had once "taken up" me in his expansive way, arousing his devotion and paying for it with the promise of excitement, with vague
hints of future benefits never precisely defined. It would all seem
plausible enough to a lay person. Even Das, so long removed from
the main stream of medicine and bemused by an attractive and
powerful personality, might induce himself to believe something
that fitted in so well with his own desires. By this time, no doubt
Martin had convinced them that nothing was impossible for him.

Suddenly Mrs. Das seemed to make up her mind to something.
She looked at me grimly, and said, "Do you mind if I ask you a
blunt question, Dr. Mayne?"

"Well—"

She did not wait for my answer. "Is it true that the Government
intends to break the encephalitis trial?"

I glanced at Das and kept my temper. He was looking miserable. I didn't think he liked me any more than she did. But he had
some conception of tact.

"As I'm sure your husband realizes," I said carefully, "this is an
extremely complex technical matter. I'm afraid it isn't possible to
discuss it in such terms."

"I see," she said disgustedly. She obviously thought I was fob-
bing her off. To emotional people accuracy often sounds like evasion. "Well, that's what the rumor is here, anyway, and I thought
perhaps it might be of value to you to know. It doesn't surprise
me if the Ministry are against the trial. It's just about the only
progressive thing that's happened on this island since Vasco da
Gama called here in 1497." She paused for a moment, brooding.
"And those priests—well, of course they were against it from the
start. That was obvious to anyone."

"Why should they be?"

"Because they're afraid of losing their influence. They've been
acting like little tin gods out there in the bush for centuries—they
ran medical missions because it was a wonderful way of bribing

people into going to church. Naturally any attempt to give proper treatment to these people frightens them to death. Any attempt to subsitute science for superstition . . ."

Das protested gently. "I don't think they're quite so bad as all that."

She turned on him. "That's typical of you, Harold. Always seeing the other person's point of view, even when they haven't got one. Everyone knows what the Jesuits are like—"

Do they, I thought. I felt the same weariness that had come over me the previous day when listening to Miss Paston talking about medicine. Once again I was the man on the inside. I felt the hopelessness of making contact with someone who had done no more than read up a few facts, probably tainted with prejudice, and then decided once for all on an attitude. The happy man is he who can appreciate the complexity of human issues and accept it without resentment. Christine Das was a born outsider. To her all issues would appear simple; any failure to solve them immediately along the lines she favored would imply at the best incompetence, at the worst dishonesty. She was the girl who worked her fingers to the bone to elect the candidate but was somehow passed over when the fruits of office came to be handed out.

She hated me. To her I represented all the forces of reaction, the pompous Ministers and M.P.s, the Strattons—the men who knew all about it, who had used their knowledge to work out a hundred reasons why nothing could ever be done. The sad thing was that my sympathies were with her. I think she was more nearly right than the Strattons of the world. Big, simple things *can* be done if you have the will and the means to do them. Compromise is sometimes right, but not always. Good and evil exist— there is not always something to be said for both sides. The trouble with Mrs. Das was that she debased moral values by equating them with political systems and with cant words like "progressive" and "reactionary"; she imagined that moral righteousness was a substitute for knowing what you were talking about.

She was, in other words, the amateur while I was the professional. We had no real point of contact and I could see that once she had given up any hope of influencing me, my presence merely exasperated her. As soon as tea was over, I excused myself and took a taxi back up the hill.

10

BACK at the house, I took a bath and sat over a drink with Barbara until Hume arrived. He was a type of man I instantly recognized—red-faced and stocky, a club bachelor, full of racy anecdotes and an insensitive, somehow almost brutal, goodfellowship. In England I could imagine him in sporting tweeds, a Home Office pathologist perhaps, carrying out post-mortems with a cigarette in his mouth and dictating facetious comments to his secretary. He would run an expensive sports car, be on good terms with the C.I.D., and be much in demand by provincial medical societies as an after-dinner lecturer (with slides)—"Identification of the Body," "The Doctor in Court," and so on.

As we drove off to Government House, he asked me, "You haven't met the old man before?"

"No."

"He's not bad. He'd like to do his best for the island, I imagine, but when it comes down to it he doesn't amount to much—his powers are limited. Besides, he's been sweating on a peerage for the last few years. He's retiring pretty soon, you know. Naturally he wants to keep on good terms with Whitehall." He grinned. "All this business is rather a worry to him."

"The trial?"

"Yes. Of course, at first he thought it was going to be wonderful. Martin really gave him the business. He was going to put Batou on the map. Wonder drugs, elimination of ghastly disease, milestone in medical research—thanks to the co-operation and support of one of our alert and most farsighted colonial administrators. Martin knew all the right sort of people—he managed to persuade the Old Man that they were even distantly related through some cousins in Shropshire. And then, of course, he had letters from Hackett. To us, Hackett may be played out. But he's the only person in tropical medicine that these old boffins have ever heard of." He paused to light a cigarette. "That was how it was then. Now he's getting a little worried. Particularly since he heard you were coming."

I said irritably, "Everyone here seems to have quite the wrong idea about me. I'm just an observer. I'm not in the least important."

"Granted," said Hume imperturbably. "But you must recognize something. This is a very small island. This is the first time anything of importance has happened here. You'll find almost everyone heavily involved emotionally, on one side or the other. Nobody believes you're here on just a routine visit. To all of them, you represent something. To the Governor, if I'm not mistaken, you represent a slight tremor of anxiety in the mind of the Establishment."

It was all too true. I changed the subject. "Is the trial still going well? Is he getting plenty of volunteers?"

Hume took his eyes off the road to look at me and then said carefully, "I believe he's getting plenty of cases. And I suppose you might call them volunteers—he doesn't actually drive them in at the point of a gun. The villagers are pretty primitive you know. They haven't the remotest idea what it's all about. How could they?"

"I see what you mean."

"Personally I think they're damned lucky to have a chance of treatment with the stuff. Nothing else does much good. But really I don't know very much about it. You ought to ask Farrell himself. Or Das—he's done quite a lot of work on the clinical side. Have you met him?"

"I had tea with him this afternoon."

"Nice little chap, isn't he?" said Hume rather condescendingly. "Did you meet that bloody awful wife of his?"

"She isn't very attractive."

"She's a prize bitch, if you ask me." He paused and then went on. "He met her when he was a student at University College. She was at the London School of Economics. Daughter of a colonel in South Kensington. So far as I can gather they used to read the *New Statesman* together and go and sit in the gallery at the Royal Court. Occasionally they'd carry banners in a genteel little parade to Trafalgar Square. She just swallowed poor old Das, along with Brecht and Victor Gollancz and the Committee for Nuclear Disarmament. I don't think he was ever really a chap to her at all—he was just a member of the oppressed colored peoples. She married him to prove something—you know what I mean? So now here she is. She hates Batou, she's mad at Das because he doesn't earn more money, and she's got three kids without the foggiest idea how to look after them. But he's the one I'm sorry for. What he needs is a nice, fat, cheerful little wife from the islands. He could stuff her all night and she could cram him with curry all day and they'd be as happy as hell. As it is he doesn't know where he is. A lot of people would like to be friendly with him but they can't stand her at any price. I don't mean just the British. The islanders don't like her, either."

"Why not?"

"She's always going round telling them they're backward. Granted, she assures them it's not their fault—it's all due to the exploiting British government. Still, nobody likes to be told they're backward, do they?"

He turned the car off the road into a private drive. I could see the white pillars of Government House through the trees. Before we stopped Hume said, "Did you tell Das you were coming here with me this evening?"

"No. Should I have done?"

"No. Better not, really. He might have thought the Old Man ought to have invited him as well. You know how touchy these chaps are."

The Governor was small and wiry, with a pink face and a white military mustache. He spoke in short, staccato sentences and seemed to find it hard to keep still. While we were talking, he wandered about the room, glass in hand, occasionally stopping to brace his shoulders back and pull his stomach in. It was as if his movements were controlled, puppet-fashion, by wires from the ceiling. Hume stayed long enough to introduce me and take a single glass of sherry. Then he mentioned a dinner appointment and asked to be excused. As I got up to join him the Governor said, "I'd be obliged if you would stay a little longer, Dr. Mayne, if you can spare the time. I have a few things I'd like to discuss with you. My chauffeur will drive you home. I hope that's convenient?"

"Of course." I sat down again.

After Hume left the room there was a short silence. The Governor paced the room, as if not very sure how to begin. Eventually he said, "I hope you'll enjoy your stay on Batou. We think it's a very beautiful island." Before I could say anything, he said, "I hear you're staying with Farrell?"

"Yes." I was not sure whether this was just a social inquiry or whether it carried disapproval. His way of speaking made every remark sound like an accusation. I added, "He's quite an old friend of mine. We were students together."

"Indeed?" His interest was perfunctory. "Well, you'll certainly be a great deal more comfortable there than at the hotel, from all I hear. How long are you likely to be here?"

"I'm not sure. It depends on how long it takes me to complete my report. A few weeks, I should think."

"I've got a lot of stuff from the Colonial Office, telling me what you're here for and asking me to give you all possible facilities— which, of course, I shall be happy to do. If there's any way in which I can make the wheels go round more smoothly, perhaps you'd let me know."

"Thank you very much."

"Of course," he went on, "the medical side of all this is a matter for you doctors. I'm only a layman." He spoke as if making a frank and honest admission. "However, when you've lived in the tropics as long as I have, you pick up a certain amount of knowledge, particularly about public health." Oh God, I thought, another amateur. "Naturally, I've been keenly interested in this encephalitis trial. Young Farrell impressed me from the start." He said with an air of discovery, "He has a very quick mind."

"Yes, indeed."

"He's very keen and not afraid to learn. When he came here he told me frankly that he knew a lot about viruses but not a damn thing about the people he was going to have to deal with. That was where I was able to give him a bit of help." It was as if Martin wrote his signature wherever he went. I could picture him amusing himself with the Governor, playing the keen young man full of drive and ideas but still not too vain to take advice from an old hand. "I think I can say that most of the people on the island believe in him and are a hundred per cent behind him. It's true, of course, we're not experts. But I have a letter from Sir Francis Hackett—"

"Yes." I said, with all the delicacy I could manage, "Between ourselves, sir, there's a possibility that Hackett may have somewhat overstepped his authority."

The Governor was visibly disconcerted. "Really?"

"I'm afraid so. He omitted to consult his committee."

"Well, maybe—but that's just red tape, surely. After all, he's the great expert, isn't he?"

"He's a great man," I said tactfully. "But he's also an old man. He hasn't done much active work for the last ten years. The day when his word was absolutely final in immunology is past."

"I imagine," said the Governor with slight acidity, "that he knows more about it than a bunch of priests."

"Of course." This was going to be difficult. The Governor had obviously committed himself in support of the trial. It might have made just that difference in his quest for the coveted peerage. A little favorable publicity before retirement, the best kind of newspaper coverage (a second leader in the *Times* perhaps), and there he was, well away. And now there was talk of people dying. These tiresome priests!

"The trouble is," I said, "that the priests are here on the spot, and Sir Francis Hackett isn't. You see—perhaps I could explain the exact nature of the difficulty?"

"Please do."

I hesitated. "I don't know how much Dr. Farrell has told you about this vaccine," I said, "but according to our information this is supposed to consist of particles of killed encephalitis virus."

"Yes. He told me that."

"The suggestion is that the vaccine will help to cure people already infected. In other words, this is a therapeutic trial. Now, therapeutic trials have two main aspects, efficacy and safety. Farrell has designed his trial very well to test efficacy. He's using a technique known as the double blind."

"He did mention that," said the Governor. "But I must admit I didn't completely follow it. What exactly does it imply?"

"Well," I said, "put briefly, the point is this. It's been found that a lot of patients will report improvement on any new treatment, whether it's of any value or not. You can give them starch tablets or injections of sterile water, and they'll feel better. And a great many doctors, no matter how impartial they might want to be, will get so emotionally bound up with the success of the treatment that they'll believe them. The double blind is designed to avoid this. The way it works is that if, for instance, you're injecting two hundred people, a hundred of the ampoules don't contain the vaccine at all. They're made up to look exactly the same as the active ones, so that neither doctor nor patient knows who is getting the stuff and who isn't. At the end of the experiment you compare the hundred patients who were treated with the hundred who thought they were, but in fact weren't."

"But how do you know which was which?"

"All the ampoules have code numbers. The key to the code is held by a third person who hands it to the experimenter at the end of the trial."

"Yes. I follow." The Governor was a little impatient. He didn't really enjoy being told things. "That sounds excellent. Very ingenious."

"The only trouble is"—I permitted myself a touch of malice—"as you've no doubt realized yourself, it has one enormous snag."

"Oh?"

"Yes. It's a wonderful method for testing the value of the drug —none better. But it makes it impossible to test safety. If somebody falls ill or dies—as I believe has happened here—you can't tell whether the vaccine was responsible or not. You don't even know whether they had it."

There was quite a long silence. Then he said, "Do you honestly think there's any reason for supposing this stuff to be dangerous?"

"Father de Freitas—"

"Yes, I know about de Freitas and these two people who died. I gather he's been writing to all sorts of damn people in London. But these chaps have an axe to grind, you know. I asked Farrell at the time. He assures me that it's most unlikely that there's any connection."

"He has an interest too," I pointed out.

"Well, yes, all right," he admitted reluctantly. I was beginning to see the Governor more clearly. Vain, limited in outlook, but fundamentally honest. He would like to be a peer if he could. But he would not cheat for it. On the other hand, he was reluctant to discard his previous happy optimism. Everything had seemed so simple. He was irritated with me for introducing complexities. "Confound it," he burst out peevishly, "I don't understand this. I'm only a layman, but it would seem to me that this stuff must have been checked beforehand. Surely they must test it before they send it out? These Germans who make it—they're all right, aren't they? Everybody's always talking about how damned efficient they are."

"So far as we know, every possible laboratory test has been done, both in Germany and in England. The virus appeared to be killed. But that isn't entirely conclusive."

"You mean," he said incredulously, "that they can't be sure

whether it's alive or dead?" He seemed to indict the whole medical profession with incompetence. He conveyed that he claimed to be no more than a plain man, a mere layman, but at least he could tell whether things were alive or not.

"They're very small, you know," I said gently. "Just tiny little particles. You can't see them moving around or anything like that. It's just possible that there might be some 'hot' particles—I don't say it's likely, but it could happen. The Ministry feels it ought to be looked into, at least. They don't want people saying we're carrying out dangerous experiments on the natives."

"My God, no!"

It was as if I had unexpectedly stamped on his toe. It occurred to me that every colonial governor nowadays must go through life praying that he would reach retiring age before the inevitable racial troubles started in his particular area. "Fortunately this has always been a very stable and contented island. We've done a lot for the islanders and I think they appreciate it. But one has to be damn careful nowadays. Some of those African politicians on the mainland are looking for any excuse to make trouble."

"I suppose so. Of course," I said, "if we were really as bad as some people make us out to be, this wouldn't present a problem at all. The Russians do the most massive trials without any difficulty whatever. But there you are." I smiled. "Anyway, let's not meet trouble halfway. There's a good chance it'll all turn out to be a mare's nest." I added, "Believe me, I don't want to interfere with the trial if I can possibly help it."

"Well, I'm glad to hear it." He seemed a little reassured. "I suppose we shall just have to see what happens." He shook his head gloomily. "It's a frightful thing, you know, this encephalitis. They get headaches and paralysis and blindness and goodness knows what. Quite apart from the individual suffering, the social consequences are appalling." He mused vaguely. "Of course, I haven't any training in these matters, but I would have imagined that one of these antibiotics . . . No?"

"I'm afraid not."

"Well, I suppose you know best," he said reluctantly. "The is-

landers themselves have an herb for which they claim a percentage of quite remarkable cures. I asked Das to send some back to
England to be analyzed, but nothing came of it." I made a sympathetic noise. He went on, "I must say I never feel the Colonial
Medical Service is very amenable to new ideas. That was why it
was such a pleasant change to meet Farrell. At least he was prepared to have a go." He gave me an uneasy smile. I could see he
was beginning to regret his earlier enthusiasm. Caution was taking over. "But these priests are pretty dodgy, you know. And very
influential here. Most of the islanders are Catholics, in name anyway—the Portuguese were here for a hundred years before us. So
one has to walk warily."

He let out a deep breath that was almost a sigh, then braced
his shoulders back and pulled his stomach in. There was an aggrieved expression on his face, as if all this was something he had
not bargained for—scientists, priests, unexplained deaths, racial
implications, anxious politicians in Whitehall. . . . "Well, there
it is," he said, with an air of dismissal. He held out his hand. His
face twisted into an official smile. "Keep me informed, will you?"

✺

✺

✺

✺

✺

✺

11

MARTIN returned in the late afternoon of the following day. Barbara and I were sitting on the terrace. He was in a large Buick station wagon, which he drove at great speed up the drive and then braked hard on the gravel in front of the house. He was dressed in a shirt and slacks, and looked brown and travel-stained. After he got out of the car he glanced around through his sunglasses and saw us together on the terrace. He stood for a moment, motionless. There was something slightly theatrical about his pose, like a film actor waiting for the cameras to start rolling. Then he took off his glasses and walked toward us.

He had the same lean good looks that I remembered, the same grace of movement. He was harder perhaps, his charm less uncertain and febrile. The years had actually improved him; he looked as if he was born to be just about this age.

"Peter!" He took my right hand between both of his and pressed it warmly. "After all these years!" From the way he looked at me you might have imagined he had been living for this moment. Again, he held the pose. He was overdoing it a little and it came into my mind that he was nervous, just as I was. He had rehearsed this awkward scene. While I remained tongue-tied, his instinct was to talk, to take the initiative, to endeavor to place himself in a position of command from the very beginning. After a moment he released my hand and put one arm round my shoulder and the other round Barbara's—it was quite remarkable how we both instinctively moved into the correct positions to give full value to the gesture—and led us inside.

"You know," he said to me, "I always felt it was just a matter of time before we saw each other again. I couldn't really believe that we'd parted for good when I left St. Vincent's."

"Nor I," I said.

"I often used to wonder where you were and what you were up to. . . ."

"I wrote to you once," I reminded him.

"You did?" He raised his eyebrows. "I never got it." By the briskness of his manner I could tell he was lying. He had evidently forgotten about the letter until I reminded him. "Of course, I've been travelling around a lot." He moved rapidly on to safer ground. He was clearly determined to play it for nostalgia. He said to Barbara, "Did I ever tell you about the first time we met, Peter and I? It was at Breckenhall, outside the Prefect's Room. He was warming his hands on pipes without any hot water in them." He grinned. "Rather characteristically, I've often thought."

"And you pretended you weren't hurt when you were," I said, "also rather characteristic."

A slightly puzzled expression appeared on his face, as if he had prepared the scene for me but I had unaccountably switched the dialogue in the middle. But he recovered almost immediately. His smile returned. "I suppose we all give way to self-delusion every now and then," he said.

On his arrival, the whole household seemed to spring into activity. Two servants were occupied in unloading his gear from the station wagon; another, his gold teeth flashing smiles, was already mixing Martinis. Martin sprawled in a chair and drained most of his glass with one gulp.

"Sorry I wasn't here to welcome you," he said. "We had three of the hill villages all laid on for vaccination, and you know what primitive people are like. If you change the date, they're just as likely to refuse to have it done. Particularly," he added with some bitterness, "with all the propaganda they're being subjected to at the moment." I thought he was going to start talking about the trial immediately, without any preliminaries at all. Obviously it was the main thing on his mind. But he stopped himself. "Did Das meet you all right? I asked him to fix everything."

"Yes, he was fine."

Martin nodded and said, rather condescendingly, "He's a nice little fellow, isn't he? And a good doctor too, within his limitations. The trouble is that he's hopelessly short-staffed and he has to do all kinds of jobs he shouldn't be doing at all—"

"Such as?"

"Emergency surgery, for one thing. Rather fancies himself, as a matter of fact." He gave a little shudder. "Not quite the sort of thing you were accustomed to at St. Vincent's."

"Is he the only medical officer?"

"There are two others, but he's the senior. They can fly out a consultant from the mainland if the weather's suitable and the airfield's open, which it usually isn't. So I should watch that gastric ulcer of yours while you're here. You'd be well advised not to perforate again during the next few weeks." He swallowed the rest of his drink and said, "I was awfully sorry to hear about that, by the way—your ulcer and everything."

I almost laughed. Martin's absorption in himself and his own affairs was so complete that when he decided, as he sometimes did, to go in for conventional expressions of sorrow or consideration, it always sounded absurdly unconvincing. A man can only simulate an emotion if there is some trace of it in his own nature. When Martin tried to sound sympathetic, he was like someone who had read about it in a book. The pretense was so far from reality that it could hardly be regarded as an effort at deception. It was too naïve, like a child pretending to be grown up.

"Yes," I said, as lightly as possible. "It was unfortunate. Naturally I was reluctant to give up surgery—"

"I was staggered when I heard of it."

"But I didn't have much choice. I was strongly advised that my health wouldn't stand it."

"It must have been a terrible blow," he said solemnly.

I could see he was enjoying himself in the role of the sympathetic friend and it annoyed me. I was determined not to be trapped into self-pity by him or anyone else. If he had had any sensibility he would have known that the temptation was severe enough without giving it encouragement from outside. I said sharply, "It's not so dramatic as all that. One gets adjusted."

His manner changed, quite suddenly. If sympathy was not going over well, he was happy to discard it. He gave a laugh, affectionate but slightly contemptuous. "Good old Peter. The man who got adjusted."

Within a second, he had removed one label and affixed another. If I wouldn't be a tragic victim, then I must be a stodgy old stick-in-the-mud, too thick-skinned to suffer at all. The familiar sense of excitement at being in Martin's company again was beginning to be succeeded by an equally familiar exasperation. He seemed to be incapable of allowing human relationships to develop on natural lines. He had a way of deliberately misunderstanding the characters and motives of others so as to fit in with his own preconceptions. It was as if one were acting in a play in which he was the main figure and all the rest of us merely character parts, permitted by the conventions of the drama to represent only the crudest and simplest of emotions.

There was a curious compulsion to co-operate with him in this form of make-believe. You had positively to fight to retain your own character and to act naturally. If he had decided that you were ponderous and lacking in dash, it was useless to argue with him, since he could make the very fact of your engaging in argument seem to confirm his point. Logic could be interpreted as pedantry.

If, on the other hand, he had classified you as obstructive or muddleheaded, he had great skill in provoking you to be just that. In his play, he was the only three dimensional character, the only person allowed variation or inconsistency, the only individual seen in the round.

I looked at Barbara. She was standing apart from us, watching, with a faint, sardonic smile on her lips. For the moment, she had no lines to say; the scenes when she was a principal performer had been played years ago, and forgotten. There was suddenly something suffocating to me in the atmosphere, so crowded with old memories and shared experience. We knew each other too well, all the pretenses that make life bearable were impossible among the three of us. No matter how much I tried to preserve conventional reticence, or Martin to cast our relationship in the form of a charade, we should be left in the end with nothing to lean on but the truth. I should never have come.

Martin looked at the two of us and his face clouded for a moment, as if my misgivings had infected him and made him wonder temporarily if this situation might possibly be more difficult to dominate than he had anticipated. He swallowed the rest of his drink and said, "I have all kinds of things to tell you. But I'd like to have a bath first." He got out of his chair. "Give him another drink, Barbara. I'll be down in half an hour. Then we can go down to Charlie's for dinner." He said to me, "Charlie serves the best Chinese food on the island."

Barbara looked disconcerted. "I didn't think we should be going out. Manolo prepared a special dinner—"

He frowned, the spoiled child. "I feel like going to Charlie's."

"He did all your favorite dishes." I had a picture of another in a long line of servants, unreasonably devoted to Martin, trying to anticipate his every wish, making excuses for him when, inevitably, he treated them casually and without consideration. "He'll be terribly disappointed," said Barbara.

"Not a bit of it."

He would, I thought. But he would probably blame Barbara— or me. "He'll be delighted," said Martin. "He'll be able to share it out among those fifteen concubines of his who hang around the back door."

12

◉

◉

◉

◉

◉

◉

CHARLIE'S was an unobtrusive Chinese restaurant up a small alley near the harbor. Martin was treated like an honored customer. We were shown into a private room by Charlie himself, and served by two of his sons. Martin ordered wan-tan soup and small roast chickens with fried rice. Surprisingly, two bottles of Moselle in ice-buckets also appeared.

"I brought the wine with me from Germany," Martin explained. He tasted his glass and nodded appreciatively to the waiter. "I don't mind living on corned beef and coffee essence when I'm out in the bush, but when I come back to base I like a little civilized living." He sat back and smiled at me benevolently. All traces of fatigue had been removed by his bath. He was bright-eyed, confident, and ready for anything. "Well," he said, opening fire, "have you started your investigation yet?"

He didn't make it clear whether the question was intended as a joke or not. I took it as such. "No," I said, smiling back at him.

"You saw the Governor last night, I believe?"

"Yes. He invited me over for drinks."

"What did you think of him?"

"I was only with him for half an hour. He seemed pleasant enough. Not a person of any great importance, perhaps."

"No. He's rather pathetic really, isn't he? He sits up there in Government House playing the proconsul, but whenever Whitehall cracks the whip, he has to come to order like a schoolboy.

This was the first time he tried to do something off his own bat. 'Go ahead, my boy,' he said to me. 'Don't worry about a thing. I believe in what you're doing and I'll back you to the hilt.' That was when he pictured himself making a reputation out of it. Now he's got cold feet."

This seemed to me rather unfair.

"Oh, come," I said, "it's surely not as bad as that."

"You don't know all the facts," said Martin. "When he heard they were proposing to send you out, he called me in and asked my advice. I advised him to take a strong line and refuse to receive you."

He looked at me challengingly. I could see he was out to create tension. I, on the other hand, was determined to dissipate it. I was at an advantage, since I had no personal interest in the trial. It was no doubt difficult for Martin, heavily involved as he was, to comprehend this.

"Why?" I asked mildly.

"Because I think the whole of this investigation is nothing but a ramp. It's a smear campaign organized by the Jesuits. I'm not attacking you as an individual. It's your job, I suppose, and you have to do as you're told. For all I know, you may be entirely honest—"

"Thank you." I glanced at Barbara. She was picking listlessly at her food, not hearing a word. She was a thousand miles away.

"But if so, they're just simply using you. You know as well as I do how easy it is to put a stop to a clinical experiment if somebody wants to. You just demand a hundred-per-cent safety. Nobody can ever guarantee that. But to the public, of course, it sounds quite a reasonable demand."

There was something in what he said. I had experience of how far governments would go in order to avoid the slightest risk of trouble or criticism, no matter how ill-founded. But that was not my affair. I was instructed to make a report. How it was used afterward was nothing to do with me.

"Of course," I pointed out, "the difficulty here is in the double blind."

His lips tightened. "I suppose," he said in a hostile tone of voice, "you're going to tell me I should have done it differently?"

"I'm not saying that. But you must admit it makes it difficult to prove safety."

"The vaccine was safe in animals. Why shouldn't it be safe in humans? It's not for me to prove safety, it's for them to prove danger."

I shook my head. "The Encephalitis Committee doesn't agree."

"The Encephalitis Committee!" He spoke with fathomless contempt. "A bunch of clapped-out old ruins who haven't done a decent bit of scientific work in the last twenty years! All they know about a research project is how to kill it. If I run it double-blind they talk about safety. If I didn't, they'd attack my statistics when the trial finished and say that my results were valueless because I might have an unconscious bias in favor of the treatment. Wouldn't they?" he said fiercely.

"Very probably."

"So you can't win, can you? They have you either way. Especially if they're looking for an excuse to ditch you, as they are in my case. They've never forgiven me for fixing things up with Hackett behind their back."

"I don't know whether that was a very good idea. You've put him in a difficult position."

He was indignant. "What has Hackett got to complain of? He ought to know how to look after himself, at his age. And what sort of position do you think they've put me in? Or you, for that matter? Sending you out to spy on me—"

"Don't be a fool, Martin." I was growing angry myself now. "You know perfectly well that it isn't in the least like that." I could see that he was working himself into a familiar frame of mind, when he imagined that any interference with his plans could only be the product of deliberate malevolence on somebody's part. "I give you my assurance that there isn't any sort of conspiracy against you."

"No?" He paused for a moment, looking at me sardonically, and then shrugged his shoulders. "I was giving them the benefit of the doubt. I just couldn't bring myself to believe that they were actually taking de Freitas seriously. I imagined that control of science by the church had gone out quite some time ago."

"Oh, really, Martin," I said wearily. Martin could be more intelligent than anyone I knew. He could also, if he misjudged or underrated his audience, be more idiotic. "That sort of talk may be all very well for journalists like Miss Paston, but it won't do with me." It seemed to me that he had been associating too much of late with his intellectual inferiors. He had had too many easy victories in discussion. He was growing sloppy. "I saw the correspondence. De Freitas was very careful not to make any comment on the scientific side of the trial. He just described the two deaths and said that the circumstances suggested to his mind that they might have something to do with the vaccine. He asked if he could be given an assurance that they weren't."

"Yes, I know all about that," said Martin impatiently. "He came to me first with that line."

"And what did you say?"

"I told him to stick to his own job and I'd stick to mine."

"That wasn't very conciliatory."

"What did you expect me to say? I could tell he was only trying to make trouble." He broke out impatiently, "You're a child, Peter. I should have thought that seven years at a hellhole like Breckenhall would at least have taught you something about the ways of the Jesuits. Of course de Freitas doesn't accuse me of killing two of his parishioners—not directly. He just points out that they died and asks for a hundred-per-cent assurance of safety, which he knows damn well nobody in Whitehall would have the guts to give even if they knew what they were talking about— which they don't. I hope you don't imagine that de Freitas is genuinely worried about those two deaths." He leaned forward and said with great intensity, "I'll tell you a secret, Peter. In a place like this, people are dying all the time. The average length of life is twenty-nine years. They're dying of malaria and tuberculosis and sleeping sickness and all kinds of nutritional deficiencies—dying in thousands, avoidably, and nobody says a word.

Both those people who died were severely ill from other conditions as well as the encephalitis. I don't suppose you know that two deaths in that number of people over the period of the trial is actually *less* than the normal death rate for the island, do you?"

"No."

"Well it is. I've had it worked out. It's a crying scandal, and nobody gives a damn. But if you try to do something to help people and somebody dies by coincidence in the middle of it, we have a crisis—letters to the Colonial Office, string-pulling, M.P.s, investigations. Can you tell me why that is?"

"I imagine," I said, looking at his intense face, "that you'd sooner tell me."

"All right, I will. It's very simple. De Freitas can see the writing on the wall. He's jealous of my influence with the islanders. He's been running his potty little amateur clinics out in the bush for ten years, dishing up quinine tablets wrapped up in pictures of the Virgin Mary, until he thinks he's St. Francis Xavier. He's got a little surgery next to his church. He has a look at the patients and then promises them a bottle of medicine after they've been to Mass. He wants to buy their souls by treating their bodies." He made a grimace of disgust. "It makes me puke." He looked at me indignantly. "What are you laughing at?"

I was not sure what amused me most, the pathetic device for getting the islanders to Church, or Martin's righteous indignation about it. "And you?" I said. "What are you after? Miss Paston," I said maliciously, "thinks you're an idealist—like Dr. Schweitzer."

Suddenly Barbara, who had taken no part in the conversation, burst into a peal of laughter. "She didn't say that, not really, Peter? You're making it up?"

"She did indeed."

Now I was laughing myself, and so thank God, was Martin. For a time it was just like the old days, when we were young and lighthearted. My own amusement was partially born of relief. Only then did I realize how afraid I had been that age and increasing importance might have robbed him of his sense of the ridiculous. Now I was reassured. There was still something left of the Martin I had known and loved.

From that moment we stopped bristling at each other. He passed off the subject of the trial and Barbara's interest in the conversation revived. We talked about Batou and various personalities until we noticed that it was eleven o'clock and the restaurant was empty. Martin paid the bill and we went back to the house.

I had a feeling that he wanted to talk to me alone, and I was not surprised that when Barbara went up to bed he suggested that I should stay up for a while and have a whiskey with him. When she had left he was noticeably more at ease. He relaxed in a chair and gave me an affectionate smile. As usual, I waited for him to make the running.

He said, "It's a pleasant change to talk to somebody like you, Peter, even if we do disagree. I'd almost forgotten what it was like. To get anything done in an affair like this, one has to humbug so many stupid people. . . . If you're not careful it can become a habit." There was something disarming in the way he had guessed my unspoken criticism of him and accepted it. "With you, I can tell the truth without fear of being misunderstood. I'm not primarily concerned with the islanders—either their bodies or their souls. I'd sooner they didn't suffer, naturally. But from the experimental point of view they're essentially a series of culture media. What I'm concerned with is my vaccine." With one of those changes of mood he was able to make so effectively, he looked at me earnestly and said, "You know, I honestly believe it's the goods."

I liked him much better like this, but in the end only the facts were important.

"On how much evidence?" I said.

"Only animal studies so far," he admitted. "But we were pretty thorough. Do you know, I got those Germans at Bremen to buy me a hundred chimps—a hundred, at five hundred marks apiece. The tears ran down their cheeks." His eyes sparkled reminiscently. "As a matter of fact, between you and me, I could have done very well with fifty. But by now I have a certain amount of experience of dealing with commercial organizations. The essential thing is always to spend a hell of a lot of money right at the beginning. After that, they have an investment in you and they don't like to write it off—if they do, it looks as if somebody's made a boob. Once you can talk them into buying you a hundred chimps, you're there—at the point of no return. The other trick is to make out a budget for the estimated cost of the whole experiment. Of course, we know that it's pretty well impossible to cost out a project like this, but to them it looks businesslike. The accountants can't understand any of the details but they don't like to admit that, so they pass it. After three months I tell them the money's finished. They don't like it, but they daren't refuse to cough up any more for fear I pack up the whole experiment and they lose what they've already put into it."

"Doesn't this make you pretty unpopular?"

"Not so much as you'd think. To a businessman all research workers are incomprehensible anyway. If anything, they have rather more confidence in you if you act a little eccentric—it fits in with their idea of how scientists ought to be. And in any case they think they're going to make an enormous amount of money out of the vaccine."

"Will they?"

"Well, that's rather up to them, isn't it?" he said ambiguously. He added, "It isn't easy to patent a living organism, you know."

"Surely they've taken that into account?"

"Oh, yes." He hesitated, and then was obviously unable to resist the temptation to tell me. "As a matter of fact, they're relying on a patent they have on one stage of the production process. But I recently discovered that there's a perfectly simple way around that—somebody wrote it up in an obscure American journal six years ago." He said, with slight misgiving, "This is absolutely confidential, of course."

"You haven't told them?"

"If they don't read the literature, that's their lookout."

I could see that the rather artificial conception of commercial morality was meaningless to him. Since he observed them doing certain things that he conceived of as dishonest, he took it for granted that they were complete scoundrels in all respects and treated them accordingly. He was prepared to cheat them without mercy if it was necessary for the sake of his vaccine. The only thing he felt any conscience about was associating with them in the first place. "I never wanted to go there," he said defensively, "but what could I do? Nobody in England would give me the money. The M.R.C., London University, the Nuffield people, the drug houses—I tried the lot, nothing doing. I will say this for the Jerries, they're prepared to spend a dollar to make a dollar. But what I couldn't stand was their being so damned sanctimonious about it. They kept telling me how they weren't in business primarily to make money but to bring health and happiness to the world—Jesus!" He made a disgusted grimace. "And all that bloody shaking hands. Every morning. I can tell you, I was damn glad to get away from them."

Later, before we went to bed, he said, "Well, what's your program? What would you like to know?"

I hesitated. "To begin with, as you can appreciate, I shall have to talk to de Freitas." I tried not to sound apologetic. "Where does he live?"

"In Cajara. That's a village on the other side of the island. About sixty miles away. I'm due to go over there in a couple of days. I could take you if you like."

"That would be ideal."

"At the same time you could see something of what we're doing in the vaccination program." He grinned engagingly. "It may look a little different, close to, from the idea you had in London. Cajara's a long way from the Athenaeum."

13

✺

✺

✺

✺

✺

✺

IT was a dull, sticky morning when we set out for Cajara. There had been heavy rain during the night and the sky was still overcast. The clouds seemed to be almost sitting on top of the cliff.

"The rains are just beginning," said Martin. "We get sporadic showers for a few weeks, then it really sets in and starts pelting down. But it's a little early for the heavy stuff. I want to get as many of the distant villages done as I can before the roads become impassable. So we're pushing it pretty hard at the moment."

As the morning advanced, the sky began to clear. The forest steamed under the heat of the sun. The body of the island was formed by a series of mountain ranges, heavily wooded, with valleys in between. The road was narrow and tortuous, working its way in spiral fashion up one hill and then down the next. The Buick station wagon took up about three-quarters of the width of the road. Fortunately there was very little traffic. Martin drove very fast, skidding the heavy-duty tires around on the mud of the hairpin bends and blasting continuously on the horn. If, as occasionally happened, a car was coming the other way, one or other had to pull over into the ditch. Apart from this, it was a pleasant drive.

"Beautiful, isn't it?" he said. He swerved to miss a goat wandering loose across the road. "At least I thought so when I came here. I thought it was one of the most beautiful places I'd ever seen. I could visualize myself spending my life here. That was for the first week or two."

"And now?"

"Now I shall be glad when the trial's over and I can get back to Europe. Things like physical beauty have an enormously strong attraction for me, but it only lasts a short time." I thought of Barbara. How long had that lasted, I wondered? "You can't live for long on scenery," he went on. "At least I can't. And there isn't much else here. The islanders are mostly primitive, and as for the British—" He left the sentence unfinished. "Well, you've met some of them."

"Only one or two. I agree I wasn't too impressed. Mrs. Das—"

"Yes, she's ghastly, isn't she? I can't imagine why he married her. I suppose he was lonely or something. Men never ought to marry outside their own country—they always seem to make a hash of it. She leads him a hell of a dance. She doesn't think he's ambitious enough. I think he'd be quite happy to stay here. But Batou's too small for her. She'd like him to get a better job in one of those new self-governing areas—Malaya or Jamaica or somewhere like that."

"Do you think he will?"

"I doubt it." I thought of the promise Martin was supposed to have made to find Das a better job after the trial was over. But that was none of my business. I said, "She seems to be quite a supporter of yours."

"Oh yes, she's on our side. Most of the people out here are, you'll find, though often for the most dubious and irrelevant of reasons."

"Such as?"

"Well, it sounds progressive, for one thing. And at the same time this sort of research carries an aura of romance. Koch, Pasteur, brave young scientist risking his life—all that sort of rubbish. It's all very well for chaps like you to sneer, but you find when you want to get anything done that you have to play up to them a little. It's not for me to tell them that a boatload of good food would save more lives in a year than all the vaccine in the world."

He added, rather spitefully, "That's your responsibility, thank God, not mine."

"It isn't, really, you know," I said as patiently as I could. Like most civil servants I had tried hard to get used to being regarded as being responsible for all acts of policy of Her Majesty's Government. "Apart from the fact that the two things aren't in the least comparable, as you very well know."

Martin smiled. "You know, you really have turned into a bit of a boffin. Those measured, logical tones . . ."

It seemed that he was never able to leave me alone for long. He felt a necessity to mock and irritate, to "type" me in the part he had written for me. Always, not very far beneath his friendship, there lay a hostility I had never been able adequately to explain. It was important not to be provoked. If I allowed my annoyance to show, it always appeared to please him, as if somehow by means of it he had established himself in a position of superiority.

"Barbara said she didn't think I'd changed very much."

"Didn't she? I do. What happened to those violent opinions, those daredevil sentiments you used to voice as a student?" He shook his head mockingly. "You've lost your sense of adventure, Peter."

"To some extent, perhaps. But that's normal, I think."

"Is it? Well, thank God I haven't."

It occurred to me that one of the strange things about Martin was how little he had changed. Surely he should have changed more? An attitude that is normal at nineteen can be all kinds of odd things at thirty—absurd, pathetic, and even, as in his case, slightly frightening. One expected a slowing down of energy, a balancing of forces, which had somehow never occurred.

We drove on for another hour or so, climbing most of the time. The sky was clear now and the sun beat down on us, but at this altitude the stickiness had gone and there was a pleasant breeze from the sea. As we climbed, the roads grew narrower and dustier, the villages small and far between. We could not be far away from Cajara now, and there was something I wanted to ask Martin before I saw de Freitas. I had been putting it off because I knew it would make him angry. Any form of criticism, direct or implied, always drove him into a rage.

"About those two deaths—" I said.

"Yes?" His voice became harder, even his body seemed to stiffen up, ready to do battle.

"It was unfortunate that there were no post-mortems."

At first I thought he was not going to answer me at all, he was silent for so long. Then he said coldly, "If you'll just hold on for a few minutes I'll show you something."

He began to drive with even greater ferocity than usual. We tore across a small valley, where the vegetation was so thick that it seemed perpetually in danger of encroaching across the road and blocking it altogether—branches and creepers whipped across the windshield of the car. We crossed the bed of a shallow stream and began to climb again, steeply and tortuously. Then suddenly we were out of the jungle. The road levelled off, and far below we could see the sea again. Martin crammed on the brakes and drew the Buick to a halt. When he shut off the engine I could hear the creaking, straining sounds of hot metal in the process of expansion. The engine temperature was two hundred—very near boiling, at that altitude. We got out of the car and looked down from the top of the mountain. The view was breathtaking. It was possible to see almost the whole of the west side of the island, the indented, rocky coastline, the cliffs, the breakers far below. In one of the valleys to the north there was just visible a small cluster of white buildings.

"Pariu," said Martin. "That's where one of the deaths occurred."

I nodded, waiting for him to make his point.

"Access is by a dirt road not nearly so good as this. No telephone, no doctor, no hospital, no electricity, no refrigeration. Mean average temperature ninety-five degrees. Does that answer your question?"

"And the other one?"

"Even worse. That was in the mountains." Indignation suddenly took hold of him. "Damn it, you haven't the slightest conception of how things are out here. You've got to live with it to understand."

I was about to break in, but he stopped me. "No, let me tell you something. You remember when we were students? In St. Vincent's, particularly in the orthopedic or gynecological wards, where you had young people, if somebody died there was a hell of a fuss, practically a public inquiry. Then you went out to the old workhouse hospitals, where they put the old people with pneumonia, and not a day passed without somebody going out feet first—it simply wasn't news." He spread out his arm, taking in the whole of Batou, the lush green valleys, the mountains, the jungle, the picturesque white villages, and said with great intensity, "Well, this is the workhouse, Peter, the whole bloody island. Try and get that into your head."

14

✦

✦

✦

✦

✦

✦

A N hour later we were in Cajara. It was a smaller town than Flores, and less Anglicized. The streets were narrow and smelled of heat and buffalo dung. The inscriptions of most of the shops were in Portuguese.

We stopped at the Health Center, a relatively modern low brick building near the center of the little town. A queue of apathetic Negroes crouched on the steps outside the door. Inside, a tall, emaciated-looking Nigerian doctor was giving injections.

"Dr. Kadu," said Martin, introducing us. "Dr. Kadu is the district M.O. for this part of the island, under Dr. Das. He's been a very great help to us."

Dr. Kadu flashed his teeth in a grave smile. We all went through into a back room, where Martin demonstrated the apparatus of the trial. There were boxes of vials, each containing a few cubic centimeters of cloudy liquid; each vial was labelled with a serial number.

"Half of these contain vaccine, the other half contain some in-active substance which looks identical," said Martin. "Nobody here knows which is which. We enter the serial number on the patient's case sheet when we give the injection." He handed over a duplicated sheet of paper. "This is the standard case sheet. We record every week, for two months after injection, the status of all the symptoms and signs, putting plus or minus signs for improve-ment or deterioration. How we judge those is laid down in the basic protocol for the trial, which you'll see later. I think you'll find it pretty fair. The statistician and I spent a lot of time trying to get a watertight system of assessment. When we've used up all the vials and completed the assessment, we can break the blind. The key to the code numbers will tell us which patients had the vaccine and which didn't. We can then divide the patients into two groups and compare the results."

It was a fairly conventional scheme of its kind. I said, "Who holds the key?"

"The Research Director of Chemiefabriken. That way nobody has the slightest chance of knowing who's getting vaccine and who isn't. At the end of the experiment I shall cable him for the key." He looked at me significantly. "We have an agreement that he won't give it to anyone else."

I made no comment. I could not imagine any circumstances in which anyone else would approach Chemiefabriken for the key over Martin's head. Nor would the key be of value without access to the case records. It was a standard experimental method, and there were no doubt hundreds of trials going on throughout the world on the same basis. There was no need to make a drama out of it.

I had lunch at the Health Center with Martin and Kadu. Kadu was intelligent and charming but very inexperienced; he had only left the medical school at Ibadan six months ago. Like Das and everyone else directly connected with the trial, he was enormously enthusiastic about it. It was impossible not to admire the way Martin had managed to implant in them all a sense of mission, a feeling of being in the forefront of great events. In fact, Kadu had already in his mind jumped beyond the real purpose of the trial. He was now completely convinced that the treatment would be effective.

"I know it," he assured me. "I am watching these people all the time and I am sure. I can tell by the response which patients are receiving the vaccine and which are not. Their symptoms are less, their minds are clearer, their whole life is completely changed. It is not myself only, it is the sister also; she can tell. It is the most wonderful thing I have ever seen—wonderful!"

He banged his fist on the table in his excitement, then became confused and apologized. But his eyes remained shining with the enthusiasm of the devotee. A paralytic would have felt in duty bound to get up and walk in response to such faith.

Martin smiled indulgently and let him talk. But when Kadu had gone back to resume his clinic, he said to me, "Now do you understand why we have to use a double blind?"

I nodded reflectively.

"You see, you can't be too much of a wet blanket on a chap like Kadu. Working out in a Godforsaken hole like this, he needs to have enthusiasm to sustain him, to keep him at the job. It's easy to say he ought to be more cautious and detached, but if he *was* detached, he wouldn't be here. Of these patients we're dealing with, some are going to think they feel better to please Kadu, some because they're flattered at the attention they're getting, some because they think there's some magic in an injection. I'm quite prepared to find that some of the people who show the most dramatic improvement, temporarily at any rate, will be placebo reactors who haven't had the vaccine at all."

It was curious to hear him talk like this when I remembered his violence and resentment at Flores, his suspicions of conspiracy and interference. The difference between him and Kadu was, of course, easily apparent. He was not prepared to prejudge the experiment. Precisely because he thought it likely to succeed, he had adopted every measure he knew to eliminate bias from the assessment of the results and protect himself from criticism. Within the experiment he was prepared to be cold and careful. But as soon as anyone attacked the experiment itself, he was like a tigress with a favorite cub.

"Perhaps you'd like to go and see de Freitas now," he said. "I sent a message for him to expect you after lunch."

He showed me the way and then left me. It was not very far to the church. I had the feeling of walking across a no man's land between two cultures separated by an irreconcilable hostility. The crowd squatting around the steps of the clinic watched me all the way, with the shameless inquisitiveness of peasants the world over. The shops were shuttered, the silence of the tropical afternoon hung over the village. Only the flies buzzed tirelessly on the piles of buffalo dung that covered the road. I walked a hundred yards up the dusty street, turned left and saw the church in front of me, rather ornate in the Portuguese style, built in stone. Beside it was a small presbytery. I went up to it and knocked on the door.

It was opened by the priest himself. As soon as I saw him I knew he was a person to be reckoned with. He was slightly built, with a long, sallow Latin face. His eyes were large and brown—watchful, serious eyes. His black, cropped hair was just beginning to turn gray. He looked between forty and fifty years old.

There is no such thing as a specifically Jesuit personality, and generalizations about them tend to be mistaken. I had met a great many of them in my time; I had grown up in close contact with them at an impressionable age. I had had dealings with all types—the hearty, the gentle and benevolent, the consciously serpentine, the naïve, the ambitious. They varied as widely as other men in most respects. But they had certain common factors.

One of these was intensity. They were hardly ever casual or lukewarm about anything that mattered. Whatever it was they did or thought, they meant it. This did not mean that they were all very determined characters. But a Jesuit seems to dispose of a determination over and above that of most people—it is the determination of his Order within him. He has the strength of purpose that is founded on the strictest mental and physical discipline. His strength is as the strength of ten, not so much because his heart is pure as because his mind is firmly and irrevocably made up. His life is founded on the belief that in every situation there is a right way and a wrong way, with nothing in between. If he is not completely and obviously wrong (and he is convinced he is not), then he must be right. It is as simple as that. And if he is right, the discipline of his Order forbids that he should give way so much as an inch.

This determination is present in all, but in some very much more than others. As I looked at de Freitas, at the grave, sensitive, somehow boyish face, I was apprehensive. This was no blinking Father Brown, no whiskey priest tormented by doubts and consoling himself with dusky mistresses and the bottle. The true aristocracy of the Order was not necessarily found at Farm Street or Stonyhurst or Campion Hall. You might find it in any place or at any time—on a sledge in the Arctic, teaching arithmetic to children at an elementary school, even in a remote tropical village.

He led me along a tiled corridor into his main living room. It was a large room, barely furnished with a few threadbare rugs, a pair of cheap armchairs, a roll-top desk untidily littered with papers. The sunlight fell in shafts from the narrow windows, and the air was very still, shimmering with dust. There was an acrid smell of cheap tobacco.

De Freitas put me in one of the armchairs and himself on the swivel chair by the desk, looking down at me.

"It is very kind of you," he said, with a thin smile, "to come and see me in this out-of-the-way place."

His voice was very English, a languid public-school voice, though with a slight deliberation about it that indicated it was not his mother tongue. Born in Spain or Latin America, I guessed, and educated at one of the four English schools. Then Campion Hall. Then the Foreign Mission. By choice or upon instruction? Probably, from the look of him, by choice.

"It's part of my job," I said. There seemed little object in pretending it was a courtesy call. We might as well get to the point straight away. "I imagine you know why I came to Batou?"

He inclined his head gravely. "Yes." So far as I could see, pretty well everybody knew by this time, though de Freitas would have more accurate and detailed information than most. His superiors in London would have kept him informed. They would certainly have squeezed everything they could out of old Bainbridge. "You have already met Dr. Farrell?"

"Oh, yes. In fact—"

He said it before I could. "I believe you are an old friend of his?"

His voice carried no special inflection, yet he was making a point. Just as Martin was ready to believe that I was out here to satisfy the Jesuits, de Freitas was suspicious that I had been sent out to whitewash my friend. It was perhaps inevitable.

"That's correct," I said. "However, I don't want you to imagine that any considerations of that kind will affect my report. I can assure you they won't. My function here has nothing to do with personalities."

He looked unconvinced. "You may find it more difficult to disregard personalities than you think." He put his hand into the pocket of his gown and pulled out a small yellow cigarette tin containing a few battered-looking cigarettes. "I'm afraid they're not really State Express," he said, offering it to me. "I roll my own."

I shook my head. "Thank you. I don't smoke."

He lit one himself and took an enormous, greedy pull at it. For the rest of the interview he smoked one after the other. It was an extraordinary exhibition of self-indulgence in contrast to the obvious austerity of the rest of his life. He pulled the smoke deep down into his lungs, held it for an almost frightening length of time, even while he was talking, and then blew it out in vast quantities from mouth and nose, like a surfacing whale. It was as if this were his one permissible vice and he felt justified in making the most of it.

"I'm sure," he said, "that you have the fullest intention of acting as a purely impartial scientific observer, making an assessment of an experiment—isn't that so? But you're obviously an intelligent man and I'm informed," he smiled knowingly, "that you've received an excellent education." He paused, smiling, and I began to feel angry. It was as if he had spoken a password or made a Masonic sign or put a hand on my shoulder to claim me. Evidently he had received a dossier on me. I was theirs, they had put their mark on me at Breckenhall and could claim me whenever they wished. . . . But before I could think of a way of protesting, he had moved on. "You know even better than I do that all this talk about the purity of scientific thought is mostly nonsense. Men are no more impartial in their approach to science than they are to religion. It's possible, you know, for a man to become emotionally attached to an idea, just as much as to a woman." His eyes narrowed slightly. "In Dr. Farrell's case, I should imagine, even more so."

I was anxious to avoid a discussion of Martin's character. "I know your views on Dr. Farrell," I said rather coldly. "I saw your letter when I was in London."

He was not disconcerted. "I stick to what I said there. In my view he is totally unbalanced about this"—he made a grimace of disgust—"experiment."

"Are you sure that you yourself are not being too emotional about the matter?" I suggested.

"I haven't yet learned to look evil in the face with indifference, Dr. Mayne." He added flatly, "I thank God for that."

His self-righteousness annoyed me. "I don't think it helps at all to use words like 'evil' in this connection," I said with some sharpness. "When all is said and done, the object of the trial is to save human life."

"The end justifies the means?" He too was growing angry. "Surely they taught you better than that at Breckenhall?"

"My education didn't end at Breckenhall, Father." I was about to say more when I checked myself. He had almost succeeded in drawing me onto the moral issue, where he was at home and I was not. It was always very important with these people to stick to the point. "But in any case I don't think we shall gain much from discussing the ethics of experimentation. I am simply here to deal with the facts of this one trial. My job is to collect the facts, and also the opinions of various interested parties."

De Freitas shook his head. "I'm afraid that's quite impossible. Come over here." He led me over to the window. Outside, on the steps of the church, an old brown man twitched in his sleep. Except for this slight movement he might have been mistaken for a bundle of rags waiting for the dustbin. As he moved, a little cloud of flies rose momentarily from his face, then settled again.

"He is an interested party. Will you take his opinion?" He regarded me sourly. "He has encephalitis. He has had the so-called treatment. Or perhaps he hasn't—no one knows, do they? And if he dies tomorrow, possibly as a consequence of the treatment, we still shall not know. Not, at least, until he has been buried for some three months or so. And then," he added with magnificent scorn, "then Dr. Farrell, in his own good time, will write a letter to some scientist in north Germany, who will in due course inform him whether he has killed anybody or not. That, Dr. Mayne, is what I call insanity."

"I think you should try to understand the difficulties involved," I said, "particularly in dealing with rather primitive people. I've seen Dr. Farrell and Dr. Kadu at work. They take a lot of trouble to explain the implications of the trial to the patients. Then it's entirely up to them whether they have the vaccine or not. It's stipulated in the protocol that they must be volunteers."

"Volunteers!" His voice quivered with passion. "Look at him, Dr. Mayne! He can hardly understand a word you say."

He was quite right, of course. The "volunteer" side of the trial was unconvincing. But what was Martin's alternative? "That's the whole point, surely? So long as he has chronic encephalitis he's hardly a man in the ordinary sense at all. Isn't it worth taking a few chances to improve him?"

He walked away from the window and lit another of his execrable cigarettes. "Dr. Mayne, you don't understand these people. None of the English people here do. Once they simply ignored them; now, since the war, they feel guilty about them, and they are enthusiastic for the trial because they think it shows they are doing something for the islanders. But the islanders are not simply a problem in public health—they are people, just like you and me. They are not animals to experiment on. A death here or there—you think, what does it matter? It matters to them." He paused and then said, "I would like to ask you to do something for me. Imagine you are not in Batou but in Birmingham." He added, with solemnity, "In the sight of God that man out there is as important as a citizen of Birmingham."

This I recognized as a typical Jesuit remark. That is to say, it contained an assumption that you agreed with his own first principles, it shifted the ground of the argument in his favor, and it subtly begged the important question. The brutal truth was that Batou *was* different from Birmingham. All clinical experiments of this kind involve a necessary and calculated risk. In an area where mortality and morbidity is already high one has, statistically, less to lose and more to gain. Therefore there is a tendency to take greater chances. The trouble is that in a democracy nobody dares to admit this. And once the question of God and the individual soul are dragged into it, discussion becomes impossible.

"In Birmingham," I said, sidetracking in my turn, "the whole position would have been easier. For instance, we should have had post-mortems—"

"Yes." He paused, and then said dryly, "It was unfortunate about the post-mortems."

His tone said as clearly as if he had put it into words that he believed that Martin had deliberately avoided carrying out post-mortems for reasons of his own. His large brown eyes were soft and sad—they never looked away from me. I was reminded of a gazelle I had once seen in captivity. It had an engaging way of gazing at you over the fence and nudging you with its horns in an apparently gentle, playful manner. But if you went into its pen, it would drive you against the wall, with those same butts which now turned out to have surprising power and menace. All the time the sad, gentle eyes remained fixed on you in apparent supplication.

I could see that his mind was totally closed, and there was no point in trying to give him Martin's point of view about the P.M.'s. He had, in any case, the advantage held by anyone who is allowed to take up an entirely destructive point of view. I decided to try to force him to commit himself.

"To come down to brass tacks," I said, "what are you actually suggesting? That we ditch the whole trial and throw the vaccine away?"

He shook his head. He knew as well as I did that a statement of that kind would be catastrophic for him. It would be meat and drink for anti-Catholic journalists, who were only too ready to criticize the Church for supporting reactionary causes and meddling in matters it did not understand. "I am not a medical man. Only an expert would be qualified to decide on a matter of that kind." As soon as a difficult decision had to be taken, I thought wryly, it became a technical question again. Over to me. "All I am saying is this," he went on. "Two people have died. Perhaps coincidentally, perhaps not. I believe this is enough to warrant investigation. It seems to me that we should know whether these two people had the vaccine or not. Surely that is not unreasonable?"

"I can see that it doesn't sound so to you. But in fact it would mean breaking the whole pattern of the trial, and probably laying its conclusions open to doubt. It's a big decision to take."

"Please believe me when I say that it is an equally serious decision to leave things as they are." He frowned. "I do not wish to sound alarmist, Dr. Mayne, but I would beg of you not to forget the islanders themselves. They are an ignorant, simple people, but they should not be ignored."

It was true, I thought, that one tended to think of the affair as a struggle between de Freitas and Martin, forgetting the actual patients. On the other hand, the ones I had seen with Kadu at the clinic had seemed docile, almost apathetic. It was only too possible that de Freitas was using the islanders as a bogy to support his own case.

"You think they are really concerned about this?"

"Yes. Some of them. I don't mean the middle-class tradesmen and professional people in Flores—I mean the villagers. When you know little, as they do, you can become very suspicious, very secret. They are not easy people to get to know."

I was growing a little tired of his claim to exclusive knowledge;

as if he was the sole person who had any idea what the people were thinking.

"Oh, I don't know," I said. "Kadu's been here some little time. He seems to know them pretty well."

He shook his head. "Dr. Kadu does not know them at all. There is a curious idea among the British, Dr. Mayne, that all colored people are substantially the same." With a trace of a smile, he glanced down at his own hands. It was true, they were darker than those of a pure Portuguese. He had probably an eighth or a sixteenth of colored blood. "I can assure you that isn't so. Dr. Kadu is just as much of a foreigner here as you are."

"Or you, for that matter."

Again he shook his head. "I was born on this island—just over the mountain." His soft brown eyes held me still, between the purposeful jabs of the horns. "Nor am I a stranger to the encephalitis—my father died of it."

15

❁

❁

❁

❁

❁

❁

"WELL," said Martin, "what did you think of him?"
I hesitated. It was a difficult question to answer in a few words.
Martin gave his challenging, slightly scornful laugh. "Takes you
back a few years, doesn't it? That room of his could easily be the
Prefect's Room at Breckenhall." More seriously, he asked, "I suppose he spent the afternoon pouring poison into your ears about
me?"

"Not exactly that."

"He thinks of me as a sort of H. G. Wells character. The crazy
scientist. Dr. Moreau—that kind of thing. I suspect he spends his
long sexless evenings reading science fiction."

I was determined not to be drawn. I said mildly, "He struck
me as an able man."

Martin shook his head. "They always seem more intelligent
than they are, you know. They learn that smug enigmatic manner—it's part of their stock in trade. The idea is to sit very still
with your hands stuffed into your gown and give little catlike
smiles every now and then, as if you knew a great deal more than
you cared to tell. In reality, of course, they don't know anything
but a lot of bloody bigoted nonsense that was discredited fifty
years ago. There are as many fools in the Jesuits as in any other
Order. They just work harder at covering it up."

"I don't think de Freitas is a fool."

"He seems to have made quite an impression on you," said

Martin. The sourness in his tone was almost that of a jealous lover; he resented anybody making an impression on me but himself. He paused, trying to force me to deny it. But I said nothing. "I must confess I didn't expect you to be taken in so easily." He moved on to another tack. "Did you tell him you were a lapsed Catholic?"

"We didn't discuss religion."

"No? But I bet he knew you were at Breckenhall. And I bet he reminded you of it?"

"Yes," I admitted.

"They don't leave any stone unturned. I'll give them that. He tried the same trick on me when I first met him. When I told him what I thought of Jesuit education, he decided on the spot that I was antichrist. That's probably responsible for part of our troubles." He said scornfully, "The trouble with them is that they believe their own propaganda. They imagine that if they've had you for five years as a kid, you belong to them for the rest of your life. It may be true of most of those half-wits at Breckenhall, for all I know. But they never had the least understanding of people like you and me, Peter." It was his way of flattering you, to group you with himself; he could think of no higher honor. "I'm quite sure he thinks that because he arranged for you to be sent out here, you'll do whatever he says."

This was a little crude. Martin was on occasions surprisingly obvious in his efforts to influence people. It came not so much from a lack of subtlety in his own nature as from a tendency to underrate others. De Freitas, I thought, was much cleverer at this kind of thing.

I smiled. "De Freitas is under the impression that I've been sent out to whitewash you."

"He may have *said* that—"

"My impression is that he genuinely believes it. It's nonsense, of course, as I assured him. But, after all, I am a friend of yours, staying at your house and so on. He probably imagines that medical men are a closed guild who tend to stick by each other. It's understandable that he tried to hit back by incorporating me in *his* guild." I was unable to resist teasing him a little. "As you say, he doesn't understand us at all. He can't appreciate that you would never even try to influence me against my better judgment, and that in any case my personal feelings would never make the slightest difference to my report."

We looked at each other for a moment and I could see Martin struggling with himself, uncertain whether to take offense. Instead, to my great relief, he laughed. But to my sensitive ear there was a slight artificiality in the note of his laughter, as if he was acting it for my benefit. He could still recognize when he was caught out, but he could no longer find it entirely amusing.

It had been arranged that we should stay over the weekend in Cajara; there were a few cell-like rooms attached to the Health Center. The Center worked all Saturday and I watched Kadu doing outpatients in the morning. It was a sight to discourage the stoutest heart.

"Here," he explained, "multiple pathology is the rule. It is a curiosity to see a patient with only one disease. The presence of the main endemic conditions is assumed. If we enter up a man as having a lung abscess, for instance, it probably means that he has a lung abscess plus malaria plus trypanosomiasis plus probably encephalitis also. The average length of life is under thirty years. If we can do something about the encephalitis it may make a considerable difference."

Kadu, as Martin had said, was an enthusiast. To him the encephalitis was not simply a disease, it was a social factor of the first importance. The headaches, the lethargy it engendered, the muscle weakness, the vague sense of futility and depression, had spread a chronic demoralization through the island. When a large proportion of the population was suffering from symptoms of this kind, progress became impossible. The islanders were lazy and shiftless and irresponsible; they seemed to have no sense of responsibility or power of concentration. It was impossible to educate them. They would not practice elementary hygiene or soil conservation, no matter how much effort was spent in trying to teach them.

"We have a vicious circle, Dr. Mayne," he said. "They are diseased because they have no hygiene, they have no hygiene because they are unresponsive to education, and they are unresponsive because they are diseased. With this vaccine we can perhaps break the circle. They have been asleep for five hundred years, drugged by the virus; perhaps we can wake them up. That is, if we are allowed to." His face creased in a smile which held no amusement, only bitterness. "I think there are some people who would prefer them asleep."

"I don't really think so, you know." I wasn't sure whom his gibe was directed against. The Colonial Office? Certainly that branch of the Civil Service had a prejudice in favor of sleep. The Jesuits? It was well known that the influence of the Church was stronger in backward countries. Yet my experience was that neither of these organizations would deliberately choose to keep a whole community in a state of chronic disabling illness. Kadu, like most enthusiasts, had a tendency to oversimplify.

The encephalitis clinic was in the afternoon. It had obviously become a very routine affair, as any experimental procedure must, since the whole object is to eliminate variations from the main feature that is being tested. The patients were examined, diagnosed, and then subjected to a laborious explanation by Kadu or the nursing sister as to what was involved in the trial. Not knowing the language, I could not know what was said, but I was inclined to agree with de Freitas that the patients had not the faintest idea what was really happening. It was difficult to see how it could be otherwise. Most of them accepted the injection apathetically, as no doubt in their time they had accepted other jujus, the skin of snakes and toads and hot wires twisted round the scalp.

"We haven't much trouble getting subjects," said Martin. "The poor beggars are prepared to have a go at anything if there's a chance of it doing any good. It's the follow-up where we run into difficulties. Nearly fifty per cent of them don't come back. I don't know whether they can't see the point of it, or whether they just simply forget." He mopped the sweat off his face. It was very hot in the clinic and began to smell a good deal toward the end of the afternoon. "My next clinical research project is going to be in South Kensington."

The next morning it was Sunday and I was awakened by church bells. As they echoed across the valley I might almost have imagined myself in some small mountain village in Switzerland or Austria; only the sweat-stained bedclothes and the mosquito screens over my windows rendered any such fantasy out of the question. I got up and opened the jalousies. The sun hit me in the face; the streets outside were dry and parched, the dew already sucked up into the thirsty air. People were moving sluggishly toward the church, some of them in tattered black, the women wearing scarves or an occasional mantilla, prized possessions, their Sunday best. On an impulse I dressed hurriedly and went out. By the time I had got into the street the bells had stopped and the street was almost empty. It was eight o'clock. I entered the church under the curious eyes of the verger, who closed the door behind me. With an automatism that simulates and almost creates reverence, I crossed myself with holy water, genuflected to the altar, and knelt down in the last pew.

The church was small and dark. Through the high, slitlike windows only a few vivid shafts of sunlight streaked across the stone floor—the Portuguese had known how to build for hot climates. Within this place they had provided those things the village so signally lacked—coolness and dignity, silence for contemplation, the smell of incense rather than garbage. The congregation was very quiet and rather touchingly devout; almost all of them took Communion and I was left alone and conspicuous as they went up to the rails. I wondered if de Freitas saw me as he said Mass, in spite of his solemnity and downcast eyes. In a way I hoped he would. It would show that I was prepared to witness his act of faith in the same way as I had witnessed Martin's in the clinic on the previous afternoon.

It was a short Low Mass without music or sermon, and within half an hour it was over. I waited until most of the congregation had filed out, and then got up to leave. Just behind me there was a bench on which two or three people sat, awaiting confession. One of them looked up as I passed, and I recognized the sister from Kadu's clinic. I had thought of her as a withdrawn, almost sullen woman, but now she gave me a smile of great sweetness and friendliness. Then, before I had time to smile back, she bent her head and returned to her devotions.

During breakfast I wondered if Martin knew of my visit to the church. He made no reference to it, and talked mainly of his plans for spending the rest of the day.

"There's no point in sitting here sweating in Cajara," he said. "There's nothing to do here. The thing to do is to drive down to the coast and have a bathe. I know a very good little place."

It seemed an excellent idea. Martin arranged for a packed lunch and added two bottles of wine that he had had the foresight to bring with him from Flores. We set off about midday in the station wagon. The last two miles of the journey were over buffalo tracks overgrown with thick vegetation, but the beach was magnificent. The sand was crisp and firm and there was no sign of life anywhere, not even a sail on the horizon. There was a small torrent running down the cliff side and we put the wine bottles into it to cool. When we had bathed, the wine was ready and we drank one of the bottles with cold chicken and peaches. Afterward, we slept in the shade and then bathed again. At about four o'clock we opened the second bottle of wine.

As we sat drinking, Martin said casually, "I believe you went to Mass this morning?"

"Yes."

"Do you still go?"

"Not for many years."

He raised his eyebrows. "Then why today?"

"I don't know." I thought for a moment. What had it been, exactly? "Sometimes, in strange places, I'm tempted to go. On a ship at sea, or in a foreign country. There's something weird and rather dramatic in the fact that it's always just exactly the same, word for word, as it used to be at Breckenhall."

Martin was silent for a moment. Then he said with a sardonic grin, "Perhaps de Freitas is right. Perhaps they've got you after all, deep down. That's what they like to think. Perhaps on your deathbed you'll suddenly cry out for Extreme Unction, like the villains in those improving books we used to read on retreat." As usual, the very thought of Breckenhall seemed to arouse a kind of savagery in him. "Little Pavlov dogs weren't we, in those days, if only we'd known it. Sitting in our cages, patiently waiting to be conditioned. Ring the bell once, show the dog food, and the mouth drips saliva. Bell equals food equals salivation. Mortal sin equals eternal punishment equals fear and repentance. Confession equals salvation. Holy Mother Church equals Infallibility equals the Jesuit Order equals the First Prefect beating the hell out of your backside with a ferula. . . ."

Equalled, in Martin's case, hate. Hate enduring and everlasting.

"God," he went on reminiscently, "it's amazing how clear those days still are in my memory. Do you know, I can remember them more vividly than things that happened only a week or two ago? The smell of floor polish in the chapel, the wart on the Spiritual Father's neck, when he used to bend down to speak to me. Sometimes he'd pinch my arm, too—I could show you the exact place. It's as if I was alive then in a way that I've never been since." He paused. "I remember the day they brought me back after I ran away. I can see the Rector and the First Prefect now—looking very grim, but sort of triumphant at the same time. It was then," he said, looking at me, "that I heard you'd betrayed me."

He waited, but I said nothing. He wanted me to deny it. Then he could put on a dramatic scene, drag up the old grievance, work himself up into a frenzy of paranoid reproach. It was all very well for him. He enjoyed it, it was his favorite form of relaxation. The bitterness, the reproaches, the reconciliation. At the end he was left exhilarated and refreshed, while others were exhausted. It was too hot and I was too old and I had been through it too often before. I would not play.

"You did, you know," he persisted. "You betrayed me into their hands." He had a tendency to overwrite his own dialogue on these occasions. He said violently, maddened by my refusal to co-operate, "Are you going to do it again?"

"Martin—" I said wearily. But he interrupted me.

"I want to know. And I want you to face up to what it really means." His voice became softer. With him, pose and sincerity were never entirely separable. His genuine emotions were over-laid by a veneer of melodrama, his posturings held always a core of truth. But for a moment it seemed to me that sincerity had at last gained the upper hand.

"You know how difficult it is to break really new ground in a field like mine," he said. "Even to the best of us, it probably only happens once in a lifetime. I've spent seven years isolating this virus and trying to prepare a vaccine. I've not only had to do the experimental work, I've had to get support and raise money. I've had to talk different sets of people into backing each separate phase. I've had to charm and persuade and reassure one pack of ignoramuses after another until I'm almost out of my mind. Of course, if the vaccine should turn out to be no good, I'm done for, I realize that. But I'm not worried on that score. I'm convinced it *is* good. What I'm not prepared to accept," he said, his voice rising out of control again, "is for the whole experiment to go for nothing because of a bloody conspiracy by a pack of priests. I won't have that—I'm going to stop it. And I'm counting on you to help me."

He sat there on a rock, glaring at me, calling on every ounce of loyalty and devotion, prepared to mortgage every scrap of our past friendship. He said, "If you'll do this for me, this is the last thing I'll ever ask of you. We've known each other a long time, Peter. We've been through a lot together. You were the only great friend I ever had. Surely that's worth something?"

He was prepared to do anything, to expose himself to any humiliation, to get his way. He seemed to have no idea that he was asking something quite unthinkable, which I could not give him without becoming an entirely different kind of person. I had imagined that a scientist of his experience and ability would have known instinctively that no such bargain could ever be made. I tried to soften my refusal. "You're magnifying my importance," I said. "I'm only here to make a factual report."

"For Christ's sake, Peter." He looked at me angrily. I might have known that delicacy would be wasted on him. "You know damn well that the way you phrase your report and the recommendations you add to it are going to govern what's decided. Don't insult my intelligence. If you're not prepared to support me, at least have the guts to say so."

I clenched my teeth and counted ten. "I'm not here," I said with deliberation, "to support anyone. I'm here to say what I think. That's what I propose to do."

There was quite a long silence. The sun was beginning to go down now; our shadows were lengthening in front of us on the sand.

"Clearly," he said savagely, "our friendship means nothing to you. Perhaps I should have expected that. Well then—is there anything else I can offer? I'm prepared to pay any price you want."

It was strange how, even at a time like this, I found it impossible to be really angry with him. If another man had tried to bribe me I would probably have been outraged. But there was in Martin such a complete lack of understanding of other people's moralities as to make indignation sound merely absurd. "I don't want anything," I said patiently. "I'm not for sale."

He looked at me skeptically, as if he thought I was bargaining. Then he said, with great significance, "I suppose you know Barbara's still in love with you?"

The sun began to duck below the mountain and I felt a chill breeze blow in from the sea. I picked up my coat and put it over my shoulders. "Don't be absurd," I said.

He leaned forward, regarding me with great intensity. "I knew it as soon as I saw you together. She was in love with you when we were students, but you hadn't the guts to take her. You gave her to me. It was a long time before she forgave you for that."

I had no wish to talk about Barbara, but the blow was such a cruel one that I was unable to refrain from defending myself. "If I had taken her, you would have said I betrayed you again."

"And so you would have done. You only wanted her because she was mine." With enormous bitterness, he went on, "You're the born plunderer, the imitator, the man who sits and watches and smiles and calculates—and wins everything in the end."

I knew then, with a stab of pain, a feeling of emptiness and loss, that he hated me. And, extraordinarily, he was jealous of me. It was a weakness I had never suspected in him. When had it started, I wondered? For how many years had it been there, simmering under the surface of friendship?

"You say you always wanted Barbara," he said. He gave a curious unnatural grin. "All right, then. She's yours."

I was so full of my own hurt that I could not immediately appreciate what he was getting at. "What are you talking about?"

"Good God," he cried, "have you got so that you can't stick the truth any more? I said you can have Barbara if you want her." He added derisively, "Have I shocked you?"

He had. And as he recognized it I could see the satisfaction on his face. To shock me was something worth doing. When we were younger we had liked to think of ourselves as unshockable. We had taken a pride in speaking to each other, with what others would have regarded as indecent frankness, of anything which came into our minds. We had discussed with a kind of bravado all our most secret and discreditable desires. But, as I realized now, we had never mentioned other secrets, the compulsions of honor, the longing for tenderness and security. The game had been a fraud. When we imagined we were being most honest, we were acting, more than ever in our lives. It now seemed to me unbelievably naïve, this idea that we could ever consciously face the whole truth about ourselves.

He went on impatiently, "Barbara and I haven't had anything for each other for years. You still want her—the logical thing for you to do is to take her." His teeth flashed in a smile. "You have my blessing."

So, I thought, this was all my sacrifice had been for. He had no further use for Barbara. She was expendable. She could be tossed back to me like a bone to a dog. She was to be a bribe, a reward for my co-operation. The insult to both of us was beyond all bearing.

Looking at him, I saw on his face an expression of relief, of anticipation. Because I had said nothing, he thought I had been tempted by his proposition. De Freitas is right, I thought. He *is* mad.

I got to my feet. "Let's go back to the village," I said.

He frowned. "You haven't replied to my offer."

"Because it's a lot of bloody nonsense," I said roughly. "Barbara isn't yours to give. If I wanted her, I'd take her. You wouldn't be able to stop me."

"*Do* you want her?"

"I want to get back to the village."

It was dark now and he was a stranger, a mad stranger. I felt almost physically afraid of him. I gathered our things together and got into the car. After a moment's hesitation he followed me and got in behind the wheel. Then he turned toward me again.

"Do you want her? Do you? You might as well tell me."

"Mind your own goddamn business."

We sat there in silence for a while. I wondered if he was contemplating refusing to drive me back until I had answered his question. It was not impossible. If so, he finally rejected the idea.

"All right," he said, and started the engine.

16

❈

❈

❈

❈

❈

❈

I returned to Flores on the Monday, not as a consequence of my scene with Martin on the previous night but because there was no real object in my staying in Cajara. The rest of Martin's tour would merely be a repetition of the clinic on Saturday afternoon, carried out in various other villages, and there was nothing to be learned from watching a series of patients receiving injections. What I really wanted to do now was to study the case records of the trial, and particularly those of the two patients who had died. It was just possible that I might be able to pick up some significant fact out of this information which would throw a new light on the situation. On the whole I thought it unlikely, but it was obviously up to me to try.

Martin and I parted amicably enough. He did not refer to the previous evening, and from his manner it was hard to imagine that anything of consequence had happened. It was even possible that he had enjoyed it. Emotional outbursts with him almost seemed to take the place of alcohol in another man. It was no doubt a delight to him when I arrived. He could revive all his old favorite situations in a new and exotic context—the Jesuit situation, the "me" situation, the interesting triangular relationship between the two of us and Barbara. I suspected that one of my attractions for him was that I was at once audience and collaborator in the drama of his life. I knew the language and the idiom and the background. I was the old trouper who could always be relied on to take over a part at a moment's notice.

I drove back in the mail van. The driver was a large, voluble Negro, who shared with many others a delusion that doctors are always fascinated by any conversation dealing with disease. He described to me in profuse and unnecessary detail the loss of a pair of fingers on his left hand, lopped off by a careless neighbor while cutting sugar cane. He had received a hundred and fifty pounds' compensation and considered he had done rather well out of the exchange. His only grievance was against Das, who had treated the fingers and taken a great deal of trouble to preserve the thumb. If he had lost his thumb as well, he would have made enough compensation for the down payment on a taxicab.

I found it hard to maintain much interest in what he was saying. My mind kept revolving around the fact that in a few hours I should be seeing Barbara again. Did Martin really mean it when he said she was in love with me? What importance should one attach to last night's conversation? I was far too experienced to believe that all Martin's statements could be taken at face value. He was liable to say things for a variety of reasons, of which the possible truth of the statement was only one. He might be wishing to impress or to influence a course of action; he might even simply be bored and craving excitement.

I thought it probably true that he was no longer in love with Barbara. Indeed, I began to question whether he ever had been. I could imagine him loving the *idea* of her—handsome, rich, charming, distinguished. She must have seemed to him the perfect setting for his own personality. At that stage of life she had represented achievement. I began to doubt whether he was capable of loving anybody except as a reflection of himself. And I suspected that the truth was the very opposite of what he had claimed—that, in fact, he had not felt very strongly about Barbara at all in the beginning, but that she had become supremely valuable to him when it appeared that I might take her away from him.

It seemed to me of vital importance not to be caught in the

same way twice. These dramas he constructed were not entirely for entertainment. The play was always written with his own ends in view. Once the story had been that nothing mattered to him but Barbara, and I was trying to take her away from him. Now Barbara was unimportant. Nothing mattered but the trial, and here I was again, his evil genius, trying to rob him of his just reward.

So I went on throughout my drive back to Flores, analyzing, interpreting, speculating. The fact was that I wanted what Martin had said to be true. I wanted Barbara now no less than I had ten years ago; more, because I was more sure of myself and I could see time running away from me. I was in a hurry for happiness before it was too late. Though Martin's proposition was absurd and outrageous, the possibilities behind it excited me. When I had agreed to come to the island, had I not, deep within me, been hoping for something of this kind—that she might have tired of Martin or he of her, and that I might have a chance to retrieve my mistake of ten years ago? I knew now that this was so. And Martin knew it too. In his urgent necessity to influence me, he had picked upon it as the weak point in my defenses.

I arrived back at the house just before lunchtime. Nobody was expecting me, since the original plan had been that I should stay in Cajara until the middle of the week. As the servant carried my bags in, I asked him if Mrs. Farrell was at home. He nodded indifferently and said, "Painting room." This was the big bedroom at the back of the house, which Barbara had had converted into a studio. I left my suitcase and went up there.

I knocked at the door.

"Yes?"

When I opened the door I saw her standing in front of an easel at the far end of the room, dressed in a smock and a pair of old slacks. Her hair was a little untidy and there were smears of paint on her hands. When she turned round and saw me, she looked flustered, almost angry. She dropped her paintbrush and threw a cloth over the picture before I had a chance to see it.

"I wasn't expecting you," she said. It was like an accusation.

"No. I came back early. There was nothing left to do in Cajara."

She stood there as if waiting for me to go. I had never known her so brusque and unfriendly. My presence in her studio seemed to throw her into an agony of self-consciousness. It was as if I had walked into her bedroom uninvited and found her naked. Indeed, worse; she could probably have coped with my presence in her bedroom without any great embarrassment. I remembered how abruptly she had changed the subject when her painting had been mentioned on an earlier occasion. I wondered whether to leave, but that would only call attention to her awkwardness. Also, I was aware that among creative people this painful shyness was a mixed emotion. On one side was the fear of revealing part of oneself, however crudely and imperfectly expressed—the fear of disappointing, of being misunderstood, of being understood too well. For the agony of a work of art from the point of view of the creator is that if it fails it is boring and even ludicrous, while if it succeeds it reveals some part of the artist that he or she may have been struggling for a lifetime to conceal. Against this, insistent, compulsive, agonizing, is the desire to show, to be seen, to be appreciated.

This was why she stood there, for the moment resenting me, and angry with herself because she did not know whether she wanted me to go or stay. Now I not only wanted to see the picture, I knew I had to. It was the only way in which the embarrassment of this moment could be erased.

I walked further into the room.

"May I see your work?"

She regarded me with unimpaired hostility. "Well, I don't know, really. . . ." She waited for me to retire apologetically. When I did not, she finally shrugged her shoulders. "Oh, all right. Only for God's sake don't try to think of something suitable to say."

She removed the unfinished picture from the easel without showing it to me, and then took a pile of about a dozen canvases from a corner of the room. She put them up, one after another, leaving each one for about half a minute. I said nothing. I know nothing about the technicalities of painting and have no great natural feeling for the visual arts. I was mainly interested in the pictures as a means of gaining a further insight into Barbara herself. The most obvious thing, which might have been suspected from her attitude toward them, was that they were not merely a method of passing the time. They did represent an effort to say something that she felt very strongly. What exactly it was was not so obvious—presumably if a thing can be formulated in words, you put it into words, not into paint. The pictures were mostly landscapes; sometimes they were recognizable views of the island. But the technique, to me at least, was curious—an abnormal stillness was conveyed, an impossible clarity and exaggerated definition of objects, as if no atmosphere existed. It made the island look like another planet—it gave a nightmarish grotesque quality to the most ordinary scenes. I had no idea whether this was a method she had developed herself or whether she had derived it from someone else she admired; that did not seem very important. Presumably all art is to some extent derivative, and the interesting thing was that she should have adopted that method rather than another. One thing seemed clear. It was not an easy, happy sort of art. The whole effect was harsh, bitter, uncompromising.

When she had put the last one away, I said, "You hate this island, don't you?"

"The island?" She looked at me in surprise. "I don't know. . . . Yes, I suppose I do. As time goes on I get more and more homesick for England. It seems to be the only place in the world where people aren't trying to *prove* something all the time."

"Were they in Germany?"

"God, yes. Worse than anywhere. They have to keep reminding you how well they've done since the war, as if that somehow made up for them having started it. And here it isn't much better. The island's full of second-rate people who came out here be-

cause it's easier to earn a living here than at home. Taxation's low
and the climate's good and servants ten a penny. I don't criticize
them for that. I just wish they wouldn't bore me to death with
what a wonderful job they're doing for the islanders."

"You'd like to go back to England when the trial's finished?"

"Of course," she said, with something like despair. "But it's not
really up to me, is it? We have to go where the job is." She packed
up her brushes and wiped her hands on a cloth. "Where's
Martin?"

"He and Kadu have to do some of the mountain villages. He
said he'd probably be back by Thursday."

We stood there, more ill at ease with each other than we had
ever been. As far as she was concerned, it was probably partly
due to the paintings. But not entirely, I thought. We had three
days alone, perhaps more. It was as if we were back again where
we had been ten years before—right at the beginning.

17

❁

❁

❁

❁

❁

❁

THAT afternoon Das brought up the records of the trial and I settled down to work. There was a mass of documents to go through, and I knew from previous experience of this kind of work that it would be a long and tedious job.

Fortunately the whole project had been laid out with enormous care and skill. It was also explained at each step with far more clarity than one was accustomed to expect. It was apparent from the very beginning that here was the production of a really first-class mind. The experiment had been written up stage by stage and arranged in chronological order. First there was an account of Martin's early work on the virus, mainly confirming and at points extending and completing the work of others. Then there came his first efforts to isolate the virus and kill it, without at the same time destroying its capacity to immunize. There were the records of many false starts and failures. He wrote of his efforts to get finance to continue the project, which had ended with his moving to the laboratories at Chemiefabriken. Here the first pilot quantities of vaccine were produced. There was a mass of information on the chimpanzee experiments that had first demonstrated the power of the vaccine to control encephalitis in animals. After that there was an account, deliberately bald and unemotional, of the difficulties experienced in initiating field trials by means of the Colonial Office. Then came the trial itself.

The plan, the method of evaluating results, the control of the double blind—they were all, as one might have expected from Martin, clearly explained and meticulously carried out, even in the most difficult circumstances. The blood studies, considering the facilities available on the island, were an achievement in themselves. When one saw the amount of work that had gone into it, one began to appreciate the reason for the attitude, not only of Martin but of Das and Kadu, toward the trial. It seemed a crime to interfere with it.

The only trouble was, I reminded myself, that the actual quality of the work was to some extent irrelevant. De Freitas was not attacking on that front—he was too clever for that. He was saying: Granted that the work is competent, valuable, perhaps even brilliant, the question remains, is it safe? This was an oversimplification, of course. No experiment is a hundred per cent safe. It isn't even a hundred per cent safe to cross the road. But was the safety factor high enough to justify continuation, on the evidence available? That was what I had to decide for myself.

There were several hundred individual case sheets, and I went through them all. They told me nothing. They were all very similar to the ones I had seen in the Health Center at Cajara—history, proof of diagnosis, record of vaccination, name and address of patient, code number, progress since vaccination. There was an enormous temptation to try to guess who had received the vaccine and who had not, as there always is when checking through results of this kind—everyone likes to try his hand at solving a puzzle. But I disciplined myself against it.

I came at last to a special folder containing two case sheets— the deaths. I took a long time over these, searching mainly for some clue that others might have missed. It was unlikely that Martin and Hume would have missed anything, but not impossible. Even the most rigidly honest of investigators can at times be governed by subconscious influences. There is a tremendous inherent resistance in most people against admitting even to themselves that they have been the cause of harm to others. It is easy to turn a blind eye to unpleasant but significant facts. But I could find nothing of that kind here. There was, unavoidably in the circumstances, a lack of really good firsthand evidence about the deaths. The doctor had been called too late and the relatives were almost valueless as witnesses. All the patients had other diseases besides encephalitis, the symptoms of which tended to overlap. To the islanders, the term "fever" covered a number of diverse conditions. An obviously serious attempt had been made to get a detailed history out of a multitude of onlookers. I could visualize them crowded in their dark, flea-infested huts, looking with impatience and resentment at the foreign interloper with his endless questions, his notebook, which was in their minds inescapably associated with the police. Did he suspect them of poisoning? And if not, what was he there for? The old man was dead, wasn't he? Could anyone bring him back to life? Then let them get back to the ceremonies suitable to death, the wailing, the ceremonial feast of goat's meat, the division of the property.

After I had finished with the records I spent the next morning talking first to Das, then to Hume. Both of them were helpful; they explained to me with great kindness and patience the difficulties due to local conditions on the island. Both agreed, with every appearance of sincerity, that it was absurd to suggest that there had been any deliberate attempt to avoid post-mortems in the two cases.

I began to wonder what action I was going to recommend. I had been less than honest, as both Martin and de Freitas well knew, when I had protested that I was a mere observer whose opinion was of no consequence. That was indeed my official position. Yet, as the only expert on the spot, apart from those who might be considered to have a bias in the matter, any advice I gave to the Ministry was bound to carry considerable weight. I was not, as they considered here, an arbitrator. But I could exert some influence over those who were.

Unfortunately the information available did not leave me in a much better position to make up my mind than I had been when I first arrived at the island. It was simply impossible to tell what had caused the deaths. I was inclined to agree with Hume and Das that this lack of evidence was due neither to negligence nor to deliberate concealment but was one of the inevitable disadvantages of working in a primitive country.

It seemed to me, weighing all the available evidence, that there was one very encouraging feature. The last death had occurred over four weeks ago, and none of the treated patients had died since. It was fairly reasonable to suppose that if the vaccine had been responsible, there would have been further trouble since then. It was a close-run thing, but I thought this last factor just tipped the scale in Martin's favor. I was inclined to recommend that the trial should continue.

18

❀

❀

❀

❀

❀

❀

I told Barbara of my decision. She said, "So the trial will go on?"

"I should think so. London will probably take my advice, if only because it's the easiest thing to do."

"And de Freitas?"

"He'll be angry, of course. The Jesuits will probably take it up; there may be a question in the House, the Minister will stall. It all takes time. With any sort of luck the trial may be finished before the opposition gets under way."

"And Martin will have won?"

"Yes."

"He'll be pleased," she said indifferently.

"Won't you?"

"This winning and losing," she said, "it's a man's game. I can't really get interested in it."

There was a silence. I did not want to talk about the trial any more than she did. There was only one thing I wanted to talk about with her and I did not know how to start. Ever since I had got back to the house I had been wondering how to do it. Now I could wait no longer. But I could only think of the simplest and most obvious way.

I said, "I don't know whether I have the right to ask this, but —do you still care for Martin?"

She did not reply immediately, and I was nervous of a rebuff. I said, "Perhaps you'll say it's no business of mine—"

She looked at me gravely. "Why do you ask?"

I could not tell her the truth, that I was only hoping to confirm what her own husband had told me. I could not subject her to the humiliation of knowing that Martin had been prepared to offer her casually as a counter in an exchange.

"Because I want you to be happy," I said.

"Do you?" She gave a little mocking smile. "With him? Would you have been pleased if you'd found us perfectly contented? If we'd been so wrapped up in each other that we'd forgotten all about you? Would you have liked that?"

"I suppose not," I admitted. "I suppose nobody likes to be forgotten."

"We didn't forget you," she said. "Neither of us. You were always there. Perhaps that was part of the trouble—though not all of it by any means." She pondered for a moment. "It's difficult to say what one feels about Martin. He's a long way off from me now—much further than he used to be. I don't know quite how to describe it, but I don't seem to have much contact with him any more. I have a feeling he never really thinks about me. I might go away for days at a time and he'd never notice."

There was something in her voice, a puzzled expression on her face, that alarmed me. Uneasy thoughts that had been banished to the back of my brain came crowding back again. I remembered my conversation with the priest and the atmosphere of unreality that had hung over that afternoon on the beach. I said, "Has it ever occurred to you that he might be—" She looked at me in perplexity and I found difficulty in going on. I changed my ground. "Did I tell you that I spoke to de Freitas in Cajara?"

"No."

"He was trying to persuade me that Martin was—what he called unbalanced."

She was startled and indignant. "Do you mean he thinks he's mad?"

"So he says."

"Do you agree with him?"

I shook my head. "No, I don't. But I think he's in a highly unstable frame of mind. He's obsessed by the trial to the exclusion of everything. Nothing else matters to him—not even you. Isn't that so?"

"Yes," she said sadly. "That's true, I think. But one has to make allowances. You see, he wants so badly to succeed at something. When you come down to it, his life has been a series of failures. Breckenhall, that business of the Spanish War, his marriage to me. . . . So often he's almost pulled it off—but never quite. Now he's concentrated on his career. If success doesn't come soon, he feels he's going to miss it altogether. He's made so many enemies that unless he comes out on top they won't allow him any place at all." She leaned toward me, her hands clasped together. "Try to understand. He thought he was there this time. It was in his grasp. And then you turn up. You, of all people—the man he's afraid of, the person he always associates with defeat—"

"Oh, no, surely—"

"Yes, Peter, that's how it is. Didn't you know he was afraid of you?"

I tried to adjust myself to this new conception. The idea seemed fanciful. I, who had always looked upon myself as the follower, the disciple. . . . But I dragged my mind away from Martin. She had still not answered my original question. I said, "That's not important. Only one thing is important to me. Are you in love with him?"

She shook her head. "I don't think I ever was. Nor he with me. Of course, the times were abnormal, weren't they? Perhaps there was some excuse. Even the most sensible people lost their heads then, and we weren't very sensible." She shrugged her shoulders. "It was a fairly common story. We pretended for a time, as everyone does. Then he was sent to the East, and when he came back we both knew, immediately. It's been like that ever since."

I said, "Does it have to stay like that?"

She regarded me searchingly for a moment. "Do you mean, would I leave him?" I nodded. "Perhaps if there was some reason. I don't know. I think we're both better together than alone—"

"You needn't be alone," I said. There was a short silence. Then I said, "I love you, Barbara. I always have."

"Do you? Do you really?"

"I thought women always knew. Don't they?"

"Usually."

"That was the main reason why I came here. I couldn't help it. I wanted to find out if—" I hesitated.

"If my marriage was a failure?"

I said reluctantly, "I suppose so. It doesn't sound very good, put like that—"

"And now you know—it *is* a failure. Does that please you?"

I didn't answer. Instead I said, "I think I could make you happy. I'd try anyway."

She gave a sad little smile.

"Is this a proposal?" she asked.

"Yes."

It was only then that I was fully aware of the implications of what I was suggesting. I did not want her simply as a mistress; I had no taste for an intrigue with her. I wanted her to divorce Martin and marry me. It was the kind of momentous step I should have expected myself to think over carefully beforehand—but in such circumstances one hardly ever does. It was with a certain relief that I looked back on my own words and knew that I was committed.

She said, "Oh, Peter, why didn't you ask me ten years ago?"

"Because I was a fool. I know it now. I didn't deserve to be happy. But surely we don't have to go on living with our mistakes forever? If you still care for me—"

"There was never anybody else but you," she said. "Even after what happened—"

"I'm sorry," I said. The apology seemed hopelessly inadequate. "I can't tell you how sorry I am. Will you try to forgive me?"

"Oh, I did that long ago. I expect I was to blame as much as you. I was a selfish little prig in those days. I don't suppose I really tried to understand you."

"No, that's not true. You were beautiful and kind and gay and understanding, just as you are now." I implored her, "Please, give me another chance."

She shook her head regretfully. "It's no good, Peter. We can't put the clock back." She walked away and stood with her back to me, looking out onto the bay. "I'll tell you something. Before you came, Martin said this was going to happen. He said, 'Peter wants two things. He wants to destroy my work. And he wants to take you from me.'"

I was suddenly angry. "Surely you don't take any notice of that? You must know that he'd say anything to get his way."

"Wasn't it true?"

"No. I'm not here to destroy his work. And if I want you, surely I have a right to try—"

"Do you?"

"Yes, I do, in the circumstances."

"What circumstances?"

I was unable to answer her. I could not tell her that Martin cared nothing for her, that he had offered her to me casually as a bribe for my co-operation. I said, "I'm afraid I can't tell you. Please don't ask me. Just say you'll come with me."

I went up to her and put my arm round her shoulders. She leaned against me for a moment and then broke away.

"Not just now," she said. "Don't let's be serious. I don't want to think of consequences. I just want to play a little—as we used to, do you remember? It seems such a long time ago."

19

FOR the next few days we acted as if we had no problems. We did nothing exciting or unusual, but we took pleasure in the sunshine, in the quiet, lazy routine of the tropical day. We got up early to make the most of the freshness of the morning, when I could work on my report and Barbara on her painting. I took my papers up into her studio and we found an old folding card table at which I sat. I did not get a great deal done. When Barbara was painting, she loved to talk, about anything but the work she was doing. She did not really enjoy being alone.

"I'd much sooner have somebody here," she said. "The only thing is it's almost impossible to find the right sort of person. Either they take too much interest in what I'm doing or they get restless. Martin was impossible. He couldn't bear the thought of so much attention going on something else but himself. In fact," she added, "he's always been a little mixed up about my painting. At times he likes to pretend it doesn't exist. At others he brags about it to people, just as in the early days he used to brag about my money, as if it was a sort of indirect possession of his own. That's much worse, of course. People feel they have to pretend interest and they don't really believe that I don't want it. They think I'm being mock-modest. Most embarrassing."

Each day we had lunch in the studio. The servant who brought it was impassive and noncommittal as always; I wondered whether he had any theories about what was going on. No doubt they all knew perfectly well about Barbara and Martin, and imagined that Barbara had taken a lover. We were both too happy to care what they knew or suspected.

Martin was due to return on Thursday, but at breakfast that morning there was a letter in his handwriting.

"It's just a few lines," said Barbara. "He says he has to pay a visit to a village on the east coast called Pamao. He won't be able to get home until tomorrow at the earliest."

It was a reprieve, another whole day, and we made the most of it. In the evening, after dinner, we sat out on the terrace sipping brandy. The moon came up, large and clear and, as always in those latitudes, a little ostentatious. The air was still and full of the rich smell of frangipani.

It was a night for love; a picture-postcard, popular-romance, magazine-story night. For the first time I began to understand Barbara's dislike and distrust of the island. The simple sensuousness of it all was somehow nauseating. Like the scent of the flowers it was all too sweet, too easy. The flowers grew without struggle or pain, they opened their blooms to you and offered you their perfume as a matter of course. I could imagine the British residents sitting out on their terraces on these eternal soft summer nights, filled with a restlessness they could not explain. It was no wonder they drank too much, that they engaged in listless flirtations with each other's wives. It was almost as if the landscape itself expected it of you.

In a curious way, too, I was uneasy. I could not help thinking of Martin, alone in some small, squalid village, being bitten by fleas on the earth floor of a native hut. But I put the picture away from me. I owed nothing to him. Neither of us did. I drew Barbara toward me and kissed her.

She came to me now, without any hesitation or resistance. It was quite different from the kiss she gave me on first welcoming me to the house, the one that had embarrassed me. Now it was a lover's kiss, sensual and abandoned, and I was not embarrassed. I knew her well enough to be sure that she would not kiss me in this way unless she was in love with me. From that moment I thought of her as mine.

I have no idea how long we stayed there together. In the end my desire for her became too great for restraint. I said, "Let me make love to you."

"Tonight?"

"Yes. Now. Please—I want you so badly."

"I want you too. You know I do. But not tonight."

"Why not? We're alone here. The servants are in the other wing."

"I wasn't thinking of the servants."

"Well, then, what? Is it Martin? Do you think he might not have gone to Pamao?"

"Oh, he's gone all right. Anything to do with his trial . . . No," she said, "it's nothing like that. I don't know whether I can explain it, but I feel it would be wrong tonight. It would be—well, it would be just what he would *expect* us to be doing." She went on haltingly. "When I think about it, it seems to me that the trouble with both of us is that we allowed him to manipulate us. He told us what sort of people we were and what we would do, and before we knew where we were we found ourselves doing it, even though it wasn't the best thing for us at all. He tries to force situations on people, like a conjurer with a pack of cards. Tonight's too easy, it's too obvious. It's *his* night, can't you see? He created it. It's almost as if he were here, encouraging us. If we do it tonight, he'll look at us in a certain way tomorrow, and he'll know. He'll feel he still possesses us."

I understood immediately what she meant. I recognized now the source of my own uneasiness earlier on, before it had been extinguished by desire. I felt frustrated and disappointed, but I knew she was right. I did not argue with her. Later, I told myself, when we had proved our freedom, my time would come.

We stayed up until very late. The servants went to bed and the lights went out in the town below. The night breeze blew in from the ocean, thin, cool, tasting slightly of salt. Barbara stirred in my arms. I was just thinking it was time we went in, before it grew colder, when I heard the buzzing.

It was very faint at first, like a mosquito but deeper. Gradually it grew louder and identified itself to my ear as a car on the road below. Then it stopped.

I got up and walked along the terrace, looking across the garden. There was no sign of headlights, no sound except the faint humming of insects. The car must have stopped some distance from the house. Whoever it was would take a little time to reach us. I stood in the darkness on the terrace, invisible against the shadows of the house. It was about ten minutes before I saw a shadow moving through the trees.

"It's Martin," I said softly. Barbara was still sitting on the sofa where I had left her. She made a movement to get up, but I motioned her back. "Stay where you are," I said. "Leave this to me."

I moved carefully along the side of the house and picked up the shadow again almost immediately. Running around the whole of the first floor was a veranda onto which the bedrooms opened. At one end of the building a staircase led up to it from the end of the terrace. I could recognize Martin definitely now as he moved stealthily toward the staircase. I thought I could make a fairly accurate guess as to his subsequent movements. Barbara's room was the first on the veranda. He would look in there and find it empty. Then he would come to mine.

I went back into the house, through the living room and up the main staircase. The door of my room was open and I stepped in, standing in the shadows near the door, with my hand on the light switch. Presently I heard a creaking of loose boards from the veranda, and one of the French doors began gradually to open. A moment later Martin was in the room, silhouetted against the moonlight.

I switched on the light.

20

✦

✦

✦

✦

✦

✦

I had never seen him quite so obviously at a loss. He looked around the room, blinking in the sudden and unexpected glare of the light. His glance focussed first on me, then the undisturbed bed, then back to me again. I could see it dawning on him that he had been outwitted. Incredulity was succeeded by indignation; it always enraged him to find that others were working against him, even in self-defense. He was so preoccupied by his own manipulations as to forget that others were able to take an active part in events at all.

For a moment he was undecided as to what attitude to take up. Then, characteristically, he plunged into the attack.

"What the blazes is going on here?" he exploded indignantly.

"As you see," I said, glancing with significance at the bed, "nothing at all. Does that disappoint you?"

"I don't know what the hell you're talking about." He sounded almost genuinely baffled. Already, I knew, he would be suppressing in his mind all consciousness of his unsuccessful maneuver. It would not be long before he could convince himself that it had never been attempted, that he had come home unexpectedly by pure chance.

"What were you doing standing there in the dark? And where's Barbara?"

"Downstairs."

"Also in the dark?"

"Presumably."

He had driven me momentarily onto the defensive. He raised his eyebrows and looked at me as if waiting for some explanation of my conduct. It was admirably done. If I was not careful I should find myself offering excuses. When I did not reply, he gave a sarcastic bark of laughter. "This is a madhouse. I come home and find the place in pitch darkness. Barbara isn't in her room. When I come along to find you, here you are, crouching behind the door with your hand on the light switch—"

I hit back. "Do you usually come in this way—through the veranda?"

He replied coldly. "I imagine I have the right to do as I please."

"We could easily have taken you for a burglar."

"Oh, don't be a bloody fool."

He flung himself into a cane chair opposite the bed. He gave the impression of being suddenly bored with the whole situation. To me too it was beginning to appear a little childish. My first sense of triumph had rapidly evaporated. While I had made Martin look ridiculous, I had an uneasy feeling that I myself looked hardly less so. The honors were just about even. But he, possibly because he was more accustomed to being involved in bizarre episodes of this kind, was handling himself more skillfully.

He lit a cigarette and grinned at me. He knew what I had been thinking. He was admiring his own resourcefulness and was glad that I was there to recognize it. There was no need to say anything; we understood each other so well. What was it, I wondered, that I felt for Martin? Could understanding in itself be a form of love?

He said suddenly, "Have you made love to her?"

He was watching me carefully, hoping for me to betray myself. "No," I said.

"There's no need to be shy about it, you know. You can tell Uncle Martin." I said nothing. "The offer I made at Cajara still stands."

"So does my answer."

"You can't fool me, Peter. I know perfectly well you want her.

Whether you've slept with her during this last day or two doesn't really matter in the long run." He paused for a moment. "I'm proposing a sensible, civilized arrangement. I don't want to make a fight of it. But if you do, I must warn you I could be very awkward."

"Awkward about what?"

It was Barbara. She had come into the room through the open door behind me. Martin must have seen her a second before I did. He said quickly, "A technical matter, dear. Nothing that would interest you."

Barbara looked at me, waiting for me to contradict him, but I said nothing. I could not disclose what we were really talking about without precipitating a complete showdown, and neither of us was ready for that. She turned back to Martin. It seemed to occur to her for the first time that we might be in league against her.

She said, "I thought you weren't coming back till tomorrow."

"I had to change my program in a hurry. There wasn't time to notify you."

"I didn't hear you drive up."

"No. I left the car at the bottom of the drive. I didn't want to wake the whole household," he said, with barefaced mendacity. "As it happens, I needn't have worried." He turned to me solicitously. "I hope you got everything you wanted while I was away?"

"What do you mean?"

He smiled. "Why, from Das, of course. All the figures and so on. I asked him to give you anything you asked for."

"Oh, yes. He was very helpful."

"Did it get you any further?"

"Not really."

"No, I didn't think it would. But you can't say we haven't been co-operative, can you?"

"No."

I wondered whether I ought to tell him that I had decided to let him go ahead with the trial. This indeed would represent a kind of victory for me. I could explain to him that he had no need to charm me or appeal to old loyalties, to blackmail me or to bribe me. I had made my decision, and by a piece of good fortune for him it was in his favor. But I did not want to talk about it now, with Barbara present. It would do him no harm to wait until the morning for his good news.

He got up from his chair in a preoccupied way and stubbed his cigarette out.

"I suppose it's time we were going to bed," he said.

"Yes," Barbara held out her cheek to me to be kissed. "Good night, Peter."

As I kissed her, awkwardly, I could feel Martin watching me, observing my embarrassment. He said, "I'll be along in ten minutes, darling. I want to show Peter something."

"Show me what?" I asked when she had gone to her room.

He motioned to me to follow him. We went down the stairs and out of the house, then down the drive. Our feet crunched on the gravel path. I was slightly irritated by his air of mystery, but I could not help being curious. Martin was not a man to risk an anticlimax. We must have walked about two hundred yards down the drive when I saw the station wagon. It had been parked on a small clearing at one side of the road. Martin went up to the big double doors at the back and opened them. The car was fitted out almost like an ambulance, with a stretcher in the back. Martin pulled out the stretcher like a man pulling out a drawer. On it lay a sheet. He twitched the sheet aside. Under it was a small brown body, dusty, aged, emaciated. A sticklike arm slipped off the edge of the stretcher. Martin tucked it back and covered up the body again with the sheet.

"There you are," he said grimly. "Now you can have your bloody post-mortem."

21

◉

◉

◉

◉

◉

◉

"WELL," said Hume, "the kidneys are cheerful enough."

He held up the organ for demonstration, first to Martin, then to myself, peeling off the capsule with the slick self-congratulation of a conjurer or a cookery demonstrator. Nothing up his sleeve. Like all morbid anatomists, he enjoyed being the center of attention.

He dictated over his shoulder to his Eurasian secretary. "Strips readily. Slight inflammation in calyces—terminal, I should think. Not much perinephric fat, but then you'd hardly expect it, would you? Adrenals normal."

The post-mortem room was cooler than most places in the town. The walls were of thick concrete and fitted with powerful extractor fans. Venetian blinds over the windows protected us from the full rigor of the morning sun. But the smell of death was still with us, sickly, pervasive, proof against the finest air-conditioning. The refrigerators stood like wardrobes along the wall. The body on the slab was small, brown, wizened, the bones almost sticking through the dry skin. It was hard to believe that he had ever been alive or, if alive, ever human in the same sense that we were. The eyes were closed, the cheeks hollow and marked by two oblique tribal scars. The legs were covered with healed ulcers. On the right foot several toes were missing.

Martin and I stood in silence, watching Hume working his way deftly along the gut. His big butcher's hands hidden in their housewife's rubber gloves cut, snipped, tore, twisted, dissected. He was whistling (slightly off key) "Drink to Me Only with Thine Eyes." His technician helped him, grinning contentedly. This was a much-coveted job and he never ceased to congratulate himself on his good fortune. There was not only good money and security but great prestige, the feeling of taking part in important mysteries.

The door opened and Das came in. I felt myself, as always, reacting equally against both personality extremes. If Hume's callousness was distasteful it was no more so than Das's air of extravagant anxiety and gloom. A post-mortem is not a tea party; on the other hand it isn't a wake either.

"I'm sorry to be late," said Das. "I had to finish a clinic."

"You haven't missed anything." Martin handed him a sheaf of papers. "There are the case notes. He was injected three weeks ago but never came back for a checkup. He lived in a little village up in the mountains. When I was in Cajara I got a message that he was ill. When I got up there, it was the usual thing. Smelly little hut, a hundred chattering relatives, no light or water. He was delirious. We couldn't get a damn bit of sense out of anybody." He turned on me. "Some of you office doctors who pick holes in our results ought to come out into the country and get an idea—" I said nothing, determined not to rise to it, and for once he was too tense and unhappy to derive any real pleasure from taunting me. He said, "After I'd been there about ten minutes he went into a coma and died."

I was thinking how fortunate it was that I had delayed in telling Martin he could go ahead with the trial. I said, for something to say, "You couldn't make a diagnosis?"

"Hardly," said Martin. He added satirically, "I didn't have my cisternal-puncture outfit with me."

Das turned on me, eager to defend his hero. "It's a pity you were not there yourself. If you had stayed in Cajara instead of coming back to the coast—"

Obviously he thought I had returned for my own comfort. I did not reply. It would have been too undignified to engage in a wrangle over the dead body. Martin said, with an air of giving the devil his due, "Well, that was largely my doing," but I could see Das did not believe a word of it. He thought Martin was simply being generous. So far as he was concerned, nothing I could ever do would be right.

"Liver enlarged," said Hume. "Full of hydatids, as usual. Some fibrosis. Typical malarial spleen. Sometimes you wonder how these people get to maturity at all." He nodded to the technician. "You can start the skull now."

The technician grinned appreciatively. This was plainly a job he looked forward to. He made a deep incision across the scalp and turned it neatly down over the face. Now all semblance of humanity was lost from the body. He fixed the cranium within a series of spikes bolted to an iron ring and began to saw vigorously at the bone. Hume turned his attention to the chest.

"A few adhesions across the pleura. Hello"—he sliced across the lung and squeezed the cut surface—"plenty of fluid and some pus." He dictated to the secretary, "Bronchopneumonia."

"Bronchopneumonia?" It was impossible for Martin to keep the eagerness out of his voice. "You think he died of that?"

Hume shook his head regretfully. "You see a lot of lungs like this in people who've been unconscious. It's nearly always secondary to something else."

The heart and arteries were normal, a great deal better than any of ours would have been. At least he had been spared the penalties of too rich a diet. Hume moved up to the end of the table. The top of the skull came off like an eggshell with a few cracks of the chisel. With sudden gentleness he snipped at the meninges covering the brain. There was a thin gelatinous film on the surface of the right cerebral hemisphere. He pointed to it and said to the technician, "Swab."

He swabbed up some of the jelly and put it into a sterile tube. "Label that, will you? I'll tell you what to do with it later on."

He cut the brain carefully out of the skull and took it over to a side table. We stood behind him, waiting. He sliced away a series of sections. They meant nothing to me, but from the look on Hume's face I could see that it was not coming out well for Martin. Presently he took several more specimens and had them labelled. Then he turned to us.

"Well, he had the encephalitis all right." He pointed to one of the cut surfaces. "That scarring's old. I don't suppose he's been too bright mentally for years, with all that knocking about." He pointed to another area. "But this is a very different cup of tea. There's been a recent acute attack."

"Can you be sure?" I asked.

"Pretty well. We shall confirm it under the microscope, of course, but I've seen a lot of these cases and I haven't any real doubt in my mind." He tapped the surface of the brain gently with the flat of his knife. "This is what killed him, all right."

Martin's voice was a little unsteady. "That's a very dogmatic statement." Hume said nothing. "Can you really be as sure as that?"

"The P.M. report calls for my expert opinion as a pathologist," said Hume without resentment. "That's it, I'm afraid. Sorry, Martin."

There was a silence. I could see Martin assimilating the catastrophe, adapting himself to it, working out a course of action. It must have been a bitter experience for him, but by no means unexpected; there had always been a good probability that the man had encephalitis. He had contemplated for a moment the possibility of shaking Hume out of his opinion, and rejected it as impracticable. There was only one thing for him to do next, and I waited for him to do it.

He turned to me and said, "Can I have a word with you alone?"

Hume had been expecting it too.

"Use my office," he said. "I shan't be finished for another half hour."

22

MARTIN said, "I don't like to say this, Peter, but after all we're dealing with a very serious matter and there isn't much room for sentiment. Hume isn't really a first-class pathologist."

I wasn't going to argue with him on this point. I was in no position to grade Hume's ability in his speciality. Martin might very well be right. A first-rate pathologist would probably never have come to Batou in the first place.

"The microscopic sections will be sent back to London, obviously," I said. "The final diagnosis rests on them. Until then, his is the best opinion we've got. We have to accept it."

Again I expected Martin to fight, and again he seemed to decide against it. After a silence he looked at me and said, "So?"

"Well—" The important thing, I told myself, was to keep the discussion on a logical, unemotional basis for as long as possible. I found myself speaking with an almost exaggerated detachment.

"Either he had the vaccine or the placebo—we don't know which. If he had the placebo, that's fine. He's just another man who got an exacerbation of his encephalitis and died of it. On the other hand, if he had the vaccine, either it failed to cure him or—"

I hesitated only for a second. Then I smiled as though it was an issue neither of us were particularly concerned with. "Or it killed him."

"Two weeks after administration? Good God, man, if we'd

injected hot virus into that man he'd have had symptoms within forty-eight hours."

"How do you know he didn't? We have practically no history and you didn't see him till very late. You can't say it's impossible."

"Just about, I should say." He went on intensely, "Peter, if you're honest with yourself you know damn well he didn't die because of the vaccine. Those virus particles are stone dead. I made absolutely certain of that before I left Germany." I said nothing. He suddenly exploded. "What's the matter with you— don't you believe me? Do you think I'm lying to you?"

I became impatient. It was not a question of lying and he knew it. It was the question of the possibility of error.

"Martin, you're talking like a child."

The accusation enraged him. "You smug bastard, do you think I'm going to stand here and let you lecture me in that condescending fashion! What sort of original work did you ever do?"

"That's hardly relevant."

"It's relevant to me. This is my experiment. I've put years of my life into it. My whole future hangs on it. I'm sick and tired of being at the mercy of clapped-out old has-beens and third-rate civil servants. Everywhere I turn it's the same thing. As soon as you try to do something worth while in research you find yourself tripping over some shiny-bottomed bureaucrat who thinks he's been divinely appointed to tell you what to do."

"You may be right," I said. "To a great extent I agree with you. But if you'll stop working yourself up into a frenzy, you must see that we can't simply ignore the death of this man. This isn't just a scientific question, it's social and political as well."

"And religious," he put in sourly. "Don't forget the bloody Jesuits."

"Well, there you are. Obviously I shall have to report to London. If I don't, de Freitas certainly will."

For the moment, he seemed more reasonable. "All right then— what are you suggesting?"

"In my view it's essential to know whether he had the vaccine."

There was no point in evading the issue. I could feel for him in his disappointment but I had given him the benefit of every possible doubt. There was only one course to take now. I said, as gently as possible, "We have to break the blind."

He shook his head decisively. "No. I can't agree to that." There was a short silence while he made a pretense of considering the proposal in more detail. Then he shook his head again. "It would make the whole trial valueless."

I had been expecting this as a first reaction. Indeed, it was rather more hopeful than I had expected—at least he seemed prepared to discuss it. I said reasonably, "That's an exaggeration, surely? If we found he hadn't had the vaccine the trial could go on. It wouldn't be double blind any more, of course, but I can't feel that's an absolute essential."

He was not prepared to accept any pretensions to authority on my part. "What the hell do you know about it?" he snapped irritably. "You never saw a case of this disease until a fortnight ago. This is my experiment and I'm the man to say how it has to be done. If you cut out the blind, it'll be ruined."

I shrugged my shoulders. "Then it's ruined. We have to know whether he had the vaccine."

He thought for a moment and then said, "Wait a moment—I've thought of something. We can find out without breaking the code."

"How?"

"Those swabs that Hume took. The natural virus here is a slightly different strain from the one we used in the lab. You can tell them apart on tissue culture. If we send them to Chemiefabriken—"

I was excited by the idea. It seemed to suggest a possibility of saving the trial. But I saw a difficulty. "Better to send them to London."

"Why?"

"Because in the end the decision's going to have to come from there. From what I know of them, they won't take Chemiefabriken's word for it—especially since they know the Germans have a lot of money at stake." I added, "You can send a specimen to both, if you like."

"All right," he said grudgingly. "I can't see anything against that."

At least, I thought with relief, he had not imputed bias in advance against whoever would carry out the tissue culture in England. It was alarming to find that I had been quite prepared for him to do so. But evidently his persecution mania still had its limits. I raised the next awkward question.

"How long will it take to get an answer?"

"Not long," he said airily.

"How long?"

"About three weeks."

"Oh," I said. I was disappointed. It seemed that this was not much of a way out after all. "We can't very well leave things in the air for three weeks."

"It's the only thing we can do." He reiterated obstinately, "I won't break the blind, not for you or anybody else. You can put that right out of your head."

I began to despair of persuading him to listen to common sense. The blind appeared to have acquired an obsessional quality in his mind. He was bound up emotionally with this mathematical device, in the same way as another man might become fixated on a religion or a political creed. The blind represented the experiment, and the experiment represented not only the sanctity of science but also his position and fortunes within science. He seemed to have lost contact with the ordinary world, in which there were worries and fears and uncertainties, where men did not behave simply and logically, where it was not enough, when you were dealing with the lives of human beings, to have a good deal of logic on your side.

"You want me to tell London that?" I asked.

"If you like."

I made a last attempt at compromise. "Look—what about this? Would you agree to suspend the trial—just temporarily, for a week or two—until the swab report comes through?"

For a moment he appeared to weaken. I thought I had him. But finally he shook his head.

"Sorry. It's not possible."

It was my last chance to avoid conflict, and I knew at that moment it had failed. I was bitter against his obstinacy, his insuperable egoism. "For God's sake, why not?" I said. "You can't say that would spoil the trial."

"Yes, it would. It would throw out the whole program. It would demoralize everyone." He went on moodily, "You don't know these people. You don't know the trouble we had persuading them to accept the trial in the first place. If we stopped the injections now, just after this death, that would be enough for them. They'd jump to the conclusion that we'd killed him. We should never get them back again."

There was some sense in what he said. The only trouble was that it completely ignored the existence of any viewpoint but his own. It took for granted that the trial was the only thing that really mattered and that everything else should be subordinated to it. So long as you were honest about the experiment itself, scientifically honest, nothing else mattered.

"You'd really be happy to go on with the trial as if nothing had happened?"

"So far as I'm concerned," he said, "nothing has happened. I'm absolutely convinced he was one of the controls."

There was a long silence. I was reluctant to say the words, to precipitate the storm. It would, I knew, mean the end between myself and Martin. We had thought so before, many times, it was true, and always we had come together again, uneasily drawn to each other—by what? A strange mixture of love, envy, hate, sympathy, understanding. Always attraction struggled with revulsion. Always, in our moments of greatest intimacy, we were on the verge of breaking with each other. I could not feel that we could survive this final and greatest conflict of wills.

"I'm sorry, Martin," I said. "I can't agree to that."

It sparked off his rage, as I knew it would. "And who are you," he said with magnificent contempt, "to agree or disagree? You told me yourself the other day that you were nothing better than a tout for your masters at the Ministry."

There was something theatrical about his insults that prevented them striking deep. It exasperated him that he found me so difficult to rouse with abuse, and he explained it by assuming that I was cold and thick-skinned. In fact, my coldness was a mere protective reaction. I had a fear that if I once allowed him to stampede me emotionally, I should be lost.

"It's true the decision's up to London," I said. "But they'll obviously ask for my opinion."

"Which is—to break up the trial?"

"To suspend it for a week or two," I corrected him.

"It's the same thing." He took a deep breath and regarded me with great hostility. "Well, at least you're out in the open now, instead of hiding behind your bloody committee. So it's in your power to make or break me? I suppose I should have known which you'd choose to do." He added bitterly, "It's been the same ever since we were at Breckenhall."

"For Christ's sake," I said, my nerves beginning to fray, "can't you ever forget Breckenhall?"

He shook his head. Obviously, and rather alarmingly, he couldn't. The incident seemed to be as vivid and disturbing to him as if it had happened last month instead of fifteen years ago. He said, "That was just the beginning. Then there was Barbara. As soon as you knew I wanted her you tried to take her from me. I beat you that time. And after that I thought I'd got rid of you. But no such luck. You caught up with me in the end. It took time, but you managed it. What you lack in ability you make up for in persistence. I don't know how you went about getting yourself picked out for this job—"

"I did nothing of the kind. I was instructed to come."

"If that's true, which I very much doubt, you could always have turned the job down. Anyone with an ounce of tact or decency would have done so. You know damn well that in these circumstances they could never have forced you to come." I was uneasily conscious that he had a point there. I should never have agreed to accept. "But so far as you were concerned the opportunity was too good to miss. To have power over me, to be able to ruin my career and seduce my wife—" He was almost beside himself. When I began to protest, he shouted me down. "Don't imagine I'm a complete bloody fool! I know perfectly well what you two were up to while I was away."

There were so many absurd and unjust accusations that I was rendered almost speechless. I was anxious to justify myself but could not think where to start. Finally I hit back at the whole basis of his assumptions.

"Do you really believe," I said, "that I spend my whole life thinking of nothing but you?"

As soon as I had said it I realized that, crazy though it might sound, that was actually what he *did* believe. In the egocentric, semi-paranoid world he now inhabited, it was the obvious explanation of my behavior. If I, or anybody else for that matter, was acting against his interests, it could only be as a result of personal spite. The idea of harm being done to him accidentally during the course of pursuing some other aim was one that Martin had always found difficulty in accepting. We were all members of a conspiracy, myself, de Freitas, Barbara, the Jesuits, Whitehall, bound together by one grand design that was the entire purpose of our lives—to ruin Martin Farrell.

His next words confirmed me in my suspicion. He looked at me intently and said, "Do you know, I sometimes think you were put into the world especially to destroy me." Even as a menace, a sinister force for evil, I was still to be part of his world; he was prepared to concede me no life of my own. He asked, almost pleadingly, as if I were a demon sitting on the end of his bed, "Why can't you leave me alone?"

I made a last effort to bring him back to the world of reality. "Your vanity's almost unbelievable," I said. "Try to get it into your head that there are other factors influencing people apart from you and your trial and your interests generally. Of course I'd sooner do you a good turn than a bad one, but to be quite honest about it your welfare's a minor consideration to me. I think first of my own interests, then my duties as far as my job is concerned, Barbara—"

It was as if he had not heard or not understood a word I said. There was no contact. Only the name called him back from his thoughts. He said, "You *were* making love to her, weren't you?"

So far, I had managed to keep my temper fairly well. But this was too much.

"Don't pretend you give a damn about Barbara," I said.

He regarded me contemptuously. "You miserable, coldhearted, *careful* bastard. If I was in love with a woman, I wouldn't hide it; I'd want the world to know—whatever the consequences. But you're not saying anything, are you? I can hear you saying to Barbara"—he adopted a curious whining voice that he used indiscriminately for caricaturing those whom he regarded as his enemies—"'Keep it quiet for the moment; it wouldn't be advisable to tell him just now, he might turn nasty. Let's wait until this affair's over, when I've managed to break the trial and fix him.'"

At last he had hurt me. He had got through the armor. His eyes were shining with triumph. There was just enough truth in what he had said to hurt and humiliate.

He went on, following up: "But don't delude yourself with the idea that I shall just sit here and accept the situation. I'm quite capable of defending myself. If you want trouble you can have it. If you're counting on my keeping my mouth shut and behaving like a gentleman, you can put that right out of your head. And you can remind Barbara that I'm a Catholic and I don't believe in divorce."

I walked toward him, my hands clenched. I could think of nothing to do but to hit him and go on hitting him, to beat in his face and stop him talking somehow. We had reached a point beyond the reach of words.

If he had tried to defend himself I think I would have hit him. But he miscalculated. The look of anticipation on his face was just noticeable to me even through my anger, and I realized his intention just in time. I drew back.

"Aren't you going to hit me?" he said, grinning slightly.

"No."

He shrugged his shoulders. It had been worth trying. It would have meant, of course, the total destruction of my strong position as an impartial Ministry observer. I could not be sure how much he had deliberately planned such an outcome, how much it had been the result of instinct and improvisation. Probably he did not know either. The sweat broke out on my forehead when I thought how nearly he had succeeded.

"Well, I got you to feel something, anyway," he said with satisfaction.

23

I got into a taxi outside the hospital gates and told the driver to take me up the hill to the house. I told myself that this was the end. I could not tolerate Martin for another moment. My one idea was to get away from him and restore myself gradually to some semblance of sanity. He would drive me crazy if I let him.

Obviously the first thing to do was to move out of the house. When I got there I told the taxi-driver to wait, and walked inside, intending to make straight for my bedroom. But Barbara intercepted me in the hall.

I must have looked a little wild. She said, in a worried voice, "What's happened?"

I didn't feel up to telling her all the details just now. I simply said, "I have to leave. I can't stay here any more."

"Why not?"

"Because I'm finished with Martin—finished for good."

She looked relieved, as if to say, is that all? "Again?" she said.

"This time I really mean it. If he wants to ruin himself, that's his affair. I don't take any further responsibility. He can go to hell, as far as I'm concerned." I began to walk up the stairs. "I'm moving out."

"Where to?" she asked, following me.

"The Clanricarde." Anticipating her protests, I said, "All right, I know it's lousy but there's no alternative. I can't stay another night in this house."

I went into my room, dragged my suitcase out of a cupboard and began to throw clothes into it. Barbara said, "Nallia will pack for you."

"I'll do it myself." I needed the activity. It did not fit in with my state of agitation to sit placidly in the living room talking to Barbara while my clothes were packed for me. On the other hand I was too emotionally disturbed to pack intelligently. I emptied the drawers while Barbara knelt down by the suitcase and began to arrange things in some sort of order. She was accustomed to accepting difficult and illogical behavior from men.

As she helped me she said, "You still haven't told me what happened."

I gave her a brief and disjointed summary of events. I could not bring myself to go into too much detail and in any case I thought she would not be very much interested in the purely medical aspects. I was also in a hurry to get away in case Martin might come up to the house. It was important to avoid meeting him again if at all possible.

At the same time I was harassed by the sense of obligation to Barbara. When my suitcases were packed, I kissed her and said, "This doesn't make any difference to us."

In a way it might even help us. Once I had broken with Martin and was no longer living under his roof, my sense of disloyalty might be diminished. I should feel freer to persuade her to leave him for me. I felt confident that in the end she would agree. As for the divorce, we would meet that difficulty when it arose.

"I'm sorry to leave you like this," I said, "but I couldn't bear to meet Martin again just now. And I've got to send my report off to London today—it's become terribly urgent. I'll get in touch with you."

Suddenly, I wondered how. It would be awkward if I rang and Martin answered the telephone. The same thought evidently occurred to her.

"No, I'll ring you," she said. "That may be easier. Then we can arrange to meet somewhere."

"Fine. And in the meantime don't believe anything Martin tells you. He's in a highly abnormal state."

She nodded her head but said nothing. I was too harassed to pay as much attention to her as I should have done. She followed me down the stairs. In the hall I put down the suitcases and kissed her again. She pressed herself toward me and clung to my shoulders. Her eyes were half closed. Suddenly I saw the houseboy behind her. His face showed neither shock nor any great interest. Perhaps he thought it was the same sort of kiss with which she had greeted me on my first arrival. It was not for him to speculate on the curious customs of Europeans. He simply picked up my bags and waited.

I stepped away and said, "See you soon, darling."

She nodded her head again. She could not, I thought understandingly, say very much with the servant listening. I gave her one last affectionate glance and went out to the taxi. Barbara stayed in the house.

The taxi-driver made a great parade of putting the suitcases in the luggage compartment. I breathed more easily. I was almost away. In my relief I grinned at the houseboy and felt in my wallet for a tip. There was nothing there but a wad of traveller's checks.

I swore to myself and told him to wait by the car. Then I rushed back into the house.

I found Barbara in the living room. She was sitting in an armchair with her back to the door, and I could only see the top of her head. I said hurriedly, "Look, sweetheart, I'm sorry to bother you with this but I've been dreadfully stupid. Do you think you could possibly lend me a couple of quid? I got out to the car—"

As I spoke I was moving toward her. She raised her head with a start and suddenly I saw, before she looked away again, that her face was covered with tears.

"Barbara—darling—what is it?"

"Nothing." She hid her face and dabbed at it with a handkerchief. The sight of Barbara, the dignified, the self-possessed, abandoning herself to solitary grief, caught at my heart. It occurred to me that if it had not been for the merest accident I would never have known. How many times before had she wept secretly in this fashion and then appeared afterward smiling, elegant, seemingly invulnerable? How many times had she been wounded before, by me, by others, and been too proud to admit it?

I could not bear to see her crying. I forgot about the taxi and the necessity of getting away, everything but her obvious misery, for which I felt myself to blame. I took her in my arms and began to comfort her.

"Tell me," I said. "Tell me, please. What is it? What have I done?"

"It's nothing," she repeated. "Just foolishness." When I waited, she went on haltingly through her tears. "It just seemed to me— as I saw you walking to the car—that you might go away and never come back."

"But we arranged—"

"Yes, I know." She made an attempt at a smile. "I told you it was just foolishness. I'm a hysterical woman."

"No."

Whatever she was, she was not that. But it came to me now that I had underrated the strain to which she had been subjected. Within a matter of weeks Martin had succeeded in driving me almost to distraction. She had lived with him for ten years. There was no knowing what subtle cruelties he might be capable of, what complex emotional gyrations within the intimate framework of the marriage relationship.

I had been misled by her pride and self-control. I had imagined she could stand up to anything and take care of herself under all circumstances. This is true of nobody. The trouble with understatement, I thought, is that people are apt to believe you. You say, "It's nothing," and they take it that it *is* nothing—especially if it is more comfortable for them to do so. This mistake could be made even by people like myself, who knew the language of understatement, and used it, and were misunderstood themselves in the same way. How many times had Martin accused me of coldness because I refused to make a parade of my emotions?

I stroked her hair and tried to kiss the tears away from her face. "I'm sorry, my darling," I said. "So sorry . . ."

At that moment I was conscious of somebody else in the room. I looked up and saw Martin, standing in the doorway.

I felt a sense of utter exasperation, as if this was more than any man could reasonably be asked to cope with. I released Barbara and looked at him disgustedly. "Oh, God," I said, "you again."

He raised his eyebrows. "It's my house, damn it," he pointed out with surprising mildness. "And my wife too, if it comes to that." But he did not seem in a mood to make an issue of it. He said, "Incidentally, there's a taxi outside eating its head off."

"Yes, it's mine. I'm leaving."

He regarded me curiously. "What on earth for?"

"I hardly think there's any need to explain."

He made a pretense of thinking, and then suddenly coming up with an idea. "You mean on account of that little altercation we had down at the morgue?"

I gritted my teeth. Evidently he was going to take the attitude that nothing much had happened, that it had been just the ordinary vigorous give and take of controversy. He had done this to me before—it was a favorite trick of his. It left you with the frustrated feeling of having gone through an exhausting ordeal to no purpose whatever.

"Yes," I said shortly.

"You take yourself too seriously." He said lightly to Barbara, "You'd be surprised how worked up he got. I swear he almost punched me on the nose."

I told myself I would not stand for this deliberate deflation of the incident. He, after all, had blown it up. Now he wanted it down again. He had had his big scene, his orgasm, and was in a pleasantly relaxed mood. He would like to discuss the whole situation over a drink, casually and flippantly. But I was of a less mercurial temperament.

"I'm going down to the Clanricarde," I said.

Martin looked at Barbara again as if enlisting her as an ally. "Is he serious?"

"Yes, I am," I said firmly. "Thank you very much for your hospitality up to now—"

"Oh, don't be a bloody fool," said Martin. "You've no idea how pompous you sound."

"All right, I'm pompous." I had got to the stage when I was indifferent to insults. I didn't care what he thought of me—or pretended he thought of me. "But I'm going just the same. I should never have come here in the first place."

"You should have stayed in London in the first place," said Martin tartly. He added, "You realize that if you move now it'll be all over the town in a couple of hours?" I said nothing. "Oh, all right," he said. "If you're determined on your hair shirt . . ."

"Before I go," I said, "I want to make it absolutely clear that I'm going to recommend to London that they suspend the trial. Don't come to me later and say that I've let you down again."

"You think treachery becomes more excusable if it's notified in advance?" He said to Barbara, with exaggerated politeness, "Are you going to the Clanricarde too, or are you staying here?"

He must have learned by this time that he could always throw me off balance by insulting Barbara. I said, "Now look here, Martin—"

Barbara broke in. She was herself again now. "Peter, can't you see he's trying to bait you?" It was true, of course. I saw Martin's lips twitching in his curious, secret smile. My anger left me. I simply felt weary and filled with a yearning to get away and be alone. Barbara said gently, "I think you'd better go."

When I got outside again I realized that I still didn't have any money. But there was nothing I could do about it. I gave the house-boy an apologetic smile and jumped into the taxi.

24

THERE was no difficulty in getting a room at the Clanricarde. Indeed, it was the same room, the best in the hotel, as the manager explained when I protested. The heat was oppressive down in the town, stifling and damp with overcast skies. There was not in the least that sense of release which often accompanies a break in the weather in hot climates, no sudden cooling breezes. It seemed, if anything, hotter than when the sun was out. During the afternoon a sudden squall came up, sweeping through the town and entering the lounge of the Clanricarde in a horizontal sheet of water, as if sprayed by some cosmic practical joker from an immense hose pipe. The inhabitants of the lounge retired into the dining room and emerged when the storm had passed, chattering plaintively to each other and steaming gently. It looked as if the rains were starting in earnest.

After lunch I went up to my room and worked on my report. Most of the factual side of it was already written. Only the episode of the third death and the post-mortem were left to be described in detail, then the commentary and conclusion. This last item was not very long but took a great deal of thought. Often when one takes a crucial step one is not conscious of how important it is; one looks back later and thinks, My God, if I had only known the consequences. . . . But in this case I was well aware that what I wrote was likely to bear considerable significance. If London followed my advice and Martin refused to obey them, there was certain to be a row of the very grandest nature. Every word of my report had to be able to stand up to scrutiny and possible attack.

I ended up:

Following the post-mortem, arrangements have been made to send all relevant pathological specimens to London by airmail with the utmost urgency, and these you should be receiving within the next two days. Microscopic examinations and methods for typing the virus can then be carried out. Full details will be given by Dr. Hume concerning the nature of the specimens, and it is suggested that they be handed over to Professor H. Scott of the London School of Microbiology for examination.

This examination should show whether the vaccine can be eliminated as a possible cause of the patient's death. However, it will take several weeks to obtain a definite result. The question arises as to what action, if any, should be taken in the meantime.

My own feeling is that while I am reluctant to interfere with this experiment, there must remain for the moment some doubt as to the safety of the vaccine, and that the trial should therefore be suspended until we have Professor Scott's report. I must say here and now that Dr. Farrell totally disagrees with me on this point. He contends that any suspension of vaccination at this stage would make its resumption at a later date impossible, because of the loss of confidence that might well arise in such a primitive patient population. Nor is he prepared to countenance a breaking of the "blind," which could, of course, tell us in a matter of hours whether the patient received vaccine or not. Dr. Farrell contends that this would destroy the whole value and purpose of the trial.

I appreciate Dr. Farrell's difficulties and sympathize with his reluctance to make any modification in his very elaborate and well-conducted study. Indeed, until the last death I was in favor of continuance of the trial. But in my view the situation has now changed. I appreciate that this form of treatment may possibly, in the end, bring great benefits to humanity, and particularly to the inhabitants of these islands. I am also aware that experiments of this kind frequently carry some degree of necessary and calculated risk. The question is whether we have now reached the limit of permissible risk in this particular experiment. I think we have. Dr. Farrell does not agree.

It may be that other factors, of a social and political nature, also have a bearing on this question. On these I am not qualified to speak. However, it is obvious even to me that feeling is running high in informed circles on Batou, both for and against the trial, and this is likely to intensify when the news of the recent death becomes widespread. The point has been reached where only a clear-cut instruction from H. M. Government, backed with authoritative scientific opinion, is likely to be accepted by all parties. I, of course, have no authority over Dr. Farrell. I have requested him to take no further action until I have received a reply to this letter. However, he informs me that he intends to proceed with the trial.

I await your further instructions.

I was reading through the draft and correcting it when I heard a knock at the door. I shouted, "Come in," thinking it must be the chambermaid. But when I looked round I was disconcerted to see Miss Paston.

She walked briskly into the room, shutting the door behind her. "Good afternoon, Dr. Mayne." She added, "I was surprised to find you'd moved in here."

"Were you?"

"Yes." She made it sound as if I were hiding. "I hope I'm not disturbing you in your work." She moved toward the table, trying, I suspected, to sneak a glance at what I was writing. When I picked up the sheets and tossed them into a drawer she gave a short laugh and walked away again. She sat down in the only comfortable chair and said, "I was wondering if you could tell me something about the present situation on the encephalitis trial. I've been asked to write a follow-up story on it."

"I'm sorry," I said. "I don't think I can tell you anything at the present moment."

"Oh." She made a grimace. Then she produced a cigarette from her bag and lit it. Settling herself into her chair, she asked suddenly, "How did the P.M. go this morning?"

I was disconcerted, as she no doubt intended me to be. The question was a difficult one. I had no idea how much she knew. She might not even know that the P.M. had taken place, but merely be hoping to find out from my answer. She was in the position of the door-to-door salesman who can claim to have scored some sort of a victory if he can even get you to engage in an argument. The only possible reply to such tactics is to refuse all discussion, no matter how unco-operative it may seem.

"I'm sorry, Miss Paston," I said. "I'm afraid I'm not prepared to give any sort of press interview just now."

"I came all the way down the hill to see you."

"If you'd telephoned me first, you could have saved yourself the trouble."

She sighed and took another puff at her cigarette. She regarded me with the patient expression of a detective interrogating a refractory witness. Do we have to go through all this, her expression said. You will come clean in the end.

She said, "Everyone knows about the P.M." So soon? I wondered. But she sounded as if she meant it. "Naturally it's a matter of great concern here. Progressive circles on the island are getting a little anxious. They're afraid it may be made a pretext for stopping the trial."

Progressive circles. How wide, I wondered, was the circulation of the *New Statesman & Nation* on Batou?

"A pretext?" I said.

"I gather the priests have been hoping for something like this. Praying for it, I shouldn't wonder."

She spoke as if praying were in some way worse—exercising, so to speak, an unfair backstairs influence on events. Perhaps she believed in God after all.

"I'm sorry," I said again. "I haven't anything else to tell you."

"You're not being very helpful, Dr. Mayne." She looked at me expectantly. Don't excuse yourself, I told myself, don't explain. You have nothing to apologize for. When she realized I was prepared to sit her out, she said, rather shortly, "I'm sure you have sufficient sense to appreciate my position. I have to write this up—that's my job. So far as I can see, with my limited knowledge, there may be two sides to the question—in my experience there usually are. But if the people on one side are prepared to explain themselves and the others aren't, well—"

"Yes, I know," I said impatiently. It was a fairly standard way of getting you to talk, by suggesting that otherwise the bias might be thrown against you. I understood that she had her job to do, and I had nothing against journalists, though as both a doctor and a civil servant I had been trained to be careful what I said to them—but I could not bring myself to like Miss Paston and I could see that she, in her turn, regarded me with the gravest suspicion.

"Perhaps," I said, "I should explain my position. I regard this as an important matter. Not just simply news—a good deal of which, if you will forgive my saying so, is of no importance whatever. Here we are dealing with human lives, actual people that you might meet in the street. They have relatives and friends and dependants and hopes for the future. I try to remember that all the time, and I think you should too. I don't care a damn what you write about me personally. If it's libelous I shall probably take action, but if it's merely offensive I shall ignore it. Whatever standpoint I take up holds no advantage to me as a person. If you attack my point of view, you won't hurt me or my masters. You may, if you are successful, hurt a great many innocent people on this island."

She looked at me grimly. "This is really the Establishment talking. Mind your own business, you say, just let us tell you what to do. Father knows best. If we disagree, we're irresponsible, we're troublemakers. That's it, isn't it?" She stood up. She was very tall, and towered above me as I sat in my rickety chair by the desk. I also stood up, as much to hold my own as from politeness.

"But the truth is, Dr. Mayne," she thundered on in her booming voice, "that we don't agree on your most important assumption. We don't agree at all. I'm a big girl now, and for upward of twenty years I've been watching Father making a horse's arse of practically everything he's turned his hand to. I don't think he knows best at all. So you can keep that kind of stuff for people who are impressed by it."

At this point she made her exit, an effective one, I had to admit. I was left irritable and unsettled. She was prejudiced, ill-mannered, a bitch, in fact; yet, government being what I knew it to be, she had made a telling point. The trouble was that I was not a genuine member of the Establishment, though no doubt I seemed so to people like Martin and Miss Paston. My heart was never on the side of authority. I believed in it theoretically, I believed in the need for Order and Organization and the Taking of Responsible Decisions. It was in practice that my trouble lay. Authority had only to open its self-important mouth, and all my theory was forgotten.

Which meant, I thought, that when it came to the point I had no real belief in my job. Yet it had to be done. Despondently I sealed my report into an envelope and went down to post it in the hotel lobby.

25

I spent an abominable night. Although I had demanded, and finally obtained, a completely new mosquito net, the insects nevertheless managed to penetrate it. Stimulated by the challenge, they bit more fiercely than ever. Constantly I was awakened by the familiar high-pitched whine in my ear, and found the inevitable red bump on some fresh part of my anatomy. The room was never silent. Bats came and went from the eaves, casting fluttering shadows across the floor; cockroaches scuttled for cover as I turned on the light, hoping to read myself to sleep. Intermittent squalls of rain hammered like machine-gun fire on the roof.

At dawn the mosquitoes retired and I slept for an hour or two. Then the noises of the town woke me, this time for good. Incomprehensible arguments beneath my window, the squeaking of barrows and bullock carts, the barking of dogs, high-pitched, interminable laughter. I breakfasted in my room on tea and toast and what was by some distance the smallest and hardest-boiled egg I had ever eaten in my life. Afterward I wondered how to spend the morning. Now that my report was finished I had no further work to do. For a while I waited around the hotel, hoping that Barbara might ring. But evidently she was finding it difficult. I tried to school myself to be patient. She would certainly get in touch with me as soon as she found a chance.

But obviously I could not remain a prisoner in the hotel. There were a few things I needed to buy, and later I went down into the town for about half an hour. When I returned, the desk clerk called out to me.

"Dr. Mayne?"

"Yes."

He took a piece of paper from a shelf behind him and handed it across. "Telephone message."

In large, illiterate capitals it read, "Dr. Main Ring Peram Robat *Right Away.*"

I read through it three times, totally mystified. This could hardly be Barbara. The name seemed to bear no resemblance to anyone I had ever heard of. It had an obscurely sinister ring to it. In my imagination there was a vague picture of an olive-skinned Levantine in a tussore suit, looking down at his nails while he made unmentionable propositions. But what did he want to see me for? Why such desperate urgency?

I said to the clerk, "You're sure this is for me?"

"He said Dr. Mayne."

"But I never heard of him. What sort of a person was he?"

He shrugged his shoulders. Plainly, in his own opinion he had done well to pass on the message at all. Some people were never satisfied. "A man," he said shortly. "He said ring back right away."

"What number?"

A shifty look came over his face. "Didn't say no number."

"Oh, all right." Obviously the clerk had forgotten to copy it down. Nobody but an idiot would ask a complete stranger to ring back without giving a number. However, if he wished to speak to me he would no doubt try again later. I went up to my room in a cheerful, anticipatory mood, still speculating on the identity of my mysterious caller. He was something to enliven an otherwise empty day.

I was sitting out on the hotel veranda drinking a cup of coffee when the bellboy came and told me I was wanted on the telephone. This was it. I went into the dusty, evil-smelling cupboard the Clanricarde provided for that purpose, and picked up the receiver.

"Dr. Mayne?" It was a sharp, high-pitched, Winchester and New College type of voice. It sounded a little irritable.

"Yes."

"Pelham-Roberts here." I did not reply straight away. My disappointment was too keen. Peram Robat, so substantial and fascinating a moment ago, holding such potentialities for excitement, was dissolving in front of my eyes. "You remember me?" He sounded a little irascible. "I'm the Governor's aide."

I had a vague memory of such a person.

"Oh, yes, of course."

"The Governor wants you out here at Government House— immediately." He said confidentially, "Between ourselves, he's in rather a sweat."

"What about?"

"I can't tell you over the telephone." His voice turned brisk and official again. "See you up here."

I took a taxi up to Government House, examining my conscience on the way. I was not able to come up with anything of significance to account for the Governor's excitement. Probably, I thought from my experience of people in authority, it was all a fuss about nothing.

Pelham-Roberts met me at the door and showed me in to an anteroom.

"You're a difficult fellow to find," he said. "When you first came you were supposed to be at the Clanricarde and you went to Farrell's. Now we've got you down at Farrell's and we find you're at the Clanricarde. I wish you'd let us know where you are."

"Sorry. It hadn't occurred to me."

"This sort of thing makes my job very difficult," he said reproachfully. "I've been chasing all over for you. Didn't you get my message to ring back?"

"Well—not exactly." I felt unable to describe the misunderstanding to him in detail. "There was a slight muddle."

"I'll strangle that bloody desk clerk one of these days. I must have spelled it out to him three times." His mind moved to more immediate problems. "When we couldn't find you, the old man got the impression you were dodging him. Nonsense, of course, as I kept telling him. But he's a bit suspicious of you Whitehall characters. Blunt old soldier boy and all that."

"What's all the fuss about?"

"He's heard about your fun and games yesterday morning. Rather expected you to get in touch with him afterward and put him in the picture. He's liable to give you a bit of a bollocking, but don't take it too seriously. He soon gets over it." He gave me a consoling grin. Evidently he was not going to hold it against me that I had caused so much inconvenience. I was, after all, only a civilian. I couldn't be expected to understand about order and protocol. "I'll tell him you're here."

He went out, and I waited for something over a quarter of an hour. It was vaguely reminiscent of waiting to see the Rector or the First Prefect at Breckenhall. The British public-school system, I thought, is like a series of inoculations. One has been in all the unpleasant situations before, only more inexperienced, more defenseless. The Governor might be angry, but he had no power over me. It was rather ludicrous even to keep me waiting, since it was he who claimed to be in a hurry. It was a good deal cooler here than in the lounge of the Clanricarde. I settled down with a magazine.

Eventually Pelham-Roberts came back and showed me in to the Governor. He retired, presumably on instructions, leaving the two of us alone. The old man eyed me coldly.

"Good morning, Doctor," he said.

"Good morning, sir." I wasn't quite sure about the "sir" but I threw it in.

"I was expecting to hear from you yesterday." He was being very harsh and military, hands behind his back, rocking a little on his heels. Orderly-room stuff.

"Yes, so Pelham-Roberts told me. I'm sorry if I've committed a breach of etiquette."

I had said the wrong thing. It seemed to provoke him. "Nothing to do with etiquette," he barked. "It's a matter of administration." He adopted a simplified, get-down-to-first-principles method of exposition. "I'm the Governor of this island. That means I have to govern. I can't govern properly unless I know what's going on. Your duty, as I think I made plain to you when I saw you last, is to keep me informed. In fact, my last words to you were precisely those—'Keep me informed.' You didn't."

He set back his shoulders, beetled his brows, and glared at me. Should I apologize again, I wondered? He was in the right. I had, if the truth were known, forgotten all about him. It was very remiss of me. I could see he would have dearly liked to give me some mild punishment to teach me better manners.

"I'm really awfully sorry," I said. "I do realize now—"

"Fortunately other members of your profession have more sense of responsibility." Who, I wondered? Hume? Martin, getting his blow in first?

The Governor cleared his throat and opened fire from another angle. "I shall be interested to know if you have been equally casual with your masters in Whitehall," he said sourly. When I made no reply, he went on, "Have you been in touch with them yet?"

My answer was almost apologetic. "I've written a report. . . ."

"Has it gone off?"

"Yes."

He breathed deeply. After a further moment's inspection he suddenly looked away from me as if he couldn't bear the sight of me for another second.

"There seems to be an idea in certain quarters," he said through his teeth, "that we people on the spot are just so much window dressing. That the function of a colonial governor is to give cocktail parties and read the lesson in church and make arrangements to look after any functionary who takes it into his head to come out from England after twenty-five years' experience on an office stool and teach him his job. I'd like to make it plain to you that I don't subscribe to that view at all. So long as I'm Governor, I'm governing Batou. Not some professional politician who wants to make a name for himself in Parliament, not some clerk in Whitehall who's never been within a thousand miles of the place—me."

He tapped himself on the chest to clinch the identification. "Is that quite clear?"

I nodded sympathetically. I knew how he felt, just as I knew how Martin felt when he raved about government interference with scientists. I represented to their minds, however inappropriately, the bureaucracy. All true and good men, in this age at any rate, hate the bureaucracy, even many of those who find themselves living within it. And all of them, including those living within it, feel powerless against it. None more so than the Governor. Brave words, I thought. The only trouble was that they were not true. As the colonial empire grew smaller, the interest taken by Whitehall in the remaining parts of it grew proportionately more intense. There was a time, no doubt, when Batou was so small and insignificant that the Governor could do more or less as he thought best. Those days were gone. The old man was living in a dream.

However, this was no time to tell him so. He was after me again, on more specific grounds this time. "Perhaps you'd like to tell me," he said, "what was in this report you've written to London?"

I told him. When I came to the crucial question of what was now to be done, I could see him calming down and becoming altogether more thoughtful. He made no interruption. When I had finished, he grunted and sat down behind his desk.

The time for blowing off steam was now over. We were down to something serious. I knew it and he knew it. The disadvantages of the attitude he had taken up were apparent to us both. I imagined that the speech about who was in charge on the island was a fairly stock one—he had delivered it with too much glibness.

But perhaps today had not been the best of times to make it. If he *was* in charge, the ball was in his court. What was he going to do?

It was obvious to anybody that this was precisely the sort of decision to avoid if at all possible. Whatever was done, there was almost bound to be trouble of some kind, either with the islanders, the Jesuits, the politicians, or the scientists. He could hardly hope to please them all. It must have been an intimidating prospect.

As he sat there, I could guess at the workings of his mind. Bitter as it was for him, I knew that there was only one attitude for him to take. He was not stupid enough to risk butchering his own career just to cut a figure in front of me.

"Of course," he said after a long interval, "I'm only a layman." I remembered him using this phrase at our previous meeting, but it had been quite different then. It had been, "Of course I'm only a layman but—" and then a chunk of do-it-yourself medicine. Now he said it with a sense of relief. It was an escape from responsibility. He was for once damned glad he was a layman. "Obviously," he went on heavily, "with all due respect to you personally, one needs the advice of experts. This—what do you call it?—Encephalitis Committee." He was much less aggressive now, almost plaintive, in fact. "It's this confounded delay that is the main trouble. If only we could get an opinion from them immediately, if we could *know*—"

"We could," I reminded him. "We could know tomorrow if Farrell would agree to break the blind."

The Governor looked worried. "I suggested that. He says it would ruin the whole thing." So Martin *had* been to see him the previous day. "And I suppose he knows. After all, it is his experiment. . . ." He drummed his fingers on the desk. "It's damned awkward. How soon do you think you'll hear from them?"

"I don't honestly know. They should get my letter within a few days. After that, it's up to them."

"The question is whether we ought to take any action in the meantime."

The "we" rather alienated me from him. I gained the impression that after treating me as a subordinate and ranting at me about having absolute authority, he was now trying to involve me with him in what would, either way, be an unpopular decision. "There's nothing I can do," I said firmly. "My advice is as I've given it. I have no executive power over Dr. Farrell. If he says he intends to carry on, I can't stop him." With a touch of malice I added, "I suppose you could."

The Governor lapsed once again into thought. I was expecting him to say something else, but he stood up and held out his hand. He was suddenly very formal again.

"Thank you very much, Dr. Mayne. I think that's all for the moment. You'll be staying at the Clanricarde from now on?"

"Yes."

"I'd like you to be easily available at short notice. If you're going out for any length of time, leave an address or a telephone number—you know the form."

"Yes, I'll do that."

"And if anything new comes up, get in touch with me immediately. Remember?"

"I will."

He smiled frostily. "Well, then—good day to you."

There was a car to take me back. I was evidently, to some extent, forgiven.

26

❀

❀

❀

❀

❀

❀

THE Clanricarde served a particularly heavy sort of local curry for lunch, in which coconut played a large part. I washed it down with a pint of beer and felt very sleepy. I remembered that I had hardly slept at all the night before, and went up to my room for a siesta. I woke up at about teatime, jaded and covered with sweat. My mouth was dry and I had that intangible feeling of having committed the Unforgivable Sin, which always besets me when I sleep heavily in the afternoon. It was raining again. I took a bath and went down for tea. There was still no news from Barbara. I was beginning to grow anxious.

About an hour later she telephoned.

"Can I come down to see you?" It was wonderful to hear her voice again.

"Yes, of course," I said. "I've been waiting for you."

"Just for half an hour or so."

I was disappointed. "I was hoping we might spend the evening together."

"No, I don't think that would be a good idea at all. Things are rather tense up here. There's no point in creating a situation—"

"Just as you think best." She was the person who would have to stand any unpleasantness. "Is Martin there?"

"No, he's down at the hospital." She spoke shortly, as if anxious not to give too much detail on the telephone. "I'll see you in about a quarter of an hour."

When I saw her coming toward me across the hotel lounge, it was with a sense of wonder that she could possibly belong to me. She had a way of walking that fascinated and excited me. Most women walk badly. They wobble, they move stiffly from the hips, they give the impression of being corseted; it is impossible to imagine them breaking into a run. But Barbara always moved loosely and gracefully. It seemed (and was in most cases true) that beneath her outer clothing she had practically nothing on. One was conscious always of the taut belly muscles, the firm, small breasts, the whole of her brown, athletic body. She was, in a way that few of us are, physically unself-conscious. She was not unaware that men looked at her in the street, no woman ever is, but she took it as a matter of course, neither courting nor avoiding attention.

There were a few men in the lounge—a waiter, a couple of commercial travellers drinking whiskey, an Arab in a crumpled brown chalk-stripe suit and a fez—and they all looked up. The waiter licked his lips. Barbara sat down beside me.

She seemed a little tense, I thought. It was perhaps under-standable. I said, "It's so good to see you again. It's seemed like a long time." It was hard to think that it was only just over a day since I had left the house.

"Yes. For me too."

She smiled uncertainly and lit a cigarette. The lounge was small and we were both conscious of being under observation. The commercial travellers had stopped talking to each other and were watching us. Our voices dropped almost to a whisper.

To try to give an impression of normality to the conversation, I said, "I'm afraid I still forgot to tip your servant when I left yesterday."

"Yes, I know." She laughed. It was working. She was a little more at ease. "You don't need to worry about that. I gave him two pounds and told him you had left it with me for him. He was very grateful."

"Then I owe you two pounds."

"So you do."

I gave her the money and she put it in her bag, to the undisguised interest of the commercial travellers. We talked easily for a little while. When I had finished telling her about the Governor, she said, "As you've no doubt guessed, Martin got at him first. There's been furious activity ever since you left."

I could imagine it. The ship was in danger, a state of emergency declared. Martin was always at his most energetic and dangerous in a crisis.

I had not been anxious to be the first to mention his name, but now the ice had been broken. I felt able to ask her, "Does he know you're down here?"

"No. I didn't tell him I was coming."

I pondered. "I wonder if it really matters?" I asked the question of myself as much as of her. "I sometimes think that when you're dealing with a person like Martin, prudence is almost a waste of time. He'd happily say he'd caught us in bed together if he thought he could get anyone to believe him."

"Just the same," she said, "I think it's better this way." She explained ironically, "He might think of me as a spy—an agent in the enemy camp. It's all very exciting and dramatic now, you must appreciate. Last night there was a big conference at the house. Das was there, and Kadu drove over from Cajara." She paused. "They're going to press on, of course—you know that?"

"Yes. Martin told me."

"You may be interested to know that there's also been a change in policy about you. Or, I should say, a change in attitude. Before, the line was that you were a person of importance, and that it was vital, by one means or another, to get you on their side. Now you're a nobody, just a minor official. What you think doesn't count in the least."

I laughed. "That's perhaps nearer the truth."

"According to this new outlook," she continued, "there is only one person who really counts. That's the Governor—and he's on their side."

I said, "I don't think he should rely too much on the Governor."

"No?" To her it was just an amusing story. She told me because she thought it would entertain me. She had never cared about the trial. "Das and Kadu are with him one hundred per cent."

"The death didn't worry them?"

"No. They're convinced it had nothing to do with the vaccine." She thought for a moment. "I think that's all the news." She remembered something. "Oh, yes, Miss Paston. You know her? She was up yesterday."

"By invitation?"

"I rather gathered so." There was a warning in her voice. "I have the impression he's pulling all the strings he can."

"I expect so." I could imagine it all. The telephoning, the persuasion, the innuendoes, the boyish charm, the enlistment of support, the drop of poison poured into a certain ear at a suitable time. In spite of the amount he had at stake, Martin would be enjoying himself in his own way.

Seeing the amused expression on my face, Barbara reminded me, "He'll be attacking you, you know."

"Oh, certainly."

"You're very fatalistic."

"Why not? There's nothing I can do about it. Once that letter gets to London, the matter's out of my hands."

"What happens then?"

"That's up to them. Either they let the work go on or they stop it. Either way, there's no need for me to stay here. I can go home." I smiled at her. Suddenly everything seemed quite simple. "Will you come with me?"

She hesitated for a moment. Then she said, "If you're sure you want me—"

I felt a sudden lifting of the heart. It was over. She was mine now. I knew that once she had said it, she would not change her mind.

"You know I do," I said.

"It will mean dreadful trouble with Martin."

"I know that. It won't be much fun for any of us, I suppose. But in the end that's not important." For some reason I was unable to get very alarmed as to what he would do. At the end of it I would have Barbara—that was the only thing that really mattered. I said, "When shall we tell him?"

"Not just yet, please," she said. "Not until you're ready to go. Otherwise it will be unbearable."

I was disappointed. Now that the decision was made, my impulse was to rush in and get the worst of it over. "I can see you'd have to leave the house," I said. "But you could come down here—"

"And live with you at the Clanricarde?" She laughed shortly. "My poor innocent Peter, you haven't any idea what life is like on a small island. That would cause a major sensation."

"Would you mind?"

"It wouldn't be very sensible for you at the moment, would it? With everybody already in a state of semi-hysteria about the trial. It would be perfect for Martin if he wanted to make trouble— and you know he does. It would be all the proof he'd need that you were carrying out a personal feud against him. Do you seriously believe that anyone—not just Martin but anyone—would credit you as an impartial observer if they thought you were living with his wife?"

"But we shouldn't be living together," I protested.

"As far as Batou was concerned, we should." She looked at me seriously. "Darling, I'm serious about this. It would be crazy. It would ruin you. I'd never forgive myself."

I was touched that in the supreme crisis of her own life she should be thinking of me. My heart was full of love and gratitude. I took her hand in mine. Her fingers were small and delicate. She wore no rings except for a platinum wedding ring. I looked up and saw the Arab leaning forward with bared teeth. I said, "Can't we get alone somewhere?"

"Where?"

I thought desperately. "My room?"

She gave a decisive shake of the head. "No. Not in this place." I could hardly blame her, under the circumstances. She looked distastefully at the commercial travellers and said, "I should feel like a prostitute."

I let go of her hand. I had remembered something else. "Supposing he won't divorce you?" She said nothing. "He told me he might not."

"He told me too." She shrugged her shoulders. "I don't care about that."

The indifference in her voice was genuine. She was an aristocrat, as Martin was. They were impervious to public opinion, as they were to money and security. It was the one characteristic they had in common against me. I envied them their lofty and unaffected contempt for middle-class values.

"Naturally," she went on, "it's a great deal more convenient to be married, and I'd prefer it. But what about you? Your job—"

"You're behind the times," I said. "The days of Galsworthy and Pinero are over. The Ministry doesn't concern itself very much these days with the sex life of its employees."

I was distorting it a little. It was true that the Ministry would not be interested in my having a mistress. But to acquire one under these circumstances, possibly in the full glare of newspaper publicity, might well be considered indiscreet. They would not be able to do anything very dramatic about it, such as forcing me to resign. But in some obscure archives a note would be made and my subsequent chances of promotion greatly diminished. This was not a prospect that concerned me very deeply. For some time I had been getting restless—my adjustment to second-best was not so complete as it was my practice to pretend.

I was about to explain this to Barbara when I noticed that I had lost her attention. She was looking across the lounge to the swing doors, where a man had come in from the street. He was struggling out of some wet oilskins and for a moment I did not recognize him. The porter was standing by obsequiously, as he had never done for me—it must be somebody of importance to warrant such attention. The man turned, and I caught the sweep of a black gown. It was de Freitas.

He tossed the wet garments to the porter and strode across the lounge toward me. There were circles beneath his eyes and a blue stubble on his dark chin. He looked like a man who had been up all night on his knees praying for guidance, and had now come to a decision. His expression was grim and uncompromising.

I was subject immediately to atavistic and unreasonable fears that went right back to the early stages of my education. The Governor, poor old fellow, for all his great house and his aide-de-camp and military swagger, was unable to deploy such forces of intimidation as this. As de Freitas advanced on me I became for a moment a small boy, skulking in some unfrequented spot, a lighted cigarette in his hand. My hair rose, my skin contracted in obedience to a reflex set up long ago.

He stopped there, looking down at me. He was nervous and his mouth worked slightly. It did not make him any the less formidable.

"I am sorry to intrude, Dr. Mayne."

"That's all right." I stood up. "I don't know whether you've met Mrs. Farrell?"

"No." He gave a thin, courteous smile, bowed, and shook hands, regarding her intently with his large brown eyes. Plainly he was trying to place her in the context of the present situation. I sympathized with him. Her presence must have been perplexing. His chances of making a correct guess as to the complex relationship among the three of us were extremely slight.

"I don't wish to disturb you," he said, turning back to me, "but I'm afraid it is very urgent that we have a few words together. I have just arrived from Cajara."

His thick boots and the bottom of his trousers, I noticed, were soaked and caked with mud. "It was wet, I imagine," I said, trying to get the meeting onto a social plane.

"The roads are always difficult at this time of year. Occasionally one has to get out and push."

He remained awkwardly standing there. "Won't you sit down?" I said.

He looked at Barbara. "We can perhaps speak together a little later. What I have to say is somewhat personal."

Barbara stood up. "I was just leaving anyway."

"No, no, please—" He was not at his ease with women. "I don't want to—"

"Really I was." She smiled at him reassuringly. "I promised Martin I'd be home for dinner. I'm already late."

She said goodbye and I took her to the door. I said, "When shall I see you again?"

"I'll telephone. I can't say exactly when. It depends on how things are up at the house."

"I don't like leaving you there."

"It's the only thing to do. And it won't be for long. Please, Peter, promise not to say anything to Martin about us—not yet."

"All right," I said reluctantly. "I promise. But ring as soon as you can."

"Of course."

She kissed me quickly and went out into the rain. The Jaguar was standing outside the hotel and she got into it and drove off. I waved to her until she was out of sight and then went back into the lounge. De Freitas was sitting in the chair she had left.

He said, "I'm afraid Mrs. Farrell will think me very ill-mannered."

"Don't give it a thought," I said. Barbara, I felt like telling him, had been brought up in a hard school as far as male behavior was concerned. "What about a drink?"

"A glass of orange squash only."

He was getting over his feeling of awkwardness. He accepted the drink in a way rather typical of priests, as if he were somehow conferring a favor on me. Evidently he was not a man for alcohol. I might have known it. He had, after all, his own particular vice. He took out his battered cigarette tin. It was full of rolled cigarettes. I visualized him rolling them, one after another, in the station wagon all the way from Cajara. At the end he would arrive, his thoughts arranged and a stock of his poison already prepared—enough for an orgy. He lit one, looked lovingly at the others, and inhaled deeply.

I ordered an orange squash for him and a large whiskey for me. Batou and the general pressures to which I was being subjected were getting on top of me. I was beginning to feel I needed a drink or two about this time in the evening.

De Freitas looked around. The commercial travellers had gone. Evidently they had lost interest after Barbara had left. There was nobody eavesdropping now.

"I imagine," he said, "that you have probably guessed why I am here."

I have always regarded this as a particularly exasperating opening to a conversation. "No," I said.

He looked at me grimly. "A very serious situation is in danger of developing around Cajara," he said. "And not only there. I believe in anticipating disaster rather than helplessly waiting for it to happen. That is why I have left my parish to drive over and see you."

"What sort of trouble?"

"It concerns the patient who died a few days ago at Pamao. The people in my area are in a considerable state of excitement."

"I presume," I said, "that you've done everything you can to calm them down."

He did not miss the irony in my voice. His lips tightened. "Naturally," he said. "However, I am restricted in this by the fact that I have not been informed of any of the details of the case. Under such circumstances," he added acidly, "effective reassurance becomes impossible." There was a slight interval while he charged himself up with more nicotine. "I believe a post-mortem was carried out?"

I was beginning to think we would have saved a lot of trouble by publishing the post-mortem report in the Batou *Sentinel*. A lot of trouble for me, anyway.

"Yes," I said wearily.

"But the result is being kept secret?"

"Be reasonable," I said. "You can't pass a copy around to everyone who wants to see it."

This, I could see, angered him. The Church, his expression implied, was not "everyone." "I take it," he said, "that he died of the encephalitis?"

"Yes. But by itself that doesn't tell us very much." He had no official position but it would obviously do a great deal more damage to leave him with only half the story. I explained the position once again. At the end I said, "You appreciate the difficulty?"

"I do indeed." He inclined his head. "And I am very grateful to you for explaining it to me so completely." His expression of gratitude was purely formal, perhaps even a little sarcastic. The undertone of hostility had not left his voice. After a moment's thought, he said, "This will not be easy to explain to my parishioners in Cajara."

"No," I said sympathetically. "I can see that."

"Particularly," said de Freitas, "since Dr. Kadu has already resumed the vaccinations."

"When?"

"This morning."

This was bad news, though of course I should have expected it. Somewhere, I suppose, in the back of my mind was a hope that they might just go on talking, that there might be delays, conferences, arguments, and an eventual compromise. When you have a reluctance yourself toward taking irrevocable steps, there is always a tendency to believe that others will feel the same. But as soon as I thought honestly about it, I knew that Martin's reaction would be precisely the opposite. Instead of recoiling from a crisis, his instinct was to rush toward it, to get his blow in first, to commit himself utterly, beyond hope of retreat. Evidently he had had no difficulty in carrying the others with him.

I said, "Has he issued any statement about the death?"

"No. There has been no statement, no explanation." So it was to be a *fait accompli*. They were to act as if the death had never occurred. It was a bluff that might well succeed against a primitive population. But against de Freitas? He went on savagely, "It may be thought that no explanation was required. Unfortunately that is not so. My parishioners may be poor and ignorant, but they have a great interest in death. They wish to know why this man died."

"They should ask Kadu."

"Kadu is as foreign to them as an Eskimo is to you," he said contemptuously. "It is to me that they come for their explanations." He went on with great bitterness, "I am the only educated man they feel they really know. This is because I am one of them and have made my life among them. I have no interests except God and these people, and they know it. When any of the features of civilization, such as this one, touches upon them, they come to me and ask me what they should do. But it is very important that I should be honest with them. Once they find I am deceiving them they will not trust me again. They will have nobody. Then God knows what may happen. So I cannot be like Kadu or your friend Dr. Farrell. I cannot tell them a lie, or a half truth, or give them an explanation I know they are not educated enough to understand. I must say yes or no and it must be my honest belief. When this trial was first projected I heard Dr. Farrell's explanation and I said yes. It seemed to me there was great possible benefit and little risk. With the first two deaths I began to wonder. Now there is another death, and they are asking me again. They say, 'What would *you* do, Father?' I must give them some reply."

"Supposing you told them you wouldn't have any more injections?"

"That is the point, Dr. Mayne," he said triumphantly. "That is why I am here. I will be frank with you. My judgment, on what I so far know, would be to discontinue injections. I am reluctant to come out and say this if it can be avoided in any way. In the first place, I shall be accused of unjustifiable interference. That is of minor importance to me personally, but I have to consider the prestige of my Order. But there is a much more serious aspect to the matter than this. My parishioners tend to see everything in simple terms of black and white. Complex issues and chains of causation are not for them. I am afraid that if I advise them to take no more of the vaccine, they will draw the conclusion that the three people who died were killed by Dr. Farrell." He lit another of his atrocious cigarettes with trembling hands. "Do you understand now why I am so serious about this affair?

"This," he went on, waving his hand emphatically, "is why I

feel entitled to full information. This is why I regard it as utterly foolhardy for Dr. Farrell to proceed as he is doing, without consultation with anybody."

There was a silence. I felt suddenly tired, resentful of these constant efforts to involve me on one side or the other. "Look, Father," I said. "I understand and sympathize, believe me." I wasn't going to tell him that I too believed the vaccinations should be stopped, since he would obviously use this as a weapon. I was not here to get involved in island politics. There was going to be a hell of a row about this business, one way or another—the conclusion was now inescapable. "But I'm afraid it's out of my hands now. I've made my report to London and my work's finished. I am simply staying here awaiting recall. I have no standing or authority whatever."

De Freitas brushed this aside as equivocation.

"You are an expert, Dr. Mayne," he said, "and an expert is never entirely without power. A ship's engineer has no authority over the running of a ship, yet if he says that at their present speed the engines will wreck themselves within half an hour, it would be a bold captain who would refrain from slowing down." He added with some violence, "I want to remind you that we are on the verge of very serious trouble here. None of us can evade responsibility."

"I am not evading responsibility!" I said fiercely. "I have made my recommendations. I have told the captain what I think about the engines. What else can I do?"

He subsided a little. After a slight pause, he said, "And who is the captain?"

That, indeed, was the point. It was a question to which there should have been, yet was not, a simple answer. Eventually I said, "The Governor says he is. Have you seen him?"

"Not yet. I have an appointment with him later this evening. Does he understand?"

"He's had it explained to him."

"I see." He stood up. His orange squash, I noticed, was untouched. A fly swam helplessly on its surface. "Well, thank you very much for your help."

"I'm sorry I can't do more."

"Are you?" He gave me a penetrating look. It was as if we regarded each other through the grill of a confessional. Only true contrition, his eyes seemed to say, is of value. Anything else can only intensify the sin. He made me wonder for a moment whether I had done less than I should. Had I, with a bureaucrat's obsession with delineation of functions, let the better case go by default? Should I, whether it was my business or not, have fought the Governor for my point of view as Martin had fought for his? Was the situation really so dangerous as de Freitas claimed, or was he overstating the case?

He, at least, had no doubts. As I watched him striding out of the hotel I felt a pang of pity for the Governor.

27

FOR the next twenty-four hours, nothing much happened. I began to experience the sense of deflation that always follows the prophecy of a crisis. Perhaps we had all been getting the affair out of proportion, and nothing would happen in the end. I knew that logically this was most unlikely, yet explosions have a tendency to come as a surprise, even when confidently predicted. There is always the feeling that it won't really happen, that when it comes to the point, good sense will prevail, and so on. This feeling grew on me as time went by. It was finally destroyed by a telephone call from Government House.

"Dr. Mayne?"

"Yes."

"Pelham-Roberts here. Can you get up here right away?"

"Well, I haven't had my breakfast. . . ."

"Sorry, old boy. I'm afraid it's urgent. Can't tell you about it now, but we're expecting Whitehall on the telephone any moment. The old man wants you here."

"Oh, all right."

From some experience of government, I guessed that it was not quite as urgent as all that. I dressed and finished my breakfast, and took a taxi up to Government House. This time I was shown straight in to see the Governor. He was obviously extremely agitated. He sat behind his desk, drumming on it with his fingernails and baring his false teeth nervously. Pelham-Roberts was there too, trying to look unobtrusive.

The Governor nodded to me. He was too preoccupied for formalities.

"The call isn't through yet," he said. "When they come on the line, they'll probably want to talk to you as well." He brooded for a moment. "I intend to get some sort of a decision out of them this morning, once and for all."

"If we send telegrams," said Pelham-Roberts plaintively, "they simply don't answer."

"Scandalous," said the Governor, fixing me with a baleful eye. "Bureaucracy run riot. No wonder we're losing the colonial empire."

"Yes indeed."

Frustrated in his hope of picking a quarrel with me, he turned his mind to other matters. "Did you see that priest the other day?"

"De Freitas? Yes. He seemed," I said delicately, "a little worked up about the vaccination program. I referred him to you. I hope that was the right thing to do?"

"Oh, yes—yes." He brooded for a while. "A difficult fellow, that. Got the idea that he owns the island. As you know, he wants to stop the trial altogether. He tried to give me the impression that you were on his side."

"Did he?"

"He as good as threatened me. Kept saying he wouldn't be answerable for the consequences." He added, a little uneasily, "Naturally I wasn't going to stand for that. I told him to take himself off."

There was a short silence. Doubt as to the Governor's skill as a diplomatist hung heavy in the air. It was easy to see that even he was beginning to wonder if he had acted a little rashly. In an attempt at a normal conversational tone, he asked, "Did he tell you what he was intending to do if I didn't agree to stop the vaccinations?"

"No. He just said he anticipated trouble."

Pelham-Roberts gave a disgruntled snort. "That's what people always say when they're going to organize it. Spontaneous outburst of popular feeling—that's the favorite expression, I believe."

"Has something happened?" I asked.

The Governor said heavily, "We have a report of a"—he hesitated momentarily—"a disturbance in Cajara." He went on, in a deliberately unemotional voice, like a policeman reading evidence: "Yesterday—soon after de Freitas returned to the village, incidentally—a crowd gathered outside the Health Center, shouting abuse and throwing stones. Nobody came for vaccination. Windows were broken. Dr. Kadu came out to speak to them and try to make them see sense. He was pelted with filth and rotten fruit. Eventually he and some of the others had to retire inside the Health Center and barricade themselves in. The row went on for several hours but quieted down during the night, and they were able to get a little sleep. However, when Kadu woke up he found that the sister in charge and most of the nurses had left during the night. They'd never said anything—just walked out. What do you make of that?"

I remembered suddenly my visit to the church in Cajara, the silent figure of the woman in hospital uniform, praying. That would be the sister who had left. That she had given no warning or explanation was disturbing but hardly surprising. She was, after all, an islander; a few years of technical training were not going to turn her into a completely self-confident, educated North European. When she felt she must do something, she would do it. She would feel neither the desire nor the obligation to argue about it.

"How are things now?" I asked.

"Fairly quiet. The crowd collected again this morning, but so far as we can gather there's been no further violence. Of course," he added, not too optimistically, "that was an hour or two ago. . . ."

"What's happened to the police?"

"There are only two policemen in Cajara—both islanders. They'd be helpless in a situation like this. We've sent a few more from Flores under a British officer, and they should be there this afternoon. That should help matters."

"Does Farrell know about this?"

"Yes." An expression came into the Governor's face that I had learned to know. Martin's patrons passed through three distinct states of mind. Between the first honeymoon and the final, inevitable disillusionment there was a stage, always distressing to watch, when the first doubts began to appear, when the idea began to obtrude itself that the association with genius might have certain disadvantages. The Governor was beginning to feel that he was being dragged along faster than he really wished to go.

"Naturally," he said, "he's very cut up about this. One can understand his anxiety. Just the same, I think he's getting unnecessarily excited. He was up here an hour ago demanding troops. I told him I didn't think there was any need for that just yet. Might only make things worse." He banged his fist on the table. "But I'm not going to have the decent people of this island intimidated by a lot of roughs. And if I find evidence that de Freitas has taken it upon himself to organize a civil disturbance—"

"Do you really think that's likely?"

"You bet your life," said Pelham-Roberts.

"He may not be doing so directly," admitted the Governor. "I should imagine that he's too clever for that. But, as we all know, there's such a thing as tacit encouragement. He certainly isn't going out of his way to stop them, as in my opinion he should be. However, we shall see. I've told Captain Daly to have a talk with him as soon as he gets there, and put the fear of God into him, if that's the right expression. If he wants trouble he can have it."

There was a silence. I think none of us had much confidence in the ability of Captain Daly to handle de Freitas. Finally the Governor said, "In the meantime, the sooner we get a decision from your friends in London the better. You haven't heard anything yet, I suppose?"

"No."

We began to talk in a desultory way about other matters. Every now and then our eyes would stray to the telephone, as if it might hold an answer to our problems. Eventually it rang.

Pelham-Roberts darted forward and picked up the receiver. He looked up at the Governor.

"Your call to London, sir."

The Governor went through into another room. As soon as Pelham-Roberts heard his voice on the extension he put down the telephone and went back to his chair. We sat in silence for about ten minutes. Then the Governor came back. He didn't look like a man whose problems had been solved.

"There's a Mr. Stratton on the line," he said to me in rather an exhausted voice. "He'd like to speak to you."

I went through into the other room and picked up the telephone.

"Hello."

"Is that you, Mayne?" Stratton's voice, over four thousand miles away, was even drier and more metallic than usual.

"Yes. Did you get my letter?"

"Yesterday. We've circulated it to the members of the committee."

"What do they say?"

"Too soon to know, I'm afraid." As usual he seemed to take a certain satisfaction in giving bad news. "We can't convene the committee as such. Some of them are out of the country. What we find slightly alarming is that the story seems to have broken in the newspapers. I hope that's none of your doing?"

Miss Paston, I thought. I was not really surprised.

"Of course not." I had the impression that Stratton was by no means convinced.

"It's very embarrassing, as you can imagine. Somebody's put down a question in the House for this evening. The Minister asked me to speak to you about it. He feels very strongly that we should have some clear-cut policy."

"So do I," I said.

"Well, then—"

"You had my views in the report. Suspend the trial."

"That's not so easy as you think," he said peevishly. "We're under a great deal of pressure here. There are a lot of influential people who still think the trial should go on."

"Quite possibly. It's a matter of opinion."

The line was poor and I had dropped my voice. "It's what?" he shouted.

"A matter of opinion."

He adopted a curious, unnaturally hectoring tone, rather as if he were trying to make an impression on somebody else in the room with him.

"Look here, Mayne, this is a serious matter. We can't just shrug our shoulders and say it's a matter of opinion." He stopped. "One moment." After a slight pause, he said, with appropriate solemnity, "The Permanent Secretary himself would like to speak to you."

"Mayne?" The voice was brisk, authoritative, no-nonsense.

"Yes?"

"We've got to have something definite here. If we make a statement we must have evidence to back it up. Now, for instance, if you can say this man died because of the vaccine—"

"I can't. Nobody can."

A note of exasperation began to come through.

"Of course," he said, "I'm only a layman"—where had I heard that phrase before?—"but I should have thought you could have come to some sort of conclusion about that. Did you see the man before he died?"

"No. He was upcountry—sixty miles away. I didn't know he was dead until they showed me the body."

He grunted. "Well, it's all very unsatisfactory." I could think of nothing to say to this.

"I don't know whether you quite appreciate the gravity of the situation," he went on. "We anticipate some very difficult supplementaries. The Minister expects us to keep him properly briefed. I was hoping for some constructive suggestions. . . ."

I was beginning to feel I couldn't stand much more of this. I tried to change the subject. "Have you heard what happened at Cajara?"

"At where?" he said irritably. "Speak up."

"Cajara."

"Oh, you mean this disturbance? I gather the Governor's taking care of that." He spoke without much interest. Evidently nobody had as yet proposed to ask a question about the disturbance. "There is something else I wanted to talk to you about. There's some sort of rumor circulating about personal difficulties between you and Farrell—"

"Personal difficulties?"

"Yes. I don't want to be more specific." He sounded embarrassed. "I take it that's all nonsense?"

From the allusive nature of the question I guessed that he was referring to myself and Barbara. Miss Paston again, very probably.

"I think Farrell may be a little hurt because I'm in favor of suspending the trial."

"Yes, yes, that's to be expected." It was obviously not what he was referring to. "Naturally at times like these one has to be extra careful to avoid complications. . . ."

His sentence trailed off vaguely. He returned to his previous grievance. "Well, if that's all the help you can give us, I suppose we shall have to leave it at that."

It seemed hardly worth pointing out that by all reasonable standards I should be asking for help from him at this stage, rather than the other way around.

I said, "Do you want to be put back to the Governor?"

"No, thanks. I don't think that's necessary."

I rang off and went back into the other room. The Governor regarded me gloomily.

"Well, did you get any sense out of them?"

"No."

"No more did I."

In his dejection he was friendlier to me than he had been before. We were fellow-sufferers, front-line soldiers being mucked about by the staff. "It's the old story. We've just got to hang on until they make up their bloody minds."

28

SOON after I left Government House it started raining again and went on all day. The streets were awash with water and almost deserted. I went back to the hotel and sat around listlessly, waiting for news. I made an attempt to catch up on my medical journals but concentration was impossible; even a novel was too much for me. I felt lonely and dispirited, filled with a premonition of disaster. I had never missed Barbara so much.

It was around midday that news from Cajara began to percolate through, in the form of a special edition of the Batou *Sentinel*. This was the only newspaper on the island, a dashing but somewhat amateurish production, which combined progressive editorial policy with a steady income from advertisements for herbal aphrodisiacs and bust creams. There was a front-page report— "Hubbub in Cajara." When one came down to reading the story, it appeared that they knew rather less than I did, and had not yet made up their minds whether to be indignant or to discount the whole incident. Vague reference was made to "certain disgraceful incidents, the work of noisy and irresponsible individuals, which attracted no public support." There was also a tribute to Kadu, "our respected and dedicated M.O., who, it is reported, silenced his assailants by treating them with the scorn they so richly deserve."

Shortly afterward rumors began to fly around the hotel—that Kadu had fled, that de Freitas was under house arrest, that the police had never reached Cajara, owing to the rains washing away the road, and a dozen others. How securely based any of them was, it was impossible to say. To the inhabitants of Flores the news was an unexpected windfall; there had not been so much material for discussion in months. For once the bar of the Clanricarde was doing a roaring trade.

I grew tired of it after a while and retreated to my room. No doubt if I was needed they would get in touch with me there. I was half expecting to hear from Pelham-Roberts about future developments, and I was also hoping for a call from Barbara. But I heard nothing until the evening. And when the telephone did ring, it was Martin.

He opened up without preamble.

"Have you heard what your bloody friend de Freitas has done now?"

It seemed to me that whenever anyone was unpopular, he became automatically "my friend," as if to make me in some way responsible. Stratton had spoken in the same way about Martin himself.

"No," I said.

He was in a state of high excitement.

"I've just had a message from Cajara. They've set fire to the Health Center."

This sounded serious. There are certain types of violence that are particularly prone to excite people, and incendiarism is one of them. There were, fortunately, no in-patient beds in the Health Center. But there was Kadu and what was left of the nursing and domestic staff. I had visions of them, either trapped inside or fleeing from the flames into a hostile crowd, maddened by its own destructiveness.

"How about the people inside?" I asked. "Is anybody hurt?"

"I don't know," he said impatiently. "They just said it was on fire, that was all. Now the telegraph line's down. They may have cut it, but more likely it's just the rains. I gather it often happens at this time of the year." His voice rose. "All my records were in that place—half my remaining supplies of vaccine—"

I made an attempt to calm him. "It may not be true," I pointed out. "Things are very confused. You know how people exaggerate."

He was not really listening to me. "I'm going out there," he said. "I've got to find out what's happened."

"It's a hell of a night."

"I don't care."

If it had really been set on fire, I thought, he would be too late to do anything. But of course no anxious person ever thinks like that. Martin, understandably, felt a compulsion to be there, at the place and time where his fate was being decided. And so, I discovered, did I. It occurred to me that I had been waiting all day in the hope that somebody would suggest my going to Cajara, though I had not thought it would be Martin.

It was curious, I thought, that we were able to talk like this, as if nothing important had happened between us. How many of our quarrels had ended in just this way? How many times had we parted for good, to meet again in friendship only a few days later, without explanation, without even a show of embarrassment?

"Would you mind if I came with you?" I said.

"All right." He tried to make it sound grudging, but why else had he telephoned me? I knew that he had hoped I would come. I knew also that the two of us would be alone. Not Das, not Mary Paston, not even Barbara.

"I'll be down at the hotel in a few minutes."

He called for me in the station wagon. There was only a slight drizzle now. Enough to put out the fire, I wondered? But Cajara was over the mountains, and the weather might be quite different there. The road was not too bad at first, but it grew worse as we climbed. The metalled surface ended about four miles out of Flores, and after that we were in the mud. Martin was not a man, at a time like this, to adjust his speed to conditions. He put his foot down on the floor boards and trusted to his driving skill, which was considerable, to keep us on the road.

Fortunately he knew the road well and had taken the precaution of fitting storm tires to the station wagon. Just the same, it was a drive I shall never forget. The rain increased in the mountains, and the low cloud became mist. We hardly spoke at all. I was concentrating on the road and hoped Martin was too. I had no desire to distract him.

We passed through the usual villages, the streets deserted now in the darkness and the rain. Even the hens and the mongrel dogs had retired to shelter. Here and there a figure stood curiously in a doorway, or the light of a paraffin lamp flickered in the window of a house. The road between the villages was sometimes not easy to define; sticks and branches had blown down on it, water from overflowing streams and ditches made shallow lakes on its surface. Yet Martin kept going, holding the road and negotiating the corners with uncanny confidence.

It was just a village like any other; I cannot to this day even remember its name. We tore through the main street as usual, at fifty miles an hour, Martin's hand on the horn, coating the houses on either side with a spray of mud. There was no sign of life. We went out of the village, round a corner, and down a hill. There was another corner in front of us, no more difficult than a hundred others. Martin turned the wheel, skidded a little, and was just beginning to right himself when a black shadow appeared, lying diagonally across the road—a tree trunk. It was stop or swerve, and he had no time to stop. The swerve set the back wheels skidding again, the front offside wheel touched the log, and we were out of control, careering toward the edge of the road. For a moment we were in the air, our wheels spinning. Then we hit the jungle. There was an appalling, stupefying crash, an earthquake, an explosion. . . .

I must have lain there half conscious for some time—perhaps half an hour, perhaps less. When I came to my senses, I started to move my limbs, one joint after another, and discovered to my relief that, apart from cuts and bruises on my head and legs, I was unhurt. The car was lying in a deep ravine, tilted on its side and badly smashed. The rain was drumming down into the vegetation all around us. The lights had gone out and it was pitch black.

I could feel Martin crumpled up beside me but there was no

sound or movement from him. I found his arm. There was a pulse —fast and weak, but it was there. I took the flashlight from the glove compartment and shone it on his face. His head had smashed the windshield and knocked him unconscious. The steering wheel had been pushed back and crushed into his left side, wedging him against the seat. I spoke to him but he did not reply.

29

✺

✺

✺

✺

✺

✺

I have only a confused recollection of the next hour or so. Obviously Martin was very ill, possibly dying, and there was nothing much I could do for him where he was; I tried for a little while to free him from his trapped position, but it was impossible. The only thing to do was to find my way back to the village for help.

When I tried to get out of the car, I found that all the doors were jammed. I had to knock away the shattered remnants of the windshield with the flashlight and squeeze myself painfully out. The rain hit me with full force as I got out, soaking me to the skin within a matter of minutes; it drummed through the forest like something alive. My feet sank into mud and dead leaves, and I clung to the trees to prevent myself falling into the ravine. Before I started to climb I shone the flashlight once more on Martin, grotesquely propped up in the driving seat of the wrecked station wagon, his head lolling sideways. He looked like a dead man. Perhaps when I returned he would be. I hoped for only one thing —that he would not recover consciousness while I was away and find himself trapped there, alone.

It took me some time to get up to the road, and then I had to walk back to the village. When I finally got there, the few inhabitants I was able to wake up were disinclined to turn out and professed to be unable to understand what I was talking about. There was no policeman, no car, the post office was shut, the telegraph wires were down. I was in a state bordering on hysteria when I heard the sound of a motor engine. It was coming from the direction of Cajara. I turned my attention away from the villagers and stood in the center of the street, shouting, waving my arms and flashing my flashlight. The vehicle came round the corner and I saw that it was an ambulance. The driver crammed on his brakes and came slithering to a halt. I stood there in the light of the headlights, a wild, dripping figure. Two men in uniform jumped out and covered me with submachine guns. Then, more slowly, another man, dressed in the uniform of a police captain, climbed down from the seat next to the driver.

"What the devil is going on here?" he asked in a slight Irish accent.

I sat in the back of the ambulance while Captain Daly, with three men, went down to the wrecked car. He insisted on leaving me behind, on the ground that in my present condition I would be more trouble than I was worth. He was probably right—I was feeling very near the end of my endurance. I could not bring myself to imagine what I would have done if Daly had not turned up. I had been incredibly lucky. I gathered from snatches of conversation that the emergency in Cajara was over. Casualties had totalled no more than a few cut heads and one patient with burns too severe to be treated locally. Daly had decided to bring him back to Flores in the ambulance. He was lying on one of the two stretchers, swathed in bandages and mumbling quietly to himself. They had taken the other stretcher down for Martin.

Eventually I heard them returning, cursing and swearing as they pushed their way through the bushes. They had managed, with great difficulty, to extricate Martin from the car. He was still alive and seemed to be recovering consciousness. When they had got him into the ambulance I tried to make a rough examination by the light of the flashlight. He could not recognize me or answer questions. So far as I could judge, his head injury was not very serious, but there was a lot of tenderness in his flank, where he had been pinned by the steering wheel. It might be just severe muscle lacerations but it might be something worse; it was impossible to say at this stage.

We lurched along through the rain on the atrocious road to Flores. No doubt the driver did his best to keep down the jolting, but there was not much he could do. Martin groaned at first, but after a little while mercifully lost consciousness again. It must have been after midnight by the time we got to Flores. The town was dark and the little hospital was flustered by our arrival. Martin was wheeled away into the recesses of the hospital—he was my responsibility no longer. I stayed in the casualty department to have stitches put in my head. Afterward I felt utterly exhausted, and it was obviously out of the question for me to go back to the Clanricarde at that time of night. I gratefully accepted the offer of a bed in a private ward.

30

❁

❁

❁

❁

❁

❁

I was awakened by somebody shaking my arm. I looked up, momentarily confused to find myself in borrowed pajamas in a strange bed, and then remembered where I was. It was broad daylight. Hume was standing by the side of the bed. For once, he looked worried.

"Hello, Mayne," he said. "How are you feeling?"

"Not so bad," I said, sitting up. I tried to clear my head by shaking it. My brain seemed a little loose inside my skull, but otherwise all was well. "I wasn't really hurt at all, you know—just scratched. I'm perfectly all right now I've had a few hours' sleep."

"I was hoping you might be."

There was something about the way he spoke that made it more than a polite inquiry. As if it was for some reason important that I should be in good health.

I said anxiously, "How's Martin?"

"Well"—he hesitated—"not too good really. That was why I woke you up. We're all a bit worried about him. It looks as if that steering wheel may have got his left kidney."

I was not really surprised. When I had examined him in the ambulance, it had been a strong possibility. If it had got the kidney, it would probably have crushed it rather badly, judging by the degree of shock. Nor would the knocking about he had received afterward have done him much good.

"Das has given him blood, of course," Hume went on. "He's

had two pints already and he's conscious now, but there's a hell of a great mass in his left flank. It looks rather as if he's still bleeding."

I thought about it for a moment, not as something affecting my friend's life but as an abstract problem. The handling of a kidney injury is a matter that requires judgment. Usually, if the damage is not too great, the bleeding will stop spontaneously without operation. But in a small proportion of cases it will not, and you have to go in and take the kidney out. The trick is to spot the necessity for this as soon as possible. The longer you go on waiting for the bleeding to stop, the more risky the operation when you do it. It is a difficult decision, and requires experience. If one is going to rupture a kidney, it is advisable to do so in one of the centers of civilization.

"So what happens now?" I said.

"That's more in your line than mine, I believe." He paused significantly. But his beefy face was all wrong for subtlety—it conveyed nothing but the vague discomfort of a lazy man being forced for once to take life seriously. "There's some talk of taking his kidney out."

"Can he be flown to the mainland?"

Hume shook his head. "We'd need a helicopter. The airfield's under mud and it's still raining. Even under good circumstances it would take half a day. We usually handle our own emergency surgery."

I asked the question that all this had been leading up to. "Who does it?"

"Das."

There was a silence. Hume looked at me as if wondering whether to say anything further, then decided it was unnecessary. Presumably my dismay was obvious on my face. I remembered Martin's remarks about Das, the competent, conscientious physician, the well-meaning surgical amateur who "fancied himself" with a knife. It was not such a joke now.

I swung my legs out of bed. I felt a little dizzy but otherwise all right.

"Do you want any help getting dressed?" said Hume.

"No, thanks. I can manage."

I washed my hands and face, and dressed quickly. Hume sat there watching me. When I was ready, he said, "You want to go to him now?"

"Yes."

We went downstairs and across the entrance hall into the other wing of the hospital. There was only one main surgical ward, with a few private rooms along the corridor.

Hume stopped outside one of these. He did not call the ward sister, as one normally does when visiting a patient, but walked straight into the room. Martin was propped up in bed with a transfusion running into his arm. He was pale but, by contrast with the night before, looked much improved. He was fully conscious and alert. He smiled at me as I entered the room. It was a good effort but it was all from the mouth, and from that I knew he must be in considerable pain. There was a nurse sitting beside his bed. She stood up uncertainly when we entered.

Hume said to Martin, "Well, I got him for you. I had to drag him out of bed." It was the first I knew that Martin had asked for me. Hume said to the nurse, "There are one or two things I'd like to talk to you about. Perhaps we could go into the office. . . ."

She went out with him and Martin and I were left alone. We were like conspirators, I thought. I did not feel happy about what I was doing. Martin was Das's patient, and under professional etiquette I had no business to give advice unless Das saw fit to call me into consultation. But I could not allow convention to stand against Martin's life. I told myself that Das had only himself to blame. If he had had any sense he would have called me in himself.

There was no time to waste on courtesies. Das might come in, the nurse might return.

"Do you mind if I have a look at you?" I asked conventionally.

"Why the hell do you think I asked for you?" said Martin. Again the smile wavered on his lips. "This is the first chance of your doing anything useful since you came to the island."

I looked at his chart and then examined him. Ideally, to form an opinion one should do a series of examinations over several hours, but we were not working under ideal conditions. There was not much doubt in my mind as to what should be done.

"Das is right," I said. "It needs taking out."

He said, "You'll do it for me?"

I paused before replying. If he could not be transported to the mainland, I, as the only person on the island with the necessary training and experience, was the obvious man for the job. But just the same it was an unpleasant situation.

Hesitantly I said, "It's a little difficult."

"Don't tell me you've forgotten how."

"Well, after all, it *is* several years since I did any surgery." As I said it, I knew that this carried no conviction. Surgery, the purely operating part at least, is one of those physical skills like swimming or riding a bicycle, that, once learned, are never really lost. I could do it, and it was desirable for everybody that I should. When I was younger I had seen lives lost on many occasions because doctors did not realize their limitations, and their colleagues were reluctant to hurt their feelings by pointing them out. I had never thought that I might be tempted toward moral cowardice of this kind. Yet I said reluctantly, "And there's Das—"

"Fix it for me, Peter." He smiled. He knew what I was feeling, but it meant nothing to him. He had never shrunk from hurting others when he considered it necessary. He was too tired to argue and he knew that there was no need. He was in a position to demand.

"All right," I said.

Hume was waiting for me outside. "Well?" he asked.

"He wants me to do it."

"And will you?"

"I haven't much choice," I said. "But it's all very awkward. Naturally I don't want to interfere. I have no standing here. I'm not even in practice as a surgeon any more. You understand."

"Yes, I understand." Hume took me by the arm. "We'd better go and see him now and get it over with."

He took me along to the theater block. The theater sister was standing by the operating table counting out sets of instruments. I took a careful look at her. She was a woman approaching middle age, plain and lanky, with a flat nose and a dark-brown skin. She looked courteous, calm, and sure of herself. Das was also in the theater, throwing out instructions for the forthcoming operation. He gave the impression of being in a high state of nerves.

"—and if I should want a clamp, I will need several varieties, a small curved cholecystectomy one for the artery, but if I decide to take the whole pedicle in one that will not be big enough, I shall need one of those flat ones with the long handles, I forget its name—"

"I know the ones you mean, Dr. Das. I've got them all in." I admired her good nature, the way she went on amiably adding up the artery clips and tying parcels of swabs. My qualms began to leave me a little. If he was as agitated as this before the operation had even started, it was hard to imagine what he would be like when he actually had to do anything. Perhaps he would be only too pleased to hand over.

"And now, Sister, for the question of retractors. We must anticipate being at the bottom of a very deep wound—"

"Das," said Hume.

He wheeled round impatiently. "What is it?"

"Could I have a word with you in the surgeon's room?"

Das saw me and a look of hostility came into his face. "I am very busy."

"It's rather urgent."

Das shrugged and followed us into the surgeon's room.

"Yes?" he said suspiciously, waiting to be attacked, waiting to be hurt.

"I've just been to see Martin," I said. "I hope you don't mind."

"Mind? Why should I mind?"

"Well, he's your case, of course, and it occurred to me afterward that I should have asked your permission, but I was so anxious, and we are such old friends, as you know. . . ." I had an uneasy feeling that this wasn't the right approach. "Also, he sent a message asking me to come."

I was floundering. Hume tried to come to my assistance. "You may not be in the picture about Dr. Mayne—or should I say Mr. Mayne? He is a surgical specialist. Until a year or so ago he was actually a surgical first assistant at a London teaching hospital."

"Yes?"

"Naturally it occurred to us that he might be a bit of help in this particular situation."

He waited for Das to say something, but Das simply looked at the pair of us, tight-lipped, waiting for the payoff. Hume was compelled to go on. "Nobody wants to step on your toes, but I gather this job could turn out rather tricky—"

"These cases aren't very common," I put in. "At St. Vincent's I was fortunate enough to come across quite a few. If I could be of any help—"

If only, I prayed, he would take the hint and ask me to do it. I was going to have to do it anyway—it would be so much better for everyone if he would agree to pretend it was his idea. But he merely looked bewildered.

"You wish to assist me?" he asked.

"Well, not exactly."

"Well, what then?"

It occurred to me with surprise that until that moment he had quite genuinely not guessed what we had come for. But now, suddenly, he knew.

"You are asking me to hand over?"

"We thought, perhaps," said Hume, "that under the circumstances you might prefer it."

There was quite a long silence. Das seemed sunk in morose contemplation. I had the impression that he was considering the matter with great seriousness from all possible angles. Finally he shook his head.

"I am sorry," he said. "I cannot agree to that. The responsibility is mine. I may not have the Fellowship but I have considerable practical experience in surgery. I think I shall manage all right."

"You think?" said Hume. He could see that Das was not going to be easy and it exasperated him. His tact was beginning to wear thin.

"Nobody can guarantee success," said Das. He turned to me. "Isn't that so?"

"It's a question of giving him the best chance."

He shook his head again. "I am sure Dr. Farrell would not wish it."

"It was his idea," said Hume.

I was suddenly conscious of how small Das was, how defenseless. His face worked, and I thought for one awful moment that he might begin to cry. I had known before that he was not only devoted to Martin but had fixed on him all his hopes for the future. In his mind he was the trusted friend and faithful disciple; I was the villain, the wrecker. He could not conceive that Martin in his extremity would turn to me. Now he was shown, brutally, that all that had gone before was no more than play-acting. We were dealing with serious matters now, and Martin had discarded him.

I said nothing. He hated me. Perhaps he was right to hate me, and there was nothing I could do to change it. I would not insult him by saying I was sorry. The kindest thing I could have done for him was to hate him back, but that I could not do.

He said with great dignity, "Just one moment, please," and went out of the room.

"Damn the fellow," said Hume. "Damn him. Why can't he just take it? Why does he have to *make* you hit him?" I said nothing. He went on. "God, it's no use, I can't understand these people no matter how I try. Sometimes they're so damn sensitive, other times you can't get them to see anything till you stick it right in front of their noses. How do you account for that?"

"I don't know."

"I want to get away from here," he said. "I want to get back to England. Yes, I know the weather stinks and gin costs two quid a bottle and you can't get any servants. But I want to get back to my own people. I want to be able to call a man a bastard without his making a racial issue out of it."

"Das isn't a bastard," I said.

"I know he isn't. I didn't mean he was. I don't really know what I did mean except that I'm fed up with everything being so bloody complicated. The truth is I'm not a tactful man. I'm not cut out for it." He wrung his hands. I had never thought I could have seen him so moved. "Poor little sod," he said. "He thought he was no end of an operator."

Das came back within a few minutes. I don't know what he had said to Martin or what Martin had said to him, but his face was quite dead, as if everything that really mattered to him had been destroyed. Only a rather formal courtesy, the ineradicable habit of a lifetime, remained. He inclined his head gravely.

"Would you like me to assist you?" he asked.

31

IT was not an operation under ideal circumstances. Hume, who gave the anesthetic, had no pretensions to special training, but on the island there was no establishment for an anesthetist and it was customary for the pathologist to help out when necessary. He had been brought up in the old rag-and-bottle days, when you poured ether onto a mask while the hospital porter sat on the patient's legs to prevent him jumping off the table. Fortunately Sister was good and Das was a competent, if preoccupied, assistant. Also, Martin was thin. I went down quickly through skin and the three layers of muscle. I was glad to notice that, once I had started, I felt entirely at home. I might have been back at St. Vincent's again. I had a fairly clear picture in my mind of what I might find and what I would do in each eventuality. The X-rays showed that Martin had both kidneys present, so I would not have to be forced to do a difficult repair. Nephrectomy, under favorable conditions, is an easy operation. With luck I might be out within half an hour.

Sure enough, I hit the blood clot just under the muscle layer. There it was—a great deal of it. We had no suction apparatus. I took out the clots with my hands and used large flat swabs to soak up the blood. It looked at first as if the bleeding had stopped, but as I got further down it obviously hadn't—clot was forming the whole time to take the place of what I was removing. As I got deeper in, it was more difficult to see, and the tissues were stained with altered blood. After a few minutes I decided I wasn't getting anywhere ladling out clot. The thing to do was to get down to the kidney. I picked up what I hoped was the perinephric fat and snipped at it with scissors. Then I stuck my hand in and felt. To my relief I hadn't made a mistake. I was in the right place. I could feel the kidney. It seemed to be in about three rather crumbly pieces.

It was from this point onward that I felt, rightly or wrongly, that I would be at a considerable advantage over Das. He could probably have done the approach as well as I had. He could possibly even have found his way to the kidney as easily. But the next step depended heavily on training and experience. In surgery it is a good rule always to be able to see what you are doing. But there are some situations in which you are never going to be able to see what you are doing, no matter how much you try. Attempts to get a sight of the area will do no more than waste time and possibly endanger your patient's life. It is essential to recognize such situations immediately.

What I needed was a clamp on the kidney pedicle to stop the bleeding. Then I could have a look around at my leisure. In the end I used three separate clamps, one for each torn segment, and I put them on by touch. I put similar clamps on the fragments and divided between them. Then I took the fragments out.

So far, so good. I was not feeling too displeased with myself. I mopped out the cavity, very, very gently, with swabs. The bleeding was controlled, all except for a slight ooze. There wasn't a lot to see. The hole was conical, with my three clamps bobbing up and down with each breath, their points invisible in the tissue at the bottom of the wound. I put in some deep retractors but it still wasn't very satisfactory, largely because of the movement. I began to yearn for a little modern anesthesia. The only other way to increase my view of the pedicle would have been to pull gently on the clamps, and this I was not anxious to do, since I might possibly pull one of them off. Kidney vessels, if you once lose them, have a tendency to retract completely out of reach.

All I had to do was to get strong, reliable ligatures around each clamp, then gently take the clamp off. Then come out and sew up. There was nothing to it. I took a little breather and examined Sister's ligatures. I had opted for No. 2 catgut. I tested it. Strong but springy, not so thick it wouldn't bind on the knot, not so thin as to tear the vessel wall. A double one around each clamp—I would take no chances. I started with the lowest because it looked the easiest, and it was. Then the middle one. Double ligature, off with the clamp—gently, gently. Everything fine. Dry as a bone.

The top one was at a slightly awkward angle, and I seemed to have taken a little bit of extraneous tissue in, as well as the pedicle. But I got my ligature around, good and tight and sound. It seemed all right. I took the clamp off.

I knew immediately it wasn't right. There was a blackish ooze and one of the ligatures floated up in it. What had happened I didn't know. The vessel might have been torn along the side, my ligature might have ruptured the wall, it might have been too near the clamp. There was no point in worrying about that now. There was no pedicle to be seen, nothing but a pool of dark blood growing larger at an alarming rate.

There is only one thing to do under such circumstances. I took a handful of large swabs and rammed them down in the depths of the wound, packed as tightly as I could get them. The theory is that if you can stop the bleeding by pressure for five or ten minutes, it takes a matter of ten or twenty seconds to start up again when you relieve the pressure. This may give you time to see the vessel and get a clamp on it. So I pushed the packs hard down, stood back, and looked around. The other thing you are supposed to do at this point is to appear unperturbed.

"Finished?" said Hume, poking his head over the top of the anesthetic screen.

"Not quite." I washed my hands in the basin beside me. "One of the ligatures came off the pedicle."

"Oh." We might have been discussing whether I took sugar in my coffee.

I said, "I'm just giving it a minute or two under pressure to settle."

I saw Das's eyes staring at me balefully over the top of his mask. I knew what he was thinking. It was what all assistants think at a time like this—that it wouldn't have happened if he had been doing it. But as a rule assistants try to conceal this conviction. He was making no attempt to do so. The eyes said that I was not only an enemy of science and a deceitful, false friend, I wasn't even the surgeon I was cracked up to be. Sister was, like all good sisters at a time of crisis, pretending that it was all part of the day's work, and counting out new bundles of swabs with the runner. It took quite an effort to prevent myself talking and explaining to Hume exactly why I thought the ligature had come off.

He said, "Would you like him a bit deeper?"

I shook my head. I would have liked him a bit deeper, if the truth were known, but I had no confidence in Hume's power to achieve this, short of almost total asphyxiation. I would have to make do with what I had. At least with the present anesthetic I had the consoling reassurance that Martin was still very much alive; I could feel his heart and great vessels banging away powerfully, if a little fast, under my hand. I was not subject to that uneasy fear that one occasionally has with modern operations, that both the patient and the anesthetist have quietly expired while you are looking the other way.

The five minutes seemed like half an hour. When they were up, I got all my instruments easily within reach, and hauled the packs quickly out. For a second or two, the field was dry. I hovered, clamp in hand, waiting for the first sign of bleeding to show up the hole. Suddenly there it was and I went down onto it. By the time the blades closed, the hole had opened and the field was swimming in blood, but by the grace of God it wasn't increasing. I swabbed away, and there was the end of the great vein in the jaws of my clamp.

I handed the clamp to Das and Sister slapped the catgut into my hand. I went down with it around the end of the clamp, and tied the first half of my reef knot. I pulled it very tight.

"Now," I said to Das, "very slowly off—and close again the moment I tell you."

He opened the clamp very, very slowly. I don't know what Hume had done, but for this moment Martin was much quieter and for the first time I got a really good view. I saw the short, wide stump of the renal vein with my clamp on the end and the ligature below it. As the clamp gradually opened there was an ooze of blood, and I saw something that almost froze me with terror.

"Close it," I said sharply. Das closed it. The bleeding stopped. I stood back from the table to collect myself. This time, all three of them looked at me.

"There is," I said as soon as I felt confident that I could control my voice, "a small tear in the side wall of the vein. It's only a few millimeters long but it goes almost to the point of origin of the vein from the *vena cava*. There's not enough vein behind it to get a ligature on. With very deep relaxation and special sutures, I suppose we might try to sew it up. . . ."

It had to be mentioned, but before I said it, I knew it was hopeless. Sister said, "I'm sorry, I'm afraid we're not equipped . . ."

Quite apart from this, I knew that Hume had shot his bolt. The diaphragm was beginning to heave again, the point of my clamp had disappeared. He said despondently, "What's the alternative?"

I thought for a moment. I could think of only one. "We leave the clamp on," I said. "Then, when we hope the hole has sealed up, we take it off again. I've seen it done with success."

"Often?" asked Das.

"No," I said, "not very often."

In silence, I began to sew up the muscle layers.

32

WHEN the operation was over, I left Das to do the bandaging and went through into the surgeon's room. I changed quickly and then called back into the theater to have a look at Martin. He was in satisfactory shape. I gave final instructions to the ward sister and promised to come back and see him again in a few hours' time.

When I walked out of the theater block into the main hall of the hospital, I saw Barbara sitting on one of the benches that were kept there for patients' relatives. She was in a white linen dress and looked very beautiful.

"How is he?" she said.

"Well—" It was not easy to explain and I wasn't even very clear in what character I was speaking. Was I the God-almighty surgeon reassuring an anxious wife. Was I the lover? Had the accident changed anything? It was too much to talk about in a corridor. "Can we go somewhere and talk?"

"There's the car."

We walked out of the front door. The porter watched us curiously. The Jaguar was outside. She drove away from the town, up the hill and along the coastal road. She finally stopped in a quiet place on the cliff and switched off the engine. In the full heat of midday the road was deserted.

She said, "Will he live?"

"I don't know for certain. It's a gamble." I explained what had happened. It wasn't easy to tell what she was thinking or how she was taking it. When I had finished she said in an uncertain voice, "You'll do what you can for him?"

"Of course." The way she asked the question made me realize that she was just as uncertain of my attitude as I was of hers. We had, for the moment at any rate, lost touch with each other. Our relationship was still young. At a time of crisis we needed more than just love—we needed a knowledge and experience of each other that only time could give.

"Of course I'll do everything I possibly can to pull him through. But you understand—"

"No." She shook her head. "No, I don't really understand. Not about clamps and blood vessels and those things. I'm afraid I've never been able to raise much interest in medicine. I used to try for Martin's sake, but it didn't really work. Do you mind?"

"Of course not."

"I suppose I should have told you before. You won't be able to discuss your cases with me when you come home in the evening. Will that be a big disappointment?"

"I haven't got any cases, remember. Only this one at the moment." I laughed, a little ruefully. "Mayne's last case. I should like it to be a success."

"So should I."

She was silent for a moment. She lit a cigarette and puffed at it. Her face was very solemn.

"I spoke to him before the operation, you know. It was very important to him that you should do it. He has great confidence in you."

"Has he?" I said dubiously.

She looked at me as if wondering whether I was serious. "I thought you would have known. You were the only person, apart from himself, that he ever trusted or respected or cared for. When you weren't there any more, I hardly existed for him. I was just a body he sometimes desired—and a source of capital in time of need. It was with you that he wanted to do all the things that really mattered to him."

"Such as?"

"Showing off. Playing the genius. Quarrelling and making up. He needed you for that."

"That's not so much," I said.

"It's as much as he has to give. More than he had to give to anyone else."

"Then perhaps I should feel flattered." Flattered at having a character part, of being something more than an extra, a stand-in. But I was tired of the play. I couldn't wait for the curtain to come down, one way or the other. There was one thing I wanted to be certain of.

"Whether he lives or dies," I said, "it won't make any difference to us, will it?"

"Why should it?" There was surprise in her voice. "You think I might fall in love with him again because his life is in danger? He's still the same man, with or without your clamp inside him. And I'm the same woman. Nothing has changed. Nothing," she repeated emphatically. She clutched my arm, digging her fingers into me painfully. "Promise me, Peter—don't let him persuade you that it has."

"You think he might try?"

"It's possible. It might amuse him to beat you with your own sense of honor, to make you feel you couldn't in decency rob a sick and dying man of his wife. But if he says that, it's not true. You can't rob him of me because I don't belong to him. If I didn't go with you, I should leave him anyway. He doesn't really want me. But he'd like the pair of us hanging around forever, dancing to his tune. He'd like us to be unhappy to provide him with a situation."

"How would you feel," I asked, "if he died?" We can be honest here, I thought, on this silent road with no one to overhear. We could speak to each other the thoughts that never otherwise could find expression. One of the great luxuries of being in love is to think aloud with someone to overhear. We could say, if we wished, that we longed for his death, that he had destroyed our happiness and battened on our lives with his egoism. Or we could admit that in our curious separate ways we loved him and that to lose him would mean that life would never seem so strange and significant without him. Perhaps both might be true. I thought of those curious twisted landscapes, those agonized sunsets and flowers and trees. Would Barbara ever paint in quite the same way again?

"I don't know how I would feel," she said. "How can one know?"

One couldn't, of course. Suddenly I felt sorry for Martin. There was nobody in the world who cared for him except Barbara and myself, and here we were, in league against him. It was his own doing, he had nobody to blame but himself, but it was sad just the same.

"Poor Martin," I said. "It would be such a convenience to everybody if he died."

"To us, do you mean?"

"Not only us. The Ministry. The Governor. Even, in a way, to himself. I don't see him as an eminent old man much, do you? If this project doesn't end in disaster, perhaps the next one will—or the one after that. He'll just keep on raising the stakes every time."

She was silent for a while. There seemed to be nothing for either of us to say. Nothing to do either—except wait and see what happened. The hardest thing of all.

I said, "But whether it's for the best or not, I'm going to do my damndest to keep him alive. I may even manage it."

She smiled at me, then took a last puff at her cigarette and threw it out of the window—it hissed away into the mud at the side of the road. I leaned over and kissed her, and suddenly it was like no other kiss we had ever had. I do not know what it was that lent it so much intensity. Perhaps it was a reaction from the tensions of the morning, perhaps relief in knowing that what we felt for each other was strong enough to survive this, its hardest test. But there was something else, a kind of pure, almost desperate sensuality. We were like a boy and girl again, young and in a hurry for love. When I finally broke away from her, I was breathless and trembling. This was what we had been missing, without really knowing it. Love and respect and common interest were all very well in their way, but they were rational emotions that in their turn could be broken by reason. But pure physical passion of this kind was beyond the reach of common sense. We felt safe now. For the first time, if only for a minute or two, we had managed to forget Martin altogether.

33

✿ ✿ ✿ ✿ ✿ ✿

MARTIN must have been very fit. He came through Hume's anesthetic without even so much as a chest infection. He had lost a good deal of blood, but that was replaced by the transfusion. As far as the operation was concerned, it was basically only the removal of a kidney, which shouldn't worry a man of his age and condition very much. If I had been able to leave a nice tight ligature on that last vessel, I wouldn't have had a care in the world.

Within twenty-four hours he was not only fully conscious but had managed to persuade Sister to show him his operation notes. After I had gone through the usual preliminaries of looking through his charts, asking him how he was, and so on, he said, "How about this piece of ironmongery?"

"The clamp?" I said easily. I was naturally prepared for this question. "Sorry about that. There was a lateral slit in the renal vein and we couldn't get a ligature to hold."

"So?"

"We give it a few days and then take it off."

He took a little while to think this over and then shook his head in admiration.

"God, you surgeons. I love the lighthearted way you have of looking at these things. Would it be tactless to ask what's going to happen when you take the bloody thing off?"

"There's no need to worry," I said. "It's quite a standard procedure."

"Well, that's wonderful," he said. "I feel better already. There's nothing like a nice standard procedure."

"The walls of the vein tend to stick together after a few days," I explained.

"Yes, yes, I'm sure they do," he said, humoring me. "Don't worry. I won't embarrass you with any further questions."

He realized, of course, that his chances were no better than fifty-fifty. But I would not say so out loud, even to him. There is a great deal of nonsense talked about doctors lying to patients. The truth is a difficult thing to face, for the boldest of us. A sick man has a right to a little harmless self-deception. I would not be surprised to find Martin taking a more optimistic view of his chances than reason dictated—or perhaps even refusing to think about the matter at all. Certainly he seemed willing enough to change the subject.

He said thoughtfully, "How do you suppose that log got there?"

"The log?"

"Yes. I can remember the accident fairly well, up to the moment of going over into the ravine. There was a dirty great tree trunk lying across the road. Didn't you see it?"

"I seem to remember something in the road. It's all a little blurred in my memory."

"Not in mine. I could have got around the corner easily if I hadn't had to swerve. I'd just like to know how it got there."

"I suppose it could have been the storm—"

"Well, perhaps . . ." The same thought was in both our minds. Perhaps it was not the storm. I saw those dumb, fearful primitive faces staring at me from the doors of the cottages, as meaningless in the glare of our headlights as the faces of startled animals. Yet they were not animals. They had a collective mind, a collective will, a collective fear. It was something almost as elemental as the storm, yet as strong and as unexpected. It could fell a tree across the path of a man who aroused it. Like the storm, it held no personal malice. It was innocent.

"Daly's making an investigation," I said. "I saw him this morning."

"Do you think he'll find anything out?"

"No."

"Neither do I." He asked, "How about the Health Center?"

"It isn't much damaged, he says. The reports were exaggerated. The records are safe."

"I suppose," he said without noticeable emotion, "they've stopped vaccinating."

"Yes."

No official instructions to that effect had been given, but vaccination, by common consent, had been stopped all over the island as soon as Martin had been injured. Without his presence, the tension had dropped, the urgency of the trial had seemed to disappear. Everyone waited, either for instructions or simply to see what was going to happen.

He said, "That's how it always is, Peter. I have to do everything myself, all the way. If I turn my back for a moment"—he shrugged—"that's the end of it. Nobody has any faith."

It was quite true. He had built too much on himself and the power of his own personality. The drive to Cajara had been not only unnecessary—it had in its consequences been ruinous to his own cause. I had been reluctant to tell him the news. I had been afraid that he might work himself into a fury. This dignified attitude of resignation came as a surprise to me. He might have been talking of some affair in which he was interested from the point of view of a spectator, but not immediately concerned.

I should not, perhaps, have been so surprised as I was. I had got into the way of regarding Martin as something apart from ordinary men, largely because he had always so regarded himself. But in the last resort he was a man, and all men have certain common characteristics. In the face of death, they are preoccupied with their own immediate fate. Nothing else holds much significance for them. For the next few days, Martin would lie there and he would not think of the trial or the vaccine or his future as a scientist. He would not even think very much about Barbara or myself. These were things that could wait until more urgent matters had been disposed of.

What would he be thinking about? He would be thinking of my clamp, moving a little with each breath he took, each beat of his heart, holding his life together in its jaws. For those few days it would support him, but not for longer than that, for if I left it too long it would ulcerate through into the vein. At the end of that time it would leave him, and his life would hang on a layer of epithelium, a clot, a few strands of fibrin. The great vessel would expand and throb, pumping against those puny defenses. Perhaps they would hold, perhaps not. . . .

That was the only reality.

34

❂

❂

❂

❂

❂

❂

ON the second day he said, "When does the balloon go up?"

"Tomorrow, I think."

"I had a feeling we were getting near. The vultures are gathering." He smiled. Something seemed to have pleased him. "You'll never guess who was in to see me this morning."

"Who?"

"De Freitas. Rather cool, don't you think, after pretty well arranging for me to be knocked off?"

"Oh, come. You don't believe—"

"Perhaps not directly. But my guess is that he knew a good deal about what was going on. Let's say that he didn't concern himself officiously about my safety." He paused. "Still, I can't help admiring him in a way."

His bitterness against de Freitas seemed to have left him. It was as if the accident had wiped out the previous situation completely, and with it all the emotions necessary to its continuance. It was almost impossible to believe that a few days ago we had been living in a world of pure melodrama, with myself and de Freitas cast as villains and himself as a knight in armor battling for progress and the purity of science. Now that was as if it had never been; his supporters were forgotten, his enemies were welcomed with good-humored tolerance.

"Why?" I said.

"It must have taken quite a lot of courage for him to come."

"In a way, I suppose." I was a little dubious. I had a feeling that de Freitas probably enjoyed such anomalous encounters in the same way as Martin did. "Though in fact the worst you could do would be to insult him. And that's not so very important to a priest. Rather useful, really. Mortification of the flesh." He laughed and so did I. We were both suddenly schoolboys again, listening to pious instructions in the chapel at Breckenhall. "What did he want, anyway?"

"Well, practically speaking, he offered to stamp my passport, if you see what I mean. . . ."

"Extreme Unction?"

"Yes. I don't think it was intended as a reflection on your professional skill. It seems anyone's entitled to it preoperatively, just in case. You take it just before the omnopon and scopolamine. He told me he knew I'd been brought up as a Catholic and thought it his duty to offer it to me." He mused for a moment and then added casually, "I was almost tempted to accept."

He obviously expected to startle me, and he succeeded. I had never suspected that his change in attitude might go as far as this. "You were?" I said incredulously.

"Yes." He smiled, pleased at my reaction. He was pulling my leg to some extent, but not entirely. "As he more or less suggested, it's a useful each-way bet. If they're wrong, you don't lose anything, whereas if they're right. . . . Also," he went on pensively, "it's an experience, isn't it? Do you remember that chap at school who got double pneumonia?"

"Wilkinson?"

"Yes. A squalid little fellow with acne. Yet he always had a sort of cachet on account of having received the last sacraments. He used to make out that he felt entirely different afterward."

"Like confirmation," I said. "I used to think that when they smeared that stuff on my forehead, I should feel a sort of glow, like switching on an electric light. But nothing happened." I waited for him to say something, but he was silent. "Did anything happen to you?"

"In a sense, yes. I glowed very brightly for about a week, as I remember—too brightly, perhaps. I burned my fuse out. I've never managed to mend it since. The truth is, Peter," he went on, "that at a time like this your sort of cold pragmatism isn't quite enough. One yearns for a little magic." He shook his head in reluctant admiration. "And they know that, the devils."

"Why did you turn it down, then?"

"I don't honestly know. Mainly, I think, because I should have felt rather silly. Perhaps," he hesitated, "I was afraid of what you might think."

"I?" I looked at him in astonishment. I could hardly believe that such a thought would even cross his mind. "But why should I think anything? And what difference would it make?"

"Don't worry. I was only pulling your leg. It was no more than a momentary impulse anyway. Poor de Freitas was very disappointed. He thought he had me for a moment. As you know, it's a great romantic dream of theirs, the deathbed conversion. It would have done him no end of good with the Provincial, I expect." He sounded genuinely regretful. "It's a queer thing, after everything he's done to me, but I rather like him. Does that surprise you?"

"Not really."

"As I told him, if there's one commandment I've obeyed, it's to love my enemies. It's my friends I can't get along with."

He was not simply being flippant. There was a truth behind what he said. It had often seemed to me that Martin saw all other people in relation to his own will. If they opposed his will he respected them but they enraged him; he could love and hate them simultaneously. If they were subservient to his will, even if it was through faith and admiration, he could treat them with bitter and thoughtless cruelty, lying to them, manipulating them, abandoning them when their purpose was served. Myself, de Freitas, Barbara—in his way he loved us, while he regarded us as his enemies because he could not dominate us. But what of the faithful, the disciples? It occurred to me that he had never even mentioned Das to me since the accident. I doubt whether he had ever even thought of him.

35

THE next day I came into the hospital at the usual time. I was tense, as one always is before undertaking a risky procedure. Not that there was anything very complicated about the procedure itself. Anybody, or almost anybody, could take off the clamp. The skill was in knowing when to do it. If I had made the wrong decision, Martin would very likely be dead within a matter of seconds. It might be that the hole was so big that there was no chance of its healing before the clamp came off. But if the hole was small enough, and my judgment was good, he had a chance.

I had made all the arrangements the day before. Das would be there and the ward sister. Hume would give the anesthetic. After a good deal of thought I had decided to do it in the ward. I was afraid to move him to the theater for fear that we might dislodge the clamp.

Martin was in good fettle. He had been improving rapidly each day since the operation and looked in the pink of condition. He didn't seem at all worried at the prospect in front of him. He was a gambler at heart and risks exhilarated rather than depressed him. I had the impression that he was enjoying being the center of so much attention.

"We're almost ready to start," I said. "It should only take a minute or two. Hume's going to put you out with a shot of Pentothal."

He shook his head firmly. "No. I want to see what's going on."

I suppose I should have anticipated this.

"Now look here, Martin—"

"It shouldn't be very painful. I promise not to move. Win or lose, this is going to be one of the big moments of my life. I'm damned if I'm going to sleep through it." His voice was very determined. I could see that he was deadly serious. He was like a child who has just heard that he is to be left behind when everyone else is going to a party—*his* party. He had the same sense of injustice, the same fanatical determination to get his own way at all costs.

"You'd be much better with an anesthetic," I said.

He brushed me aside. "No, don't give me a lot of doctor talk. You know you haven't any real reason for the anesthetic, except that it's usual. All you have to do is to unhook the thing. There's nothing to it. You don't need an anesthetic for that."

"Perhaps not. But supposing I did have to do anything else that needed cutting down—"

"Don't talk nonsense, Peter. Either the vein holds or it doesn't. If it does, fine. If it doesn't, there isn't a damn thing you can do. Is there?" I did not reply. There was not much I could think of to say. He went on helpfully, "If you don't like to take the responsibility, I'll refuse an anesthetic. I'll fill in one of those little printed forms saying I went against your advice. How about that?"

"Don't be an ass." I gave in. When it came to the point, I could hardly force him. "I suppose, if you insist—"

"Excellent." Having got his own way he smiled benevolently. "And now I can have some breakfast. They've been starving me since last night. Tell them I'd like a slice of pawpaw, and two soft-boiled eggs."

"Go to hell," I said. "You'll get nothing till we've finished. Then you can have all the eggs you want."

I left him and went to make the necessary arrangements. He had two final visitors, Barbara and de Freitas. I never knew what either of them said to him. De Freitas was carrying his box with the holy oils in it, hopeful to the last. When he came out, his face was impassive. It was impossible to tell whether he had succeeded or failed. He never even looked at me as he went out of the ward.

It was time to begin and we collected in the side ward. Das stood against the wall, his mouth drawn down hopelessly, his clothes crumpled. He seemed too dispirited even to hate. When Martin smiled at him, gaily and completely without embarrassment, his mouth twitched in an attempt at a response. He wanted, I could see, to smile back, to show that he didn't really care about being rejected and betrayed, that the wound within him was not mortal. But he could not do it. He grimaced like a dying man.

Hume stood by with the anesthetic machine, just in case, and Sister with a trolley of instruments. The atmosphere was the same as for all minor ward operations, brisk and rather chatty. I put on a gown and washed up at the basin in a corner of the room. Then I came back to the bed. Sister had opened the bandages. She was cool and matter-of-fact, a true professional. She picked away the last pieces of gauze with her forceps and there was the wound. It was a long, curved one, good and clean, ugly as they always are compared to normal flesh, but very pleasing to the expert eye. There was no sign of infection. The only thing that defaced it was the handle of my long clamp sticking out of the upper end. I cleaned the surface of the skin and packed towels around. I checked the instruments. Everything I might conceivably need was there.

"Comfortable?" I said to Martin.

"Yes."

"Then here we go."

"Oh, Peter, before we start—"

"Yes?"

"Supposing anything goes wrong—" He hesitated. "Buy yourself one of those ouija boards. I'll see if I can get through to you."

"All right."

We smiled at each other and I turned back to my work. I started by unlocking the blades of the clamp. I waited. Nothing happened. Then I opened the blades slightly, very slowly and gently. I didn't move the clamp from its position and I was holding it ready so that I could clamp it shut again if any bleeding appeared. None did.

I left it like that for several minutes. The blades were wide open and could no longer be holding the walls of the vein. It was holding. It was going to work. At last I moved the clamp about half an inch. Still all right.

Hume had his hand on Martin's pulse. He would know immediately if any bleeding started, even before it got out of the wound —the pulse would begin to race. He nodded to me reassuringly.

I took the clamp out of the wound, very slowly and gradually. I held it in my hand for a moment before putting it down on the trolley. As I relaxed, I felt an ache in the side of my face, and realized that for the past ten minutes the muscles of my jaw had been tightly contracted. I let them go and took a deep breath.

Then I saw a frown appear on Hume's face. It was like watching some delicate meter from which a connection extended through his brain and his fingers and thence through Martin's body to that small break in the continuity of tissue of a certain vein on which his life was hanging. I reached for Martin's other wrist, but before I had time to locate the pulse I saw his face turn suddenly as pale as wax, his eyes bright and startled. I looked down at the bowl I had placed below the wound. . . .

There was nothing to be done. It would be over in a matter of seconds. We stood like statues, waiting for the inevitable. Martin's body became rigid, and he lifted his head off the pillow. He took one deep, jerky breath. He was gazing before him very intently, but not at any of us. His skin was stone cold, with drops of sweat. But his face showed neither fear nor pain. He seemed totally preoccupied with his own sensations. He was like a boy experiencing his first orgasm, in the grip of a new, exciting, yet at the same time frightening experience. He was like a man opening a door into a dark and secret room. The last expression I ever saw on his face was one of intense curiosity. A few seconds later, there was no expression at all.

36

I drove Barbara back to the house in the Jaguar. She had cried a little when I had brought her the news but now she was calm and almost, I thought, more controlled than I was. While I was in the hospital I was the surgeon in charge of a case, a case that had ended in fatality. It was regrettable, it was upsetting, but it happened often. There was a routine for dealing with it. That routine had held me up for as long as I was involved in it. Now, outside the hospital, I had no such support. I was no longer a surgeon, I was a man. And I had just witnessed, perhaps even caused, the death of my friend.

Barbara took my left hand off the wheel and gripped it in hers. "It wasn't your fault," she said. "You couldn't help it."

"No, it's true. I couldn't."

To feel guilty at this stage, I told myself, was childish and hysterical. I had not killed Martin. I had tried to save him. If I had failed, it was probably because success was impossible. Even if my judgment had been wrong, it was certainly the best available on the island at the time. Why should I feel guilty?

"There was nothing else you could have done."

"No."

"Then why reproach yourself?"

I pondered for a moment. "For being alive, I think. Oh, don't tell me it's not reasonable—I know that. But it was what he always said to me, you see. It seemed like nonsense at the time, but it happened. He said I'd take everything from him, that I'd been put into the world to destroy him. And now he's dead and I'm driving his car to his house, planning to marry his wife—"

Barbara said, "My car and my house. He never owned either of them. And he didn't own me either." She added slowly, "Oh, I feel miserable too, of course I do. Perhaps I didn't love him in the conventional sense. Sometimes I felt I hated him. I was prepared to leave him for you. Yet in a sense, even then he was a part of me, just as he was a part of you. Love isn't just falling in love. He mattered very much to me, but I couldn't live with him. Toward the end, I was afraid of him and what he could do to us. I had a sort of nightmare that he'd never let us go, that he'd hang round our necks in some way or other for the rest of our lives." She went on fiercely, "He's lying there dead now. It's terrible. I can't get it out of my mind. And yet"—she was suddenly crying, bitterly, helplessly—"surely we still have a right to our happiness. He hasn't taken our future with him, has he?"

"Of course he hasn't." And, I discovered with relief, in spite of everything, he hadn't. Our future was still there. He couldn't rob us of that. "Nothing's changed as far as we're concerned. I promise you."

We said nothing more. A few minutes later I turned into the private road leading to the house. Barbara dried her eyes and began to repair her face. I stopped the car in front of the house and we walked inside. A servant was waiting for us in the hall. He handed Barbara a visiting card. It read, "Dr. Klaus Halder, Chemiefabriken GMBH, Bremen."

"See him for me, will you, Peter? I can't talk to him now."

"All right."

She kissed me and ran upstairs to her room. As I went into the main living room a young man rose hurriedly from one of the chairs. He was tall and thin, with a bony, serious face and horn-rimmed spectacles. He held out a hand.

"Halder," he announced precisely. "You are Dr. Mayne, I presume."

"Yes."

"I am here under the instructions of Dr. Grune, our director of research. As soon as he heard that Dr. Farrell had had an accident, he asked me to fly out." He spoke excellent English, with a slight American intonation. "How is Dr. Farrell?"

"He's dead," I said.

"Oh." His solemnity increased. In a hushed voice he said, "That is a great tragedy."

"Yes." I didn't feel much like discussing it. I sat down. "Will you have a drink, or a cup of coffee or something?"

"No, thank you."

"Food?"

"I have already eaten, down at the Clanricarde Hotel."

"When did you arrive?"

"Last night."

"Are they making you comfortable?"

He shook his head despondently. Looking more closely I could see several mosquito bites on the side of his neck. "It is a horrible place. But that is not important. Such a cruel, wasteful accident."

I was about to tell him that it probably wasn't an accident, but what would have been the point? Even then he could not be expected to understand. The forces of ignorance, of suspicion, of panic fear—they were almost as deep and elemental as the forces of nature itself. They would say it was lightning that had felled the tree, and that would be the best thing. You could not represent Martin's relations with the islanders in terms of a struggle between individuals. He was a phenomenon totally incomprehensible to them. If he bewildered us, what can he have represented to men to whom the last two thousand years, which had produced him, were totally unknown? They could not dispute with him. When he tried to explain what he was doing, they stood before him, understanding nothing, cowering before the limitless self-confidence of civilization. There was no judgment available to them but that of their emotions, primitive, amorphous; no weapon but that of force. Or so they must have seen it. When they felt themselves threatened by him, they could think of no way out but to kill him.

"Just when his work was almost finished," went on Halder. He shook his head reverently. "He was a great scientist."

"You think so?"

"Do you not?"

He looked at me with anxiety, as if I might be in possession of evidence that Martin was a charlatan.

"I'm no judge. I just wondered."

"He had his faults, of course," admitted Halder. "Like many men of unusual talents he was not always easy to deal with. In Bremen, for instance, we had much troubles with him over money."

"Really?"

"Yes. It was all to do with some chimpanzees. I can tell you in confidence that this investigation has already gone half a million marks over the maximum budgeted cost." He stopped for me to be impressed. "Dr. Grune was often very angry with him. Sometimes we were close to breaking with him altogether. But we never did, I am glad to say. In our hearts we knew he had genius."

"Did you?" I felt overcome with fatigue. It was like listening to somebody reading an obituary notice aloud. I neither knew nor cared whether Martin had genius. I knew that he was my friend and he was dead.

"I hear that you also had troubles here. About some deaths."

"Yes."

"I am sure you believed in him and supported him as we did. It is good to know that we were both right. The tragedy is that I am too late to tell him. He will never know now."

"Know what?"

"We have broken the blind, Dr. Mayne. I am very happy to say that none of those three people who died had received the vaccine." His manner was triumphant, almost as if he had scored off somebody. But perhaps he was simply relieved at being able to take good news home to Dr. Grune. That half-million marks would not be wasted after all.

"So you see," he went on, "he was right and those stupid priests were wrong."

I said, "It's not so simple as that."

He raised his eyebrows. "No?"

I wondered how to explain to him. I wondered too if it was worth while trying. I asked, "Are you a doctor of medicine, Dr. Halder?"

"No. I am a scientist. Ph.D."

Perhaps it wasn't really worth while. He would be thinking in terms of mice, guinea pigs, cats, even chimpanzees, and in those terms Martin was right. I wondered, when Martin saw those black, sad, stupid faces lined up before him, their heads crammed with ancient superstitions, their minds dulled with ignorance and disease—was that when the trouble started, did he for one fatal moment see them as something less than human beings? Did perhaps one of them, more sensitive than the rest, less exhausted by the mere struggle to stay alive, see that look and recognize it?

"I'm very glad the vaccine was harmless," I said, "but he was wrong just the same. He didn't understand people. You can't do medicine without understanding people."

I could see Halder looking at me pityingly. I was a sentimentalist. Suddenly I remembered something.

"What will you do about the vaccine now?" I asked.

"It is proved now, I think. It is effective and harmless. We shall market it."

"Will you get back the money you spent? I believe it's very difficult to patent a virus."

He shrugged. "It is impossible." A trace of a smile appeared on his lips.

"If it had been simply the development of the virus, we could never have justified that amount of money. No, there is a process in the manufacture, a fixing agent."

I felt almost sorry for him. "Martin told me something before he died. That process was published six years ago, in the U.S.A. You haven't a chance of patenting it."

The effect was greater than I expected. He looked as if somebody had kicked him in the stomach. It came to me that probably his whole career was at stake. They would never forgive him that half-million marks. No doubt he had ambition, commitments, a wife and family to support. What had he done to deserve being involved with a man like Martin? Martin, who had been saving up this last piece of information as a cruel prank to play upon his patrons, his last practical joke. Well, I had taken that from him, as I had taken all the rest.

I was shocked to see the beginning of tears in Halder's eyes. I had not thought the question of the patent could possibly mean so much to him. Was there more than that? Wherever Martin went he sought to gain disciples, to arouse loyalty. There was no reason why it should have been different in Bremen from anywhere else. Was this another betrayal I knew nothing about? I put my arm on Halder's shoulder.

"Don't take it too hard," I said. "It wasn't just you. It happened to many people."

He looked up at me fiercely, as I remembered Das's looking at me when I landed from the boat. He did not want my sympathy. "You didn't understand him," he said.

I moved away, saying nothing. I let him bear his pain alone. Perhaps he was right, I thought. Perhaps I didn't understand Martin. Perhaps none of us truly understands another person. But this at least I could say, that I wished him well wherever he was. I hoped he existed, as himself, somewhere or other. I hoped that when he had opened that last door there had been something there and that he had not simply fallen out of existence into a pit of nothingness. "One yearns," he had said, only half joking, "for a little magic at a time like this." Well, they had offered us magic, all those years ago, and we had rejected it. I hoped, for his sake at least, that we had been wrong.